I0556214

Monstrosities

of LIFE

By: Alec Managhan

1st Edition
ISBN #: 978-0-9960126-6-9

Thank you to all the fantastic people I am so fortunate to have in my life. Special thanks to Olivia Taylen, Melody Managhan, and Rebecca Braae for your never-ceasing support and your exuberance to help me fulfill my dreams. I am so blessed to have the friends and family behind me that I do. You constantly empower me to do my best, and I am so grateful for all you do.

Thank you so much!

Contents

Chapter 1
A Life of Torment

"Tell me the truth, Martin. Did you do it?" the man in the tan suit asked me.

It was a good question, but I had no answer for it. I had no answers at all for this man. Yet, he persisted, believing me to be lying. There was no way I could answer his questions. My amnesia had taken that away from me.

Retrograde amnesia. This is what the psychologist had diagnosed. I had lost all my memories. Everything from my childhood to my infamous adulthood was gone. He told me that I may not remember what I had learned, but skills are something that stay with you. Cultural references, understanding of math and science, and even punchlines to jokes could be remembered, but no memory of how they were obtained would remain.

"Look, Martin. I'm your lawyer. You need to have faith in me. I can help you. Anything you tell me stays between us. Do you understand, Martin?" he asked me.

How I wished that I could answer him! I wished that I could know the truth. I just could not remember. What had happened to me? I wanted to know so badly.

"I understand, Mr. Lewis. But as I've told you over and over, I don't remember anything. I cannot tell you one thing that you don't already know. Hell, you know more than I do about what I've done," I answered my attorney.

"That isn't the truth, and you know that. Martin, can you seriously tell me you don't understand the consequences here? They are charging you with horrendous crimes! Destruction of a government facility, participation in an organized crime group, mass-murder! You're going to rot in solitary for the rest of your life if we don't win this! I'm doing all I can to fight off the death penalty here and I need your cooperation if you don't want to die in prison!" Mr. Lewis yelled at me.

Life in solitary. How could I be charged with these crimes? I could not even remember committing these heinous acts. I knew I did not deserve this. Whatever criminal I was before my amnesia, I was not that man anymore. Truly, it made no sense to punish me for that man's crimes.

How could they do this to me?

Mr. Lewis paced around the small, rectangular room. He arrived at the far end of the table from me and turned his back to watch the clock slowly tick. He was waiting for me to confess to him my crime, but I would not. I tapped rhythmically on the polished mahogany table in impatience. We both waited for the other to make the next move.

Mr. Lewis was a tall man with broad shoulders that made him look strong and intimidating. I had no doubt that this had helped him with his career. The man wore a suit well, and his black hair was combed neatly on top of his head. He was put together quite well, and this was what inspired my confidence in him, but I lost confidence in how he refused to believe my story. He was a smart and talented man, but he would not be able to free me.

Time did not move as both of us refused to speak. The stillness and silence of that room could make one wish for chaos and cacophony. The motionlessness was incredibly unsettling. As time stood still, I became more and more eager for Mr. Lewis to yell at me. Any sound would be better than this silence he was using against me.

Finally, Mr. Lewis let out a deep sigh.

"Fine, Mr. Yellog. If you truly wish to remain obstinate in your self-righteous stance, that is fine by me. Just know that I will have to fight much harder in the dark. Please, I beg you, Martin, enlighten me! I want to know what happened to you, too! I can help you. I'm the only one you have to tell," Mr. Lewis pleaded with me.

"I have amnesia. That is what happened to me. Now, you have the whole story," I responded coldly.

"Mr. Yellog, the jury is assembled. Your trial is tomorrow. Since you refused to work with me and take the plea bargain, I have to beat every charge against you if you ever want to leave prison! I can't do that without your help."

"You need help, but I can't give it to you."

He hit the table and stared me down. Shaking his head, his temper cooled. This temper, as well as the need to cool it, appeared to be commonplace to my lawyer. He had to deal with difficult people all the time; it was his job. With difficulty came anger. He had dealt with this anger for a long time and he was starting to devise methods to end it. He and others suffered from his anger and he knew, but he still had a long ways to go before it would be vanquished.

"If you need anything else, Mr. Yellog, don't be afraid to ask," Mr.

Lewis said as he made his way to the door.

"I want my freedom."

He was paused in the open doorway. Another deep sigh escaped him. He shook his head and turned his eyes back to mine. As much as he was frustrated with me, he really wanted to help me. He, too, wanted my freedom and he wanted it badly. This man seemed as if he were an enemy against me, but that was not the truth. He was fighting for my freedom alongside me.

"I will do everything in my power to get you your freedom, Martin. Believe me, I will," he responded and walked out the door.

The door closed behind him, and I was left in the room by myself. The guards would enter soon and take me back to my cell. I stared into the wood of the table. If only I could spend some more time here. I desired to read the many books on the shelves that surrounded the room. That cell was the worst place I had yet experienced. I did not want to return.

That place was where there was no escape from fear. At all times, I was forced to be consumed by the greedy eyes that surrounded my cell. They lusted for my misery. In the cell, I could do nothing to stop them. They were without mercy, and I had no power over them. It was like hell living in that cell.

Sure enough, the door opened, and in walked Troy, a prison guard whom I had learned to respect these days. I had seen him put an end to anything my fellow inmates threw at him. This man was hardened by his job, and it showed. He wore a stern expression at all times, and his body was rigid, never relaxed. This was a man that could not be caught off guard. I made sure to do as he said.

"You have a good talk there, Martin?" he asked me, putting his hand on my shoulder.

"As good of a talk as any, I suppose. What do I know of pleasant conversation?"

"I think you're about to be reminded how nice a conversation you just had. The people where you are going don't behave the same way as Mr. Lewis," Troy responded with a chuckle.

I quickly realized how I had not taken full advantage of my time here. It was already time to return to the horror. How had I let the time slip away from me?

"Please, Troy, give me another minute in this room. Don't make me go back," I pleaded.

"Sorry, but that's a no can do. I didn't take this job to not do it. You're due back in your cell, so that's where we are going."

"30 seconds, please! That is all that I ask of you!"

"Let's go, Martin. Back to your cell," he told me with no emotion.

He unchained me from the table, and off we went towards the certain malfeasance of the detention center. Back through those infamous halls we walked to my misery. Closer and closer, the suffering would soon come. I had to walk straight into it and face my fear.

Prisoners stared me down as we walked by their cells. I saw them licking their lips just at the sight of me. I could see the wheels turning in their heads about how they would torture me today. They sought my anguish and they would have it. They were predators, and I was their prey.

"In you go," Troy said, pushing me into the cage.

He removed my handcuffs and had me move to the back. When I had done so, he closed the door with a bang. He then locked me in there to suffer. Troy walked away from the cell, whistling.

I lay in the bed and tried to forget where I was. If only I had forgotten this part of my life! Only then could I be a happy amnesiac. What joys had I forgotten so that I could learn such suffering? I had thought amnesia to be a curse in totality, but forgetting this place could only be a blessing.

This cell was identical to all the others on this block. There was a bed, two shelves, and a toilet in every cell. The only difference between my cell and the others was that I kept mine considerably cleaner. The beasts in the cages surrounding me did not quite care about sanitary conditions. Their only concern was whom they would stalk today.

A quiet tapping sound could be heard outside my cell. I knew what would happen if I were to glance outside the cage. They were waiting for me out there. They needed me to acknowledge them if they were to have any fun with my torture. I could not grant them even acknowledgment.

The tapping persisted, and I became more and more curious with its origin. It could be as simple as an inmate tapping his finger on a bar of his cage or it could be something else entirely. Whatever it was, I wanted to know. I knew how idiotic it would be to find out the cause of a simple sound and then to suffer the consequences that followed, but I had to look.

My head turned to the bars, and I saw the beast in his cage, rapidly tapping the long fingernails of his first two fingers on the bars of his cell. Upon seeing this, my eyes went to the beast's. I did not mean to do this, but I could not help it. He had seen my acknowledgment, and now my torture would begin. I had been a fool to let my gaze leave this cage.

"Hey, Yeller. Here, Yeller Yeller Yeller. Here, Yeller. Here, boy. Hahaha!" the beast across from me whispered from his personal dungeon.

Yeller was what I had been nicknamed here. They called me that because I had introduced myself as Martin Yellog. That was what the officers had told me my name was during the booking, and I was still getting used to it that day. The nickname came about after the first night when, after being tortured by my stalkers all night, I yelled for help. Yeller was a good cowardly name.

"Yeller, they gonna send ya way from us. I sure hope they don't. I been liking watching you sleep!" the beast taunted.

"My trial is tomorrow. That is when I shall be free from this place. Free from you," I retorted.

Laughter burst from him as well as from the rest of the block.

"Boy, Yeller, you clueless piece of shit! There's a reason you here, boy! They ain't never gonna let you go free. Not somebody like you," the beast laughed.

"I'm innocent. They cannot convict me," I responded, flustered.

"Oh, yeah, right. Hey, everybody, you guys innocent too, right?" he shouted out.

A resounding affirmation came from every cell. Their voices made my legs tremble. The beast glared at me through the bars. His grin was overwhelming. The maliciousness emanating from his cell and every other cell was so apparent. I hated it here.

"You gonna be my bitch for the rest of your life, Yeller. You gonna be all our bitches!" he cried.

The threats from the monsters echoed throughout the block. I closed my eyes and bent over in the bed. I slammed my hands over my ears so I could not hear their tortuous screams. It was to no avail, though. I could not escape the terror that would be my fate for the rest of my life.

Even as the sun set outside my barred window, they continued to cry out. It never ceased as I tried desperately to sleep so that I would have just a little strength to face them tomorrow. It had to be at least 2 am before I finally overcame my insomnia.

Never did the tormenting stop. Even in my dreams, they hunted me. There could be no refuge from the beasts except that of my trial and the meetings with my attorney that came so rarely. There was no safety here and even less in my dreams, where they found passage through the bars so much easier.

The days before my trial drove me to my knees every day. My meal was luckily served in my cell, for I was a dangerous criminal. No contact with the prisoners ever had to be made. This was one horror that I had avoided. The beasts could not harm me in my cell, but they surely tried.

How could human beings be brought down to such depths? These creatures no longer even resembled anything that could support kindness and compassion. They were void of any virtue and they were ever-searching for more vices. By the second week, I could not even look at them. My eyes remained in my cell at all times. I never dared to peek. Yet, when my eyes were forced outside the cell by curiosity, I regretted the decision immediately. There was no humanity outside my cell.

These days would have profound impact on my life. Here, I learned what true, unfiltered evil looked like. For the rest of my life, I could so easily identify it. Even the slightest sign of malice was now obvious to me. At least, the beasts had given me something.

Eventually, I forced myself to watch them. They were curious creatures, and, as much as I was afraid of them, I was interested in their habits. Every action they took appeared to be in the interest of bringing others down. They never sought to raise themselves up, but just to bring the deprecation of their foes. It was strange to me, but perhaps they believed they could not get better.

If they truly thought they were without hope, then I could understand their desire to attack everyone around them. They were so desperate for escape, exactly as I was. I would do anything for escape, and they were doing the same. Only, while I wished to escape this prison, they wished to escape their own inadequacy. Seeing themselves so low, they could only justify it by seeing others as low as they were. If you cannot climb, knock those around you down. This was their mentality.

Was this what made people into these beasts? I was not sure because of my lack of memories, but I believed it to be somewhat true. With no way to reach the top, they had to redefine the top. By bringing the top lower, it appeared as if they were equal with it. Whether or not they knew what they were doing, I believed this was their motivator.

So they fought for freedom as did I. With this frame of reference, I was more easily able to find sympathy and understanding for the beasts. They were as I was. Were we not all human? Still, they treated me so poorly, I could not forgive them without difficulty. We were both searching for freedom, but something told me that they would not find it.

I knew I would not receive my freedom either. I understood that, but I desired an escape so badly that I could not let go of the hope. I knew that freedom was as far away as regaining my memory, but still I hoped and hoped. I needed it, not desired it, needed it.

Chapter 2
An Impossible Task

I woke to the sound of Troy's jingling keys. He stopped outside my cell and began to unlock it.

"Hands to the wall, Martin," he commanded me.

I complied, and then he entered. After he had searched the cell to his liking, I gave him my hands, and he cuffed them. We left this dark place, but were chased out by the voices of the beasts. I so dearly hoped that this would be the last I heard of them.

There was still a chance that I would have to return. It was a small chance, but I feared it all the same. With prisons filling up because of the overwhelming increase in crime and the promise of the reward of a bounty for turning in criminals, my options for prisons were limited. Being that the max-security prisons might be too full, they might decide to send me back here. Truly, a max-security prison would be a hundred times better than my return to this horrendous dungeon. Even locked up in solitude, I could be so much happier. Oh, how I wished that I would not have to come back here!

Outside the detention center, I could breathe once more. All the fear left me, and I was happy again, or at least, as happy as I could be in this prison. I filled my lungs with free air and breathed it out with great satisfaction. It was a good feeling to be out of that place.

Troy walked, whistling, in front of me. I contemplated catching him off guard and attempting escape, but did I have the strength? Who was I to actually escape? Many, many people had attempted this before, and so few had made their way to freedom. Why should I be any different? I had no chance at escape, however much I tried. I was a man just as they.

Troy signed me out at the front desk. When he was done, he gave me a look that I comprehended with no problem. This was the last time he would do anything for me. He grabbed my arm and led me to the outside. Doors were opened for me, and I was pushed into a truck that would transport me to the trial. I was joined by two guards, neither of which looked half as friendly as Troy had been to me.

I gave Troy a slight nod before the doors were closed and he returned to the prison. This man who had protected me inside those cursed walls was now out of my life. Even though he was only a guard and he never showed any emotion to me, I knew that I would miss him. Maybe he was not significant to others, but to me, one with so few memories, he was incredibly significant. He was a good man, and I would miss him.

As the truck made way to the courthouse, I received a thorough covering from the eyes of my companions. They said nothing, but there was no need for words. They understood that I knew what they were doing. That did not matter, though. I was lost in my own thoughts and barely spared a glance for either guard, anyway.

Here I was, possibly on my way to freedom. I would meet with my lawyer, and we would discuss our battle plan for this case. I had nothing to offer to Mr. Lewis; he held all the information. I could not do a single thing to aid him in this case. He would do everything for me. He alone would defend me. I wanted to fight, but I was not the one fighting. Mr. Lewis was.

I knew I could not defend myself in court. I barely understood the court system, and, even with basic understanding, the opposition could still tear you apart. Trial court was a dangerous place and the outcome here would decide the rest of my life. Whether I spent my days behind bars or out in the sunshine was completely reliant on the performance of my lawyer. I was thankful for the support I received from Mr. Lewis.

Mr. Lewis may have been rather hostile towards me, but it was only because he really wanted to help me. Without my cooperation, he would be fighting blind. I wanted to help him, but I could not. He thought me to be lying, but I truly could remember nothing. I felt bad for him, fighting with nothing to support him and his cause. He was a smart man, but I did not believe he was smart enough to win this case alone.

I did not want such a burden on his shoulders, but the court had appointed him to me, and he was a man who wanted to defend those who could not defend themselves. He would gladly take the burden just so he could see me in a better situation. Still, attempting to fight off the charges on me would be the hardest task Mr. Lewis had been assigned. To put it accurately, it was an impossible task. He probably was having a hard time sleeping just thinking about the tremendous responsibility he was given.

Perhaps it would not be all negative for Mr. Lewis. If he won this case, he would be heralded as an exceptional attorney all throughout the country. If he failed, he would be tossed aside and forgotten. Even with loss, there came little damage. With victory came such great rewards. This was definitely a risk Mr. Lewis should take, even with the high possibility of failure.

Would he fail, though? From what he had told me when I spoke to him before, he was incredibly intelligent. Mr. Lewis had been an attorney for almost six years now. He had won almost all of his cases. He knew what he was doing and could handle himself in court with ease. With that experience backing us up, I felt more confident in Mr. Lewis' abilities.

However, my faith was still wavering. I doubted our victory every second. This doubt was crippling and brought down a veil of pessimism over me. I could not see an outcome where I was permitted freedom. I could not see it. Without faith in my success, I only saw failure.

How I hoped I would not fail today! So far, my life had only been disappointment. I woke up on the ground before a building I allegedly destroyed. Immediately, I was thrown in jail by police officers who looked all too happy to throw away my life. I was tossed into a cell that was perpetually under siege by monsters that only wanted to witness suffering. This had been a terrible start to a life for which I had so much hope.

Victory here would only bring about more failure. I thought about where I would go after the trial. My name could not really be cleared of this ordeal. Employers would still see me as that domestic terrorist that somehow got away. Who would ever want to hire that man? Anyone I met would know of my crimes. No one would want to be around me. Everyone would fear me. Even with success, failure was inescapable. Was this the life I would have to live?

I was cursed to this life by my former self. All the evil I had done was now coming back to haunt me. I was forced to endure so much suffering for deeds I could not remember. I felt that it was so unfair, but perhaps it was the most fair outcome. If I was as bad as people kept telling me I was, then losing my memories and being plagued by torment was a fair fate for me. I deserved everything through which I was going.

That was not what I wanted to believe. I hated this life boundlessly and I desired forgiveness with everything I was. I did not want to be that man. I coveted the idea of change. I wanted to be better. If only I could be forgiven for what I had done!

My reflection came to a halt with the truck. The metal doors opened, and I was led out of the truck and into the courthouse. This structure towered above me as we entered through a door in the rear of the building. Inside, the courthouse was very beautiful. Expensive paintings and impressive architecture were the main features I noticed as I entered.

This was a marvelous place.

I walked the marble floors to the room where my lawyer was. I could not wait to hear his plan of attack. I anticipated a brilliantly constructed opening statement accompanied by a genius defense and a witty closing statement. I wanted to know how he would defeat the prosecution in the case of his life. All this was for what I hoped, but doubt was blocking my belief that he would have anything at all.

The door was opened for me, and I entered, no longer with my acquaintances. There sat my court appointed attorney, with dissatisfaction on his face. The look alone sent a chill down my spine and crushed my hopes. My doubt had won.

"Sit down, Mr. Yellog," Mr. Lewis said to me.

I took a seat across from him, and he looked into my eyes with intent.

"I don't know how to tell you this. We are about to lose this case," Mr Lewis told me somberly.

"We sure as hell will if you give up now! Look, I'm innocent! There is no way a jury could convict me. We just have to convince them that I'm telling them the truth!" I argued with my defender.

"There are so many pieces of evidence to convict you with, Mr. Yellog. Surveillance video, eye-witness..."

"That is evidence from another man! I am not he! Convict that man!" I shouted, angry with the injustice of my life.

"Let me finish, Mr. Yellog. There is no hope. Let me repeat that. There is no hope. Okay? We will win this case when hell freezes over. Do you understand?"

"Stop speaking to me as if I were a child! You are a cowardly fool! You know that this case could be won, but not by you. Trust me when I say that we can win this."

"No, Martin, shut up! You know why you're going to spend the rest of your life in jail? Because you won't give me anything to go off of! Because you didn't listen to me when you pleaded 'not guilty' in that hearing! I cannot win this fight without your cooperation, and you know it! Just tell me what happened before we have to go in there in half an hour and you're sentenced to your death!" he yelled, his cool lost due to frustration caused by my stubbornness.

"Why can't you believe me? What is so hard to understand about amnesia? I can't remember anything at all! Do you understand?!"

The door flew open, and the guards entered in alert. They approached me, ready to restrain me at my next move. I did nothing but sit there and stare disappointingly at my lawyer.

"It's okay, gentlemen. Everything is all right here. Please, leave us," said Mr. Lewis, staring back at me, angry.

The guards nodded to Mr. Lewis, but kept me in sight until the door was closed. They knew I was a threat and they took no chances with me. I knew I was not a threat, but my opinion did not seem to matter these days.

"As I was saying, Mr. Yellog, we just can't win. And I want you to know that I *am* sorry. I'm very, very sorry, but I can't save you," he said and fell into his seat.

"I understand. But I will not give up, and you can't either."

"Know that that isn't what I'm telling you. I will fight for you...but I won't win. But if you give me something..."

"Nothing. I can give you nothing. For the last time, I have amnesia."

"Mr. Yellog, I cannot help you any more than I have. I'm sorry. Truly, I am," Mr Lewis sighed.

"I have told you everything I know. I am sorry that you can't believe that. Truly, I am," I responded.

He leaned on the table and closed his eyes to think. His breathing slowed and his heart rate dropped. Mr. Lewis then regained his composure and looked me in the eyes.

"Then...all that is left for us to discuss is what I am going to do in there. Do you wish to hear my defense for you?" Mr. Lewis asked me.

"Sure. Maybe you can inspire me with a little bit of faith in your abilities," I answered sarcastically.

For the remainder of our time left in that room, Mr. Lewis told me everything he planned to do and to say. He informed me of every little detail he could use to help me and of every weakness that the prosecution would use against us. He left out nothing, for he wanted us to be on the same page. Even though he believed I was withholding information from him, he withheld nothing from me.

"...and even after all that, I tell you that I don't think we will win. In fact, I have no confidence whatsoever that we will win. I'm sorry, but that is just the truth. But don't think that I am going to show it out there. They will see a man defending you without a doubt in the world. They will see no fear in my eyes. They will not see me tremble. My words will be solid and no one will see my lack of confidence. That is all I can offer you," spoke my defender.

"For that, I thank you. I, too, have no confidence, but I shall do my best to hide that from them. I cannot give up hope. Please, tell me that you won't either," I said, making an honest request to the man whom I knew I had to trust.

"I cannot stop hoping...for your sake. No, I won't give up hope."

"Thank you. I must apologize for how I have spoken to you. I know you want the best for me. Just understand that this injustice angers me so quickly. I am sorry for how I have responded to your attempts to help me."

"I understand, Mr. Yellog. And don't worry, I've been yelled at by others much angrier than you," he said with a chuckle. "I know the hatred of injustice. It is what fuels me more than anything. I will do all I can for you."

"Thank you, Mr. Lewis. What you are about to do means a lot to me. I probably won't see you anymore after the trial...so...thanks. Thank you for trying," I said, granting a smile to the one for whom I only had anger before.

Before Mr. Lewis could respond to my gratitude, there was a knock on the door. We both knew what it meant. My legs began to tremble, and the fear of what was about to happen became so much more real. Judgment was coming.

The door opened, and a guard entered.

"Martin Yellog?" the guard asked, looking down at a clipboard he held.

I nodded to him to confirm my identity.

"Yes, this is Martin Yellog. And I'm his attorney...Mr. Lewis," my lawyer said to the guard, pointing out his name on the clipboard.

"It is time. Come with me," he told both of us.

I looked to Mr. Lewis for encouragement. I believe he looked at me for the same reason. His face granted me no more courage than I had. I could offer none to him either. Mr. Lewis looked at the guard and then slowly turned back to me.

"Are you ready?" he asked.

"Let's go," I answered, ready to accept my fate.

Chapter 3
Judgment

The guards held my arms and pushed me through the halls towards my judgment. Apart from the two holding me, there were another two in front of me and another two behind. They all were armed, and there was nothing I could do to escape. This judgment would be final.

The doors opened, and we stepped into the courtroom. I was led to Mr. Lewis, who was already sitting at the defense's table. I sat down next to him, and my guards stayed right behind me. Handcuffs locked into place, forcing me to stay in my seat. I was stuck.

I could see the prosecution on the opposite side of the room, staring me down. In fact, it seemed as if every single person in the whole courtroom was looking right at me. It made me very uneasy to have so many eyes on me. Ignominy attracted the attention of so many in this room.

Flashes of light almost blinded me. Photographers captured my image for their newspapers. T.V. cameras sent the live, exclusive footage of inside the courtroom back to their respective news channels. All over the country, people were watching me. Everywhere, people were judging me. Millions upon millions of eyes focused on me. I could not escape.

I searched for an escape, but such a feat was as impossible as Mr. Lewis said winning this case was. Guards were at every single exit, just standing there, waiting. I would not try to run, anyway, especially carrying a chair with me. Even escape from this building would result in nothing besides my execution.

Heavy footsteps announced the presence of the bailiff. He walked out in front of everyone and he stood straight before speaking.

"All rise for the honorable Judge Erdman," said the bailiff.

I stood as did everyone else. In came Judge Erdman. She wore a stern expression, and her solemnity was disheartening. She looked very wise in her black robe, and I could tell that she strove for justice. If she truly did strive for justice, maybe there was a small chance for my freedom.

"You may take your seats, everyone. Good afternoon," Judge Erdman said.

The judge glanced down at the mass of papers before her. She then turned to the bailiff and nodded. The bailiff turned to address the court.

"The charges against Martin Yellog are as follows: one count of mass-murder, one count of destruction of a government building, 16 counts of assault on an officer, 23 counts of assault on an officer with a weapon, and one count of participation in a criminal organization," read the bailiff.

My crimes listed to me, I could feel nothing but shame. While I thought I would never be the kind of person to commit such acts, I was just told I was. I felt trapped by evil. I did not want this. It was forced on me by my previous self. I was angry and ashamed. How could I have done these things to myself? What had made me wish to do such wrong?

As Judge Erdman was preparing the trial, my attention fell from the case. It rested instead on who I was before my amnesia. This evil man had condemned me to be here. While I believed myself to be separate from this evil, perhaps I was not. If I had fallen before, I could fall just the same. I had not been given a new life, but a new perspective. I had a chance to turn from the evil man who had brought me to this place. I was given a chance to change.

Realizing this, I vowed to change. Yes, I was being judged for my past, but that did not mean that I should let the past make me who I did not want to be. I would live for a better future. Whether it be in a cell or in the outside world, I would devote myself to destroying the evil man I was before. My amnesia now appeared as more of a blessing than a curse.

I glanced back up to the judge. She was still addressing the jury, informing them of the rules of the court. Although Judge Erdman spoke with a certain intensity to convey the importance of her words, the jury seemed to not even care. None of them wanted to be here. I could predict the plans of every single one of them. They would go back to their room and immediately decide that I was guilty. That would be the fastest way to end this trial. They would rather throw away my life than waste any more of their precious time here.

Judge Erdman's gaze suddenly returned to me. Instead of what I expected from this judge, judgment, she looked at me with pity. She knew her instructions to the jury had no effect on them. They did not listen because they had already made up their minds. She saw that I was not going to get a fair trial here and she pitied me for it. It was not a good feeling knowing that I was going to lose.

Her eyes then turned away from me. She had to let it begin. It was her job to start this trial, however unjust it was going to be. Her eyes returned to me for a brief second, and then she turned them back to the prosecution.

"You may begin, prosecution," Judge Erdman said with the slightest hint of regret.

"Thank you, Your Honor. I want to start off by showing the jury some of Martin Yellog's handiwork," the prosecution's attorney said, clicking a button in her hand that controlled a slide show that was projected above the judge.

The lights in the courtroom were dimmed, and an image of the burning ruins of some building appeared for all to see. I recognized the picture, for Mr. Lewis had waved it in my face quite a few times. This was the Vaillancourt.

"In this first picture, you can clearly see the rubble of a structure formerly known as the Vaillancourt Hotel. Mr. Yellog along with his accomplice, Tyler Ishler, destroyed this hotel, bringing about the death of every man, woman, and child in it. It is believed that Mr. Yellog and Tyler Ishler accomplished this by planting multiple explosive charges in many different rooms on many different floors," said the prosecution, feigning disgust for my unfathomable actions.

She clicked the button again, and a new slide came up. This time, it was a picture of a very similar scene. This was the hotel formerly owned by a family of four who had built it out of nothing. To me, it was just another flag of infamy.

"In this next slide, you can see the remains of another hotel that was named Shepards and Sheep. Many innocent lives were lost that day. That day it was blown to pieces with no regard for human life. It is believed that they, Mr. Yellog and Tyler Ishler, used the same strategy as with the Vaillancourt to destroy this building and take all those lives."

I heard the click of the button again, and the picture changed. The scene was not too different from the previous two. The smoldering remains of the L.I.F.E. Organization's headquarters was shown to all. Another building I had allegedly destroyed. I was beginning to sense a pattern.

"This next slide shows Mr. Yellog's most recent attack, the L.I.F.E. Organization facility. This facility is used for research into projects that will progress and improve the human race. It is an organization that has saved many lives and enhanced the lives of everyone in this beautiful country. As shown in this slide, it has been crumbled the same as every other building Mr. Yellog has set his sights on. It is unknown if Tyler Ishler had any part in this scheme, but he is now presumed dead. The general consensus is that he died in the same explosion Mr. Yellog used to destroy the facility. Strange how Mr. Yellog managed to escape the blast, though. I wonder why Tyler Ishler was unable to make it out as well," the prosecution said, maliciously attacking my character, but Mr. Lewis remained silent.

The new slide showed me with a group of men that was believed to be in the West City Mafia. It was strange to see a picture of myself taken before I could remember. Even with this evidence against me, I had difficulty believing that I had been in this illegal organization.

"As for his participation in a criminal organization, this picture shows Mr. Yellog with numerous individuals who were known to be in that organization. Mr. Yellog has also assaulted many federal and state officers...with and without a weapon. In conclusion, Mr. Yellog has done terrible things that number so many it is hard to count them. Mass-murder, destruction of a government building, assault on officers with and without a weapon, participation in a criminal organization. These are the charges against the man sitting there in that chair, and we believe he is guilty of all of them. That is what we aim to prove. Thank you."

The prosecution's attorney sat back down and the anxiety was clear on the face of Mr. Lewis, but only to me. The slide show was deactivated, and the lights were thus activated. Judge Erdman nodded at the prosecution and turned her gaze to our bench. I could tell she was curious of what Mr. Lewis was going to say.

"Defense. You may now begin," she said, showing interest even though she knew the jury had none.

Mr. Lewis stood, all signs of nervousness gone. He marched to where the prosecution had stood so confidently and he filled the space with the same level of confidence. He turned to the jury and began.

"Thank you, Your Honor. Now, I don't have anything like a slide show for you today; I don't need it. I can tell you with all honesty that this man is not guilty of what he has been accused. My client is a victim of retrograde amnesia. In layman's terms, he has no recollection of anything that has been shown to you the past few minutes. My client is lacking the most important element of any crime: intent. He is a victim and cannot be held accountable for such crimes that he had no intent to commit. This man in court before you never intended to blow up those buildings or take innocent lives. He couldn't possibly intend to do so because he hasn't even heard of these events until this trial. Martin Yellog is completely innocent, and I'd like you to think long and hard before you even consider throwing an innocent man in jail for the rest of his life. That's all I have to say. Thank you."

Mr. Lewis showed his true abilities that day. He had just given such an excellent defense for my case. My freedom was not yet secured, but I felt a whole lot better about it. Mr. Lewis was on my side, and that was the best advantage I could have.

After that, many witnesses were called upon to testify for and against me. They would either speak of my unfathomable crimes against humanity or they would discuss the injustice of my injury. I was deemed both evil incarnate and helpless victim. I was yelled at and spoken to softly. The two sides of the argument were always so different that they could not possibly be telling the same story. If I could ever learn anything about my past, this place would not be where I would learn it.

I struggled to follow the events of the case, having no understanding of the law or of my actions that had brought this upon me. Overloaded by unknown faces of anger and pity, I found it difficult to even watch as my future was decided before me. Already trapped in a world of unknowns, I was being thrust even further down into the muck of mystery.

There were no witnesses who were recognizable to me, save one. When Officer Nick Turnbull took the stand, I did not fail to pay full attention. This was the man who had brought me in so zealously. He took immense joy to see me finally in position to be crushed by brutal, yet honest, justice. There was no way I could not be interested in what this justice-seeker had to say.

"I do," answered the officer, being sworn in.

He sat down and was then approached by the prosecution. She looked into the eyes of the officer and then quickly turned to the jury. Seeing that all the members were paying full attention, she returned her attention to the man who would condemn me.

"Officer Nick Turnbull, you have a lot of experience dealing with the defendant, do you not?" asked the prosecution.

"Yes, I have had to deal with Martin for the better part of the last three months," answered Nick.

"And during the ordeals brought on by the defendant of those three months, what was your biggest concern? Did you fear he would keep killing? Did you fear his attacks would only become more and more violent? What did you expect Mr. Yellog to do?"

"I expected the worst from him and I never stopped looking for him. I knew that if he was not brought to justice, he would only continue to take innocent lives."

"Now, personally, what kind of conflicts have you had with Mr.

Yellog?"

"I actually had him in a cell once, not too long after the Vaillancourt Incident. I thought it was over, but, somehow, he had influence over those who were above me, those whose judgment I was not allowed to question. They made us release him, but I would not stand for that injustice. I vowed to bring Martin in...whatever the costs. I would not stop fighting to take him down until he was put behind bars for good," Nick said, staring angrily into my eyes. "Sadly, I did not fight hard enough to bring him in...and he returned for vengeance on the police. We still had his friend Tyler Ishler locked up in the station, and Martin wanted him out. So Martin barges into the station and shoots down five other officers and myself, then releases Tyler and escapes. That's when I knew what kind of man Martin Yellog was. That's when I knew that I would have to bring him to justice."

"Mr. Yellog is currently trying to avoid life imprisonment with the defense that he has amnesia. What are your thoughts on that, Officer Turnbull?" the prosecution asked with a grin that knew that I would not escape the judgment that awaited me.

"That man is a liar, and I would not believe a thing he says. He's incredibly smart and a con man of the highest caliber. I have no doubt that he is tricking the psychologists into believing his story and diagnosing him with amnesia. There is no way that is true, and I can only hope that the good men and women of the jury know this. That they are not fooled by him. That would be the greatest injustice of all."

"That's all, Your Honor," the prosecution said to the judge before taking her seat.

Judge Erdman looked over to our bench and nodded at Mr. Lewis. He stood and approached the officer who hated injustice as much as I.

"Officer Turnbull, is it true that you knew Martin before he began his alleged crime-spree?" my attorney asked.

"Um... Yeah, that's true. I knew Martin before I knew anything about what kind of man he was going to be," answered Nick.

"How did this meeting come about?"

"He brought in a mugger who had been at large in Alemande. He had beaten him badly, and the mugger was barely conscious. It was a strange meeting because he looked like he wasn't a day over 18, but he had beaten and captured an infamous criminal. I didn't know what to think about it and I gave him the bounty money, and he left."

"What were your first impressions of Martin?" my lawyer asked, hoping to revive my character by some miracle.

"He seemed like a fellow justice-seeker to me. I thought he was a good guy, but now I know that I was wrong about that. He must have beaten the man for reasons other than justice. That would be much out of character for him."

With that answer, my character was still headed down the drain, but I could see that Mr. Lewis was not yet done. He would give it another try. He had to show the jury that I was not a complete monster.

"Is it not possible, and this question goes out to everyone in this room, that Martin did turn in the mugger for justice? Is it not possible that Martin was a good man who only was violent in the name of justice? Do we not encourage our citizens to make arrests against criminals? Why else would we have enacted laws to award bounty to anyone who could bring in criminals? In this day and age, we are up to our necks in crime. So is it not possible that my client was fighting crime just as Officer Turnbull does? Is it not possible that Martin Yellog is a good man?" Mr. Lewis asked, moving back to address the whole room.

"There is not a doubt in my mind that the answer to all those questions is no, Mr. Lewis. Martin Yellog is not a good man and he deserves death. But I'll settle for him rotting away behind bars for the rest of his miserable life," answered Officer Turnbull.

Applause sounded from the jury box and only grew louder and louder as the whole room joined in. There was no way we would win. Every single person in this courtroom was dead set against me. As the applause grew even louder and Mr. Lewis motioned to Judge Erdman that his cross-examination was done, I knew that it was all over. He sat next to me with sorrowful eyes. He had failed, and we had reached the end. It was time for my judgment.

The time between the jury being released and the jury returning was even faster than I had predicted. The foreman took up his spot and announced that I was to be rotting away in a cell for the rest of my life. I could see the smiling faces behind the foreman, ready to be done with this case after only several hours. They had judged me and were done with me. It was time for them to get back to their much more important lives.

Judge Erdman accepted the verdict, and her mallet slammed down. The sound of it almost killed me. That whack filled me with doubt and fear so quickly, I could not stand when prompted to by my guards. They lifted me from the chair and began to carry me out of the courtroom. I was being dragged to my doom.

I looked at Mr. Lewis before they had pulled me too far away. His eyes were sorrowful and full of apology. He was so sorry. I just shook my head. It was not his fault; it was mine. I was receiving due payment for my evil. I was doomed from the start.

As the guards pulled me through the doors, the applause from the courtroom began to fade away. All of it began to fade away. Just as they were fading, so would I fade from their minds. They had judged me and they were finished with me. In their eyes, I was worth nothing but cheap entertainment. I was only there so they could condemn me as evil. They used me to see themselves as better. At least, we are not as evil as that man, they would think. They were so wrong.

The doors closed, and all of it faded away.

Chapter 4
Life in Prison

They marched me off to the truck once again. This time, I would meet my sentence. They would lock me away for the rest of my life for everything I had done in the past. Punished for evils forgotten.

I was once again pushed into that truck with the ever-watching guards, and all I could do was wait. I contemplated escape, but how? There was no way I could fight back against such force. I was just a man, and one man could not defeat such adversaries.

The one thing that was able to bring me joy in this low time was the conversation I heard between the driver of the truck and an official from the courthouse. The official had instructed the driver to take me to a federal prison that was about an hour away. This was a new prison. From my current perspective, it would be a better prison than what I had suffered before.

I was glad to hear that I would not be returning to my previous prison. That news alone brought a smile to my face. There were still many things that could go wrong, but I knew they would be different challenges. At the very least, I would receive new tests and not suffer through the previous ones.

Yes, I could not be sure what awaited me. I fully doubted that it would be a pleasant experience, but I could make good out of it. I would be forced to find at least a little good if I was to survive there. I had to make the most out of every bit of good I could find. This was my game plan as I sat in the back of the truck that would take me to my new permanent home.

When I finally arrived in the federal prison, I was sent through such trials that no one should have to endure. An extremely thorough and invasive search was where it started. Next, I was given my bright orange suit that I would wear for the rest of my life. I was pushed into my designated cell, and the door was slammed shut.

I, fortunately, had no cellmate. I was deemed too dangerous, and they feared I would kill anyone trapped in a small space with me. This was entirely untrue, but no one cared to listen to what I had to say, anyway. Another pleasant part of this cell was that it faced a balcony that overlooked the lower levels of cells. These cells did not have another cell directly across from them. This spared me one torturous detail that I had combated before my trial. I was happy to live alone.

If only I truly was alone. Again, I was surrounded by the vile beasts with which I had suffered in my past prison. These ones, though, were completely different animals. Instead of being all threats and obscenities, these were just aching for that chance to snap your bones. Anything they could do to you was worth any amount of punishment. All for which they lived was my suffering.

Every day, I had to walk with them. I feared for my life not every minute, but every second. I felt their eyes on me, waiting for their chance. If only they were slightly closer, surely they could snap that flimsy neck of mine. But then, where would be the fun in that? Of course, there would be more to torment, but would any ever be as good as Martin? These thoughts were all that I believed went through their heads and kept me alive another day.

I had few actual friends here. One resided in a cell right above mine on the fourth level. He was a large and fat man who seemed a bit off. His name was Griffin, but that was not what the beasts called him. To them, he was Blood Tooth. Why was he called that? He was named that because he killed his wife and drank her blood. He told me himself as he was introducing himself.

"The grub is crap here. Isn't it?" he had asked me while we stood in line to receive our food.

"Yeah, there's absolutely no taste to it. It's bland and dry," I responded as a pile of beans was slopped onto my tray.

"Exactly. I, too, prefer my food with a little more...flavor," he said.

"I'm Martin by the way," I said, looking back.

"Griffin," he motioned to himself, "but you can call me Blood Tooth."

"Why?" It was a fair question to ask.

"Because I just love that feeling when it flows between my teeth."

"It? Do you mean blood?"

"Of course, I do, Martin. Specifically, my wife's."

"I'm guessing that's why you're here."

"I'm here because of what I did to her boyfriend. They never found out what I did to her."

"Sounds like she deserved it," I said as I took my usual seat in the cafeteria.

"I'm no animal, Martin. I know what I did was wrong. But that doesn't mean I didn't enjoy it," he replied and dropped himself into the seat across from me.

"If you're truly not an animal, does that mean I can trust you?"

"Nope," he responded bluntly. "But you have to choose someone to trust in here, Martin. You'll not make it far without some kind of friend."

"Will you be my friend?"

"What's this?! Kindergarten?" he burst out laughing, way too loudly.

"Shut up! You know what I meant!" I growled in a whisper.

He did not seem to like being told what to do. I saw a sudden flare of rage enter his eyes. His huge hand launched at my throat and squeezed tight. In shock, I pulled away, and he lost his grip. He tumbled out of his seat and onto the floor. Guards directed their vision to me and readied a response. All Griffin did was chuckle.

"That's a pretty slippery neck you got there, Martin. What you doing oiling up your neck like that?" he chuckled from the floor.

"Goodbye, Griffin," I said as I took one more bite of food and got up from the table. I left Blood Tooth laughing on the floor.

Another friend of mine was named Hailie. She, obviously not a prisoner because she was a woman, was a guard whom I saw a lot. She passed my cell every day, making sure I was in there. Whenever I saw her, I noted that solemn look in her green eyes. After a month of her silently passing by my bars, she decided to speak to me.

"What are you doing in there?" she questioned me.

Totally absorbed in the book, I barely heard her question. "Um... Reading," I responded, holding up my book and shifting my position on the bed so that I could talk to her.

"You're the only one I see who consistently has a book. What's that one your reading?" she asked, pointing to the book.

"It's called *The Lost Flock*. I've been reading it for the past couple days. It's a pretty good book if you want my opinion."

"I didn't come here for your opinion on the book. I wanted some information on the Book Man. And specifically on the guy they call 'Mr. Finder'."

"By Book Man, I assume you mean the guy passing out books each night. And if that is the case, I have told you everything I know about him. As for 'Mr. Finder', I have no clue who that is."

"How could you know even less than I do? You must be lying."

"I tell you the truth. I do not know Mr. Finder."

"Regardless, I need you to ask the Book Man about Mr. Finder for me."

"Why? Why can't you do it?" I said, taking interest and setting my book on the bed.

"I'm just a guard. He'd never talk to me. But you're a prisoner. He will definitely listen to you."

She was getting impatient. She was not allowed to talk to prisoners like this. If anyone saw her, she would be in big trouble. "What's in it for me?" I asked.

"It can always help to have someone with more authority than you as a friend. Keep that in mind. I have to go. I'll be back here tomorrow."

She walked quickly away, continuing her route. She wanted me to talk to the Book Man for her. This was something that would be one easy task in this difficult place. Even if I received no reward from completing this task for her, it would be worth it. I needed something on which to focus.

The Book Man was a lucky prisoner who was allowed access to all the books in the prison's library. With this privilege came the job of passing every cell, asking if one of us wanted to borrow from his humungous collection. Apparently, he knew Mr. Finder. Through the Book Man, I would make contact with Mr. Finder for Hailie.

That night, the Book Man passed my cell. I heard that same squeaking that I heard every night as he approached. His cart passed, and I whistled for him, as was the norm.

"Yes? What is it you wish to borrow?" the old man said, barely above a whisper.

"I need information on Mr. Finder," I said much louder than he had been speaking.

Sudden shock and anxiety filled the old man's eyes. He came much closer, almost pushing his head through the bars.

"Shh! What do you think you're doing?" he asked me, quietly and angrily.

I apologetically shrugged my shoulders, and he grumbled something that I could not hear.

"Here, take this," he said, throwing a book to the floor of my cell.

"What's this? *What Lives In The Mountain*? What does this have to do with anything?"

"It's an appointment. Be there. And next time, ask for the finder. It's a little less suspicious," the Book Man said and then began pushing his cart down the walkway again.

Opening the book, I found a note.

It read, "Cafeteria, R1, C2. 11:30. Tomorrow."

This was my appointment with Mr. Finder. Was it mine, though? Or was it the guard's? I decided that it could be dangerous to go to this meeting without understanding into what I was walking. I would wait for the guard to pass by the bars of my cell tomorrow.

The next day, I skipped my appointment. I elected instead to traverse the yard, even though that was the one place I had avoided in fear of attack ever since my very first day. I feared this Mr. Finder and I refused to even risk being seen by him. I waited patiently; I knew she would come.

It was about 6 o'clock in the evening. Lying in my bed, I heard the quickened footsteps heading in my direction. She stopped right at the door to my cell.

"Did you see him?" she asked.

"No, but I have this," I said, handing her the note through the bars.

She read it. Her fists clenched with anger. She tore up the note and threw the pieces into my cell.

"The meeting was today! Why didn't you go? Everything could be ruined now! I can't wait any longer. I need you to help me!" she cried, but she did so very quietly.

"I don't know what to ask for. What is it you need?"

"I need...I need... I don't want to tell you."

"I cannot help you without knowing what I am to ask for. What is it you need?"

She sighed. She knew that my help was completely imperative. She looked me in the eyes to answer.

"Heroin. I need you to get me heroin. I only need ten grams. I will pay whatever it takes. He can get it for me, and I need it."

"Heroin?! Why would you expect me to help you get heroin? Ask another inmate for help with your addiction. There is no way I'm getting that for you."

She fell to her knees and sobbed against the bars. Such behavior showed true desperation. To even get within a foot of the bars could result in a guard's death. Her hair was inside my cell.

"Stop before someone sees you. Stop! You have to get up!" I attempted to persuade her.

"You can't help me. It's over. You are the one prisoner I've seen who might actually help me. You have refused, and now he will surely die."

"Die? What are you talking about?"

"A gang has been terrorizing my father for weeks. They say he took some drugs from them when he didn't. They kidnapped him two days ago and are demanding I return what he stole. They say it was ten grams, but I'm not sure why they would kidnap him for such a small amount."

I realized to what she had been brought. Her only chance to save her father was to have heroin smuggled into the prison, just so she could smuggle it back out. Mr. Finder must be quite skilled for such a thing to happen.

"I...can help you. And if I truly am the only one to whom you can go, then I don't know how I could turn you away. You have my help."

She looked up into my eyes. Pure joy shined from her face.

"Thank you! You cannot understand how much this means to me. Thank you so much!" she said, standing once more.

"I shall arrange a second meeting. You can count on me."

"Thank you, thank you! But there is still a price to be paid for such help. I will make sure you are rewarded for this."

"There is no need. I understand your trouble. Your father's rescue will be my reward."

"You are too kind to be what they say you are. I don't understand. How could you be so evil yet so compassionate?"

"I'm not what they say. Everything they tell you is a lie! I'm not that man! At least...not anymore."

"I understand. At tomorrow's meeting, tell Mr. Finder that he will be paid out of Hailie's locker. Tell him I expect the drugs to be put in there as well."

"I shall. Now, you must go. You have been here way too long."

"Thank you...Martin."

She returned to her route as quickly as she could without raising suspicion. There she went, the one I could save. Maybe I could slowly regain my lost glory. Whoever this man from before my memory was, he had taken my good name. I could redeem myself and I would.

Hours I waited only so I could have another chance to meet the mysterious Mr. Finder. The Book Man, why did he have to pass by so late in the day? When would I hear that horrible squeaking wheel of his book-crammed cart? I do not think I had ever wanted to hear such an obnoxious sound so much in my life.

As the sun set outside my barred window, that squeaking wheel was heard. How the seconds felt like hours as he approached! I whistled as soon as I could see the worn front of the cart he pushed. He came to a halt, looked in, and knew exactly what I wanted. He threw in a book.

"Don't skip out this time. Or else," the Book Man said and pushed his cart away.

I opened the book and shook it out to find my note. The tiny piece of paper fell to the ground and only remained for fractions of a second, for I snatched it up so eagerly.

It read, "Cafeteria, R2, C6. 12:00. Tomorrow."

Here was my chance. Mr. Finder, I would meet him tomorrow. With his help, I would save Hailie's father and perhaps redeem myself somewhat. All would occur tomorrow. Tomorrow, I would pursue my redemption.

Chapter 5
Mr. Finder

As night came and passed, I waited. This was not eager waiting, but was instead fearful waiting. Mr. Finder was a dangerous man. This man smuggled for his living. Weapons, drugs, pornography, food, alcohol, and anything you could want. It was yours...for a price. This man, the power he possessed was incredible! I did not joyfully await his presence; I was terrified in anticipation of it.

For breakfast, I ate a good meal of toast and sat far away from where I was scheduled to meet Mr. Finder. Even though my appointment was not until lunch, I feared seeing him here. I only ate because I needed the food for energy. I choked down the toast as quickly as I could and then went out into the yard where I spent the rest of the breakfast period.

Lunch, its approach felt as if it stalked me throughout my cell. All I could do was stare into its eyes and accept my fate. Here it came, so close. It would overtake me, and I could do nothing.

I knew nothing of how Mr. Finder would act in my presence. Knowing what little I did about him, I felt as if he would demand my highest respect and obedience. Since I had skipped our previous meeting, I had already denied him to what he felt entitled. I felt as if he was going to be angry, but I could not be sure. I did not know what was going to happen. That was what scared me more than anything.

Currently, I was facing a specific type of fear. It was fear of the unknown. This fear has to be the most common type of fear. We as humans desire to know everything, and a lack of knowledge puts us on edge. We seek power over our circumstances. We seek control. If we do not understand what we are about to face, we fear it. I was overcome by this very fear.

When that buzzing sounded the arrival of the dreaded lunch, I froze. As the cell doors opened and the other inmates stepped out into line, I remained in the cell. My mind was telling my legs to move, but my legs were surely not moving at all. I could not rise to meet my fate.

"Cell 108! Step into line!" yelled a guard.

All the inmates looked at my door, waiting as I had waited so long. Now that my patience was done being exercised, I was not ready. Mr.

Finder could mean my death. I did not know into what I was stepping. This line led straight to his presence.

I could go to the yard instead, but I had dodged him once already. Another dodge would chisel my name in a tombstone much faster than the meeting would. I had to face him. I had to do this for Hailie.

"108! Step into line! Now!" the yell came again.

Seizing whatever courage I had inside me, I rose from my bed and stepped out.

"I'm sorry. I was asleep," I answered the guard sheepishly.

He grunted angrily at me, but said nothing. The line moved, and I came closer and closer to Mr. Finder. To the cafeteria, where everything would change.

As we marched the halls under heavy supervision, I did not fear my inmates to my front and back. I could not have even pondered what evil thoughts ran through their heads at this very moment. I was too afraid to think about such minuscule and unimportant things. My thoughts were plastered on that table in the cafeteria. On one man, Mr. Finder.

The swinging doors to the cafeteria opened, and the line entered. I had the option to separate as soon as we entered, but I would have been seen by then. I had to accept that there was only one option. I had to go forth and face my fear. Here it was at last, my fate.

I entered the bustling room that smelled of beans and something horrible that was indistinguishable. My eyes failed me as I tried to force myself to look at the table. My head moved so slowly that I almost had to physically force its direction. Eventually, my eyes were set upon the table.

There he was at row number two, column number six. He was alone. In fact, there was no one at any of the adjacent tables. I approached him without even going through the line to get food. I knew how important this was and how I could not put it off any longer. I sat down with every ounce of courage in my body.

Mr. Finder was a strange sight in this dungeon in which I resided. He was incredibly clean. There was not a hair out of place on his head and not a single hair on his face. A gold watch glistened on his wrist. His sophistication was only fought by one aspect of his person: the orange jumpsuit. While the rest of him seemed so elegant and terribly upright, the jumpsuit brought him down a level and stole his overwhelming atmosphere of importance. In it, he almost appeared to be a normal prisoner the same as myself.

"Are you the man from 108?" Mr. Finder asked me, keeping his eyes to the table the whole time.

"Yes, I am. I believe we have something to discuss," I said slowly, close to stammering on every syllable.

"Indeed, we do. But first, a question. What..." he said, immediately stopping after looking up.

Now, the awe of his power faded completely. He stared at me in bewilderment. Mr. Finder was struck speechless. His posture suddenly took another shape. It formed to one that honored my presence. What was happening?

"Martin? Boss, is that you?" Mr. Finder whispered, awe-struck.

"Boss? What do you mean? I'm Martin, but... Do I know you?" I responded, confused.

"Boss, it's me. It's Brandon. My god, I haven't seen you since the Vaillancourt! You look so old!"

"I don't know who you are. Vaillancourt? What's going on?"

"How can't you remember me? The mafia. I was one of your soldiers."

"I don't remember the mafia. I don't remember any of that! I have amnesia... I'm sorry."

"What?! Amnesia? Boss, I apologize. I didn't know! Whatever you want, it's yours. With Don Sanzano gone, you're next in charge. I work for you!"

Mr. Finder, the man upon whom I had feared to even look, had just offered his absolute servitude to me. I had been in such terror to meet him, and here he was, not my enemy but my employee. What just happened? Whatever it was, it was good. Very good.

"Tell me about the mafia. That is your first order," I commanded Brandon.

"Okay, where do I start? You joined in the summer of 2013. The head of the West City Mafia, Keir Sanzano, wanted you after you had killed three armed men in a subway train. He released you from the prison, and you quickly jumped up the ranks. You were as high as the boss after your first day!"

My charges were correct. I truly did participate in a criminal organization. I had thought that maybe these accusations had been false, but I was wrong. I had led men to crime, but perhaps I did not commit these acts myself.

"What kinds of crimes did I commit?" I asked.

"You did it all. Bank robbery, vandalism, murder, drug trafficking, all kinds of stuff. You even led us into battle against a rival gang. And you were the one that killed the most of them. I was amazed. You were awesome! A killing machine!"

A killing machine. That was what I was. It really was true. Charges of mass-murder had condemned me justifiably. I deserved all the punishment I had been given. I was as evil as I had feared. How could I have taken part in such atrocities? I did not know the answer to that question, but I had another answer. I would never be that man again.

"And that brings us to the Vaillancourt Incident," Brandon continued.

"Yeah. What happened? What happened to the Vaillancourt?"

"The Vaillancourt was a luxury hotel that was in the heart of West City. After you had been in the mafia for a good while, we attacked the rival gang I spoke of. They were the Pirates and they controlled the second largest part of the city. We had the first largest and, to have the whole city, we needed their part. So we killed them. But as we celebrated their defeat in the Vaillancourt, some stragglers came to the hotel, planted bombs, and blew the place up! Luckily, I had gone out to take a smoke and was a few blocks down when it exploded. The mafia was destroyed in a fell swoop! I was out of the job, and the police force was beefed up to take back the city from crime. They found me not two days later and put me in here. I've been waiting ever since," Brandon told me.

It seemed that the accusations that I had blown up the Vaillancourt were false. A rival gang had destroyed the hotel. Yet, it was all blamed on me. Knowing that I was one of the only people to survive the blast, it made sense to be suspicious of me, but they had gone too far to come to the conclusion that I had actually blown it up. As it turned out, I was just as lucky as anyone else who had survived.

"So the Pirates won in the end. But I'm alive today. How did I survive?" I imposed.

"That's exactly what I was going to ask you. I saw a news report not too long after the Vaillancourt Incident that said you guys were alive and on the run. I couldn't believe it!"

"Wait. Guys? Who else do you mean?"

"You and Little Ty. They had the T.V. on in the prison when I was captured and they gave an alert to watch out for you guys. That's how I knew that you had to be alive. But I never expected you to come here. I didn't think you guys could ever be caught by the police. You guys were good."

I guessed that this Little Ty was actually Tyler Ishler. It made sense because the bombing had been blamed on both Tyler Ishler and me. Since Little Ty had escaped with me, it was quite probable that he was Tyler. Aside from those facts, their names were very similar. I was not entirely sure, but I believed myself to be correct.

"Tell me who Little Ty is."

"Little Ty was in the mafia when I joined. He was just about ten years old then, though. He was practically raised by the mafia. He was one of the highest ranked right beside you. And he was one crazy freak! I'll tell you that much. I never knew if he was actually insane or not!"

"Little Ty was just a nickname, right? What was his real name?"

"Little Ty? I only knew this from the news report, but his real name was Tyler Ishler."

Little Ty was indeed Tyler Ishler. This was the man who had allegedly helped me to destroy the government facility and hotels. Somehow, this had led to my amnesia. I could not be sure, but it was possible it also had led to Tyler's death.

"Do you have any more information for me?" I asked.

"Nothing. I mean, all you have to do is ask me another question, Boss. I will try to answer to the best of my ability."

Here was my salvation before me. This powerful man was willing to give me any and all information of my past. Through him, perhaps I could recover from this amnesia. I could learn all about who I used to be. All I had to do was seek this info. All I had to do was ask, and it would be given to me.

"What kind of person was I?" I questioned.

"I didn't really know you when you first joined. To me, you were just another recruit. But after your first real job, the robbery of the largest bank in West City, you established yourself throughout the entire organization. Every single member knew your name."

Brandon paused and remembered. He chuckled almost in disbelief. He shook his head and looked back to me. He had a respectful and admiring smile on his face.

"You asked me what kind of person you were. You were the craziest thing I have ever seen. Fantastically strong, incredibly smart, and more fierce than a wild beast. Yet, you were so merciful. You spared lives whenever possible. Don Sanzano said you left them alive to spread your reputation and bring fear to every home in the city, but I knew better. You could have killed them all so easily...but you rarely did. You killed only when it was completely necessary. A merciful master. That's what kind of person you were."

I had been told by the guards, the police officers, the judge, the witnesses, and even my own lawyer that I was a cold-blooded killer. Here, I was told that I was merciful. I was a killer, but I did not thirst for blood. My opinion of myself rose.

"You said that the report on T.V. said that Tyler Ishler and I were together. Why would that be? Did he and I have a good relationship?"

"You and Little Ty were quite close. You and him as well as Mr. T were all caporegimes. You were equally second under the don. So, yes..."

"Who was this Mr. T? You have not mentioned him before," I cut him off.

"Mr. T was an older guy that was tough as nails. I think he was about sixty or something, and he still fought every chance he got. He loved where he was in life. I know he enjoyed every day that was spent in crime beside you, Boss. You guys were very close, too."

It seemed as if I had a good life in the mafia. I had a great influence on it, and it on me. The mafia had strengthened me. However bad my actions in the mafia were, they had fortunately helped me to learn and go further in life. Another question came to mind as I pondered my time in the mob.

"How long was I in the mafia?"

"You joined around June of 2013...and the Vaillancourt Incident was sometime around...uh...sometime around May of 2014. So you were in the mafia about eleven months."

Eleven months? I was only in the mafia for eleven months? Brandon also had said I was a killer from the moment I first joined. What made me so strong before?

"Why was I so strong before I joined? Did I have some kind of prior training with this kind of thing? Was I in another gang or something?"

"No. Absolutely no gang affiliations or anything like that. Don Sanzano did extremely thorough background checks on anyone who had any connections to his organization. There is no way you were in another gang before you joined."

"Did Don Sanzano tell you anything about what I did before the mafia?"

"All he told me was about how you killed three men in the subway and seriously beat up people in the Vaillancourt's Fight Arena. He did tell me about a fight you lost in the Fight Arena as well, but he didn't seem to care about that at all."

"Tell me about the Fight Arena."

"All right. The owner of the Vaillancourt, Miles Vaillancourt, was a strange kind of fellow. I guess that's what helped him launch his hotel into such great success. But, anyway... Miles liked to watch fighting. So he had an arena built in the center of his hotel. Each day, audience members would get their chance to fight the Vaillancourt's hired fighter. If they won, they received 500 dollars and a free stay in the hotel for a week. That was quite the prize because the cost of a night at the hotel was somewhere in the area of 2,000 bucks a night! And those were the cheapest rooms!"

"That's horribly expensive. Why did anyone stay there?"

"Luxury sells, Boss," he said, tapping the gold watch on his wrist with his finger. "Rich people are always searching for the next bit of luxury they can partake in. I guess that's why we liked it so much."

"We stayed there? Why?"

"We had a strangle-hold on Miles, and he could do nothing to stop us from staying there and doing whatever we pleased."

This group of which I was a part surely was extremely powerful. We did what we pleased and killed anyone who stood in our way. The bond of brotherhood had made us so many times stronger than any force we ever faced. To think that it was all ended with a single bombing.

"What about the fights you mentioned? You said I seriously beat some people up. And that I lost a fight. What was that about?"

"From what I gathered from the don, you worked for Miles Vaillancourt right before you joined the mafia. You were the hired fighter. The don said something about how quickly your fights ended the first night. Many sudden, vicious attacks is what he recalled. But the next night, you fought much longer than usual...and only once. Someone named Jack Lamb fought you and beat you quite severely. So much so that the don actually approached Jack first! But the guy turned him down and, as the don put it, 'would not join without a fight.' So Don Sanzano forgot about him and found you the next day. I think he was kind of pleased that you lost, actually. He did not want to be turned down again and he knew you were in a difficult place after losing your job. You were ripe for the picking."

"So I lost a fight and lost my job? From what you've said about me, this Jack Lamb must have been an extremely strong guy."

"The don didn't say much about him, but that's what I think. Anyone would have to be to beat you in a fight," Mr. Finder chuckled.

"Oh! And I killed three men in a subway?"

"Yes, that's what I was told. Keir wasn't there himself, but the police report and eyewitness statements all said that you attacked the men with no provocation. I don't believe that for a second, but that's what I was told. Make of it what you will, but I couldn't ever see you killing three random guys on a train for no reason."

"Exactly. Why would I..." I started to say, but was interrupted by a loud buzzing.

It was the bell informing us that the lunch period was over. We were to line-up and then be led to our cells until dinner. I did not want to leave this place. I did not want to leave Mr. Finder and his answers.

"Crap! You have to meet me here for dinner. I need to discuss something with you," I said frantically as we both stood and moved towards the line.

"Of course, Boss. I'll be here. Whatever you need is yours," Brandon responded.

We took our places in line, and the line moved forward, back to our designated cells. I had run out of time to ask for the heroin this time, but I had another chance in several hours. I could not fail Hailie and her father. At least, I knew that Mr. Finder would cooperate with me.

I entered my cell and sat down on the bed. The cell door slid closed and locked. I was stuck here until dinner. How could I wait? Brandon was the most influential aspect in my life right now. He held the keys to my past and would unlock the door to the forgotten truth.

Another meeting awaited me. This one I was eager for and wanted it to approach as quickly as possible. With it would come further understanding and the fulfillment of a promise I had made. I lay on the bed and stared at the ceiling, waiting.

Chapter 6
The Three Friends

That annoying buzz could not have come sooner. My cell door opened, and I eagerly stepped out. I stood at attention, perfectly upright at my place in line.

"Glad to see some cooperation this time, 108," said the guard who had accosted me for my tardiness this afternoon.

I nodded to him, but he did not see because he had turned to the guard next to him to say something. The other prisoners took their places as well, and the guard's eyes darted through us. He said something else to the other guard, and then we started moving towards the cafeteria. I would get the opportunity to learn about my past once again.

This slow march varied much from the one I took this afternoon. Deep hesitation was replaced with overwhelming impatience. I wanted to ask if we could speed up a bit, but I knew that would be a stupid thing to do. Both the guards and prisoners would be annoyed by such a request. I pushed the idea out of my mind. Not that my mind was then unoccupied. All I could think about, aside from how slow the line was moving, was what I would say to Brandon.

When the doors swung open once more, the anticipation was almost a deathblow. Brandon would be right where he was last time, waiting for his boss. I would go to his table, and he would welcome me as his superior. This powerful man would reintroduce me to my memory, and I would learn the truth. How lucky had I been to stumble upon this man! Now, I would meet him again, my fate.

Entering, my eyes could not have hit him sooner. There he was, just the same as he was during lunch. He looked down at the table intensely, refusing any kind of eye contact with any person. Emotionless and motionless, he emanated a presence of control, and I was the one who controlled him! I practically ran to the table.

"Hello, Mr. Finder."

"It's not good to starve yourself, Boss. Go ahead and grab some food. There is no doubt in my mind that you have to be hungry. I can wait," he said, looking up into my eyes.

"Uh... All right then. You're probably right. I do need to eat. Thanks."

I joined the dinner line as fast as I could. This line moved exceptionally slowly, especially because Brandon was within my line of sight now. As the beans fell to the tray at the end of the line, I thanked the cook. I spun around and made my way to the table.

I slammed down my tray and jumped into the seat. With great anticipation, I stared at Brandon and waited for him to address me.

"You seem rather anxious, Boss. Anything wrong?" Brandon said to me, looking up.

"I'm fine. Tell me about Don Sanzano."

"Didn't you have something you had to tell me?"

"Just tell me about the don."

He sighed and looked down. His eyes remained fixed on the table for a second, but then rose to meet mine again.

"I guess I'll start where he started. Keir Sanzano became the don in the spring of '95. His father started the mafia his own 23rd birthday, so on Keir's, he gave it up to him. Since Keir inherited his father's organization, he didn't really have to do too much work. Everything was already set up for him. Now, that doesn't mean he was a bad leader...because he wasn't. He was fantastic. When he recruited me, I was terrified of him. And that was good. I wouldn't have joined him otherwise! But what I did for him helped him to launch his empire so that he controlled half of the city within four years. I was in charge of import and export for the mafia and, man...did I supply that man with enough weapons to conquer any city he wanted! He was a frightening man to tell you the truth. So much wealth and power in one man. It was pretty scary."

"So you controlled import and export. No wonder you're Mr. Finder in here."

"Exactly. I have so many contacts who are still loyal to me and are connected to this prison. That was just luck. But because of it, I can get whatever I want in here."

"Then, why don't you escape? You have all the tools. It wouldn't be too difficult."

"No offense, Boss, but you've never broken out of prison. Even when you're outside the walls, they will still be looking for you. No way I'm doing that. That's not the life for me."

Brandon painted such a bleak picture for something as beautiful as escape. It seemed so fruitless to even contemplate an attempt of escape, but could I really spend the rest of my life here? I knew I did not want to; who would? There sadly was not another option for leaving this place.

They would never let me out willingly. With no options, I would remain here until I died.

With Brandon on my side, though, maybe life could be better than I imagined. He could get anything I wanted in here. That assured me safety. I was practically a rich man in this prison with the help of Mr. Finder. Having him below me gave me power. His ability could lead to a better life for me with life imprisonment.

I could rise to the highest ranks of this prison as I had done in the mafia. I could make something for myself here, but was a life here, even a good life, really better than what I could experience on the outside. With my life, maybe it was better to stay confined. Outside the walls, it was not as beautiful a picture as I had painted.

Then, I remembered. "That thing I needed to talk to you about. I need your skill to help me out a little bit. It's just a small favor."

"Whatever you need, I can get it, Boss," Brandon said, perking up.

"I need you to get me heroin."

"That will be very simple and will only take until tomorrow. But I never imagined you to be the hardcore drug type. Seems kinda out of character for you," he said, genuinely surprised.

"That's the thing. It's not for me. It's for a guard who works here."

He seemed shocked. Brandon glanced around himself. His head lowered, and I mimicked the movement. His gaze met mine, and he did not seem happy.

"Why would you work with them? Are they threatening you? Or is it a bribe?" he whispered.

"Neither. The guard needs it for her father. If she doesn't get it soon, a gang might kill him."

"She? Now, I see the motivation," he chuckled.

"It's not like that either. I just want to help her. I...I...want to redeem myself for everything I've done."

Brandon leaned back as did I. I saw the wheels turning in his head. It would be easy to get the drugs, but there was hesitation in helping any person who had kept him trapped in here. I saw that hesitation, but it did not matter, for I was his boss. He owed it to me.

"How much?" Brandon asked me, ditching his reluctance.

"Ten grams. It's a small amount. I don't think it will be any problem for you. But you need to have it delivered to Hailie's locker. She said that payment would be in there for you as well," I answered, trying to make the job seem worthwhile for him.

"That is a small amount. But it still comes at a price. Do you know what she's paying me in?"

"I have no clue, but I'm sure it will be worth the effort."

"Of course, it will be. I would do it for nothing if you just asked me. But the reward is to be given, and I will receive it."

"Thank you. When will it be done?"

"Tomorrow. I can have it done by dinner of tomorrow."

"I shall make sure to tell her. I'm meeting her tonight," I said, finally taking a bite of my food.

Brandon nodded and ate with me. I could see that he knew he was doing the right thing by helping this guard, but his animosity towards the guards made it difficult for him. It was a challenge to help those whom he believed brought such weight down on his shoulders, but he would do it. He would do it for me.

We ate the rest of the food before the bell buzzed and we lined up to return to confinement. I did not bring up anything more of the past, and neither did he. I had a lot about which to think. Namely, what I would say to Hailie now that she would get what she needed. I was very glad that I was going to be able to give her good news.

The door slammed and locked, and I was stuck once again. I had about an hour until she showed up here again. I could not wait. Some people wish they had more time in life, but I felt like less would be mercy for me. All my time spent in this cramped cell was spent waiting. What torture it was! I had to pay for my crimes somehow, I guess.

I suddenly heard a clanking coming from above me. I moved to the bars to look for the source of the noise. A can with a string tied to it appeared from the balcony above me. It lowered slowly until it was at my eye-level. It then started swinging back and forth. After it had gained some momentum, the can fell off the string and the can clattered to the ground right outside the bars.

The noise attracted a guard who was on the same level as my cell but on the other side of the gap that separated the balconies of this level. He squinted to see if something had happened over here. Not able to see anything out of the ordinary, he commenced an investigation that would start at my cell.

I dived to the ground to retrieve the can. I grabbed it and pulled it in. The can was a soup can that had held a type of cream of mushroom. Now, the contents were reduced to only a simple note. I stuck my hand in and took the note out. Knowing that being caught with this can could get me in trouble, I placed the can outside the cell and returned to the bed.

The guard reached my cell and found the can. He picked it up and looked it over. His eyes then strayed into my cell.

"This your can?" he imposed threateningly.

"Nope. I don't know where I'd get something like that."

The guard did not trust me, but he continued his route carrying the can. It was not worth it to investigate further. If I had a can, so what? Other prisoners probably had more dangerous items than I. His time could better be spent patrolling near their cells.

With the absence of the guard, I could now read the note.

"Hey Slippry Neck its me Blood Tooth. Have'nt seen you at lunch for about 3 days now. Are you sitting some where different? Are you avoiding me? No worry I know we are still friends. Anyways someone told me they saw you with Mr. Finder. What ever you are getting from him you should share you know. Since we are friends and all. Just saying. Keep that in mind," the note read.

It appeared that Blood Tooth had not forgotten me. It had been about a week since he and I had spoken at lunch. It was good to have friends here, but this friend only seemed to be looking for a handout from me. Also, he was one of the scarier people I knew in this place. That was saying something.

"Got your message," I said to the person awaiting a response from above me.

"We still friends, Slippy?" he asked down to me.

"You could say that, but that doesn't mean we share everything. Got it?"

"What good are friends then, anyways?"

"Better than an enemy, I guess. You do not have to fear me."

"Ha! I never did, Slippy!"

"You will soon, Blood Tooth," I said and returned to my bed. I could hear his laughter above me. He would not laugh if he knew how much power I had now. He would be so happy to be my friend if he only knew.

"Hey! Did I hear you saying something in here?" said a guard that had approached the cell unnoticed.

"Uh...no! You heard someone else. I..." I said, but, looking through the bars, I saw Hailie. "You are much earlier than I thought. What are you doing here?" I whispered.

"I'm making sure you did your job. When do they arrive?" she asked in a hushed tone.

"Tomorrow by dinnertime. That was the best I could do."

She heaved a tremendous sigh of relief. Hailie looked through the bars at me. It was the first time I had ever seen her smile. This little action filled me with joy.

"Thank you! Thank you so much! You've saved me and you don't even know how much! Thank you!" she whispered happily.

"You are very welcome. But don't think it was any trouble for me. And I wanted to do it."

"You're not what they say you are at all. You're different. You really are."

"Sadly, I used to be what they say I am. But I have changed and I won't be returning to that way of life any time soon."

Hailie then looked around herself to make sure no one was watching her.

"I've got to go," she whispered. "Thank you."

She moved away from the bars and once again looked around. She took a deep breath, and her smile disappeared. She then turned back to me with a stern expression.

"I don't want to hear you making any more noise. Understand?" she said loud enough to be heard by other guards.

"Yes, ma'am," I responded respectfully.

She flashed a smile after my response and then turned to leave. Hailie left my presence without raising any suspicion. My job with her was done. I had saved her father. I did good. I actually helped someone. It did not make up for all the evil I had done in the past, but it was a start.

"Friends with a guard, huh, Slippy? Maybe I should fear you a little bit. But I suppose she would probably be your only friend. I guess there really isn't anything for me to worry about then," Blood Tooth said from above.

"Just know that you have nothing to fear, not because I am not a threat but because I am your friend."

"I'll keep that in mind, Slippy. You have a good night now."

"I'll do that, Blood Tooth. You have a good night as well."

We did just that. We had a good remainder of our night. Blood Tooth did not speak to me for the rest of the time I was awake. I tucked myself into the bed and closed my eyes. I was ready for a rest. My job was done, and I had a partner in this fight.

Actually, I had three. I had Mr. Finder, one of the most powerful prisoners in here, Hailie, the guard, and I had Blood Tooth, a maniacal murderer. Maybe my team was not perfect, but at least I had some friends. Life in this prison would not be as bad as I thought. No more long nights of torture. No more slow marches spent in fear. I had nothing about which to worry anymore.

I rose from the bed and went to the wall opposite it. There were the tally marks I had made with a small rock I had found on the floor of my cell. I took up the rock as I did every night and I put a mark next to the other 42. I set the rock back on the ground and retook my place in bed. I fell asleep not too much later, content.

Chapter 7
The Visitor

I woke to the buzzing sound of the breakfast bell. The daily routine had commenced once more. It was understood that this repeated pattern would eventually numb my mind in its entirety, but I would not resist it for now. How could I avoid it, anyway? I got in line, and we moved to the cafeteria.

I grabbed some food and sat down with Blood Tooth because Brandon was with a client. Blood Tooth crunched biscuits and slurped gravy in front of me. I was all right with this. Although he was more insane than I could comprehend, he was one of the safest people with whom to eat in here.

"What are you doing there? Pretending the gravy is blood?" I asked Blood Tooth jokingly.

"What else would I be doing, Slippy? Why don't you try it?" he responded, looking up with gravy dripping from his mouth.

"I'm good. I get enough blood," I answered with an uneasy chuckle. "What have you been up to lately, Griffin?"

"I got a new pool table in my cell. Been doing a lot of that."

"Sure you have. I know Mr. Finder would tell me if he got something like that in here."

"Slippy, I believe that as much as you believe I have a pool table in my cell!"

"You should trust me more. We are friends, aren't we?"

All he did was laugh at me. Waiting for a response from this man proved fruitless. He quit laughing not much later, but he never answered my question. As simple and easy a question as it was, I still thought it deserved some kind of answer. We may have been very different, but I counted this man as a good friend. I wanted to hear a similar statement from him, but I did not. After finishing my breakfast, the buzz sounded, and we returned to our cells.

At lunch later that day, I sat and discussed prison life with Brandon. I did not have any more questions pertaining to the past left, so this was about what I wondered. It was good to have another man's opinion on the struggles we faced in this place.

"Life's good for me, Boss. I don't really have anything to worry about. No one really comes after me because they fear me. I also have many different prisoners who pledge their allegiance to me. They have to if they want their cigarettes!"

"My life is not too bad either. Ever since I met you, I haven't really been too afraid. And hearing about my past has made me more confident as well."

"That's good. But keep in mind, if you ever want anything, I can get it for you."

This was a very good point. I did not have a thing in my cell. I was not yet permitted to work and receive payment for my work. I could not buy things from the store that was available to the "good" prisoners. I did not need that store. I had my own free supply of anything I could ever need.

"You know, I'm good for now...but I will remember that. Thanks, Brandon."

"No problem, Boss. It's my job."

The bell buzzed again, and off we went to detainment. A slow march back to boredom was all the fun I was allowed to have before I would be trapped. The doors slammed and locked, and I lay on my bed as I always did. I grabbed *What Lives In The Mountain* from the bed and began reading it. This would be my fifth time reading this book.

When dinner came, it was the same story. I talked with Blood Tooth for a while until I said what was apparently an insult to him, then left when the bell buzzed. Line-up, return to cell.

After dinner, I waited for Hailie. It was an hour until she passed. She did not stop this time, but, instead, dropped a small package of crackers and continued past. I grabbed the miniscule package and read the note on the back.

"My father will be safe tonight. I already called the gang and told them I have the drugs. They will release him tonight when I give them the drugs. I have no doubt that everything is going to work out! Thank you so much!" it read.

This was great! I had saved a life from within prison! I was overjoyed as I ate the crackers and threw the wrapper out of my cell. It floated down to the next level of cells and could be traced to neither Hailie nor myself.

I slept happy this night. I was proud of what I had accomplished. I was a good guy. I was not shackled to my past of crime. I could change. A new life was in front of me, and all I had to do was take it. It would be good, indeed.

The next day, I continued through the monotony the same as I did yesterday and was greeted by another package of crackers and a note from Hailie.

"He's home! Thank you, Martin! I owe everything to you! I will not forget you," this second note read.

Her father was home. I was very glad to hear this. After all through which she went, she had her father back. She had come to me and asked for my help. It was this help that I could provide that had bought freedom for her father. I was glad to give my assistance. I had made a new friend and saved her father. All in a day's work for Martin.

This was the last significant event for many days. After that note I received from Hailie, nothing changed. She even dropped a package every single night. Wake up, eat, cell, eat, cell, eat, cell, crackers, sleep. This was my daily routine. It did not fail to bore me day after day. The pattern was slowly killing me. I wanted some kind of change.

I never thought there would be a dull moment in this place. Before, I was terrified of everyone all the time. Now, I felt secure with where I was. Hailie constantly kept an eye out for me, and if any problem came up, Brandon could get me a weapon. I was safe and bored.

Only one event broke the pattern I faced for months. A new guard arrived at my cell door after lunch.

"Hey! 108, you have a visitor," she said, looking in from outside the bars.

"A visitor? For me?" I said slowly with uncertainty.

The guard said nothing in response to my confusion and grabbed the keys from her belt. She unlocked my door and instructed me to face the far wall. I did as I was told. She grabbed my arms, pulled them back, and cuffed me. I was then guided out of the cell and down the walkway.

I had a visitor. Who could it be? I did not think that I had any surviving family since none of them had shown up at the trial. An old friend, perhaps? I honestly did not know who this could be, but the mystery was quite refreshing after dealing with the unbreakable pattern for so long.

The guard led me into a room where many other prisoners were conversing through glass windows using phones hooked to the wall. I sat down on a stool before one of the glass windows and grabbed the phone.

Behind the glass was a young woman who I suspected to be in her twenties. She had long, curly blonde hair and was about average size for a woman. When I looked at her face, I could tell that it had been devoid of a smile for a long time. She looked strong enough to take it, though. She, in fact, looked quite hardened by her trifles and appeared to no longer be affected by them. As I analyzed her, she grabbed the corresponding phone, and her blue eyes met mine.

"Hello, Martin. My name is Mikaila," the woman said through the phone.

"Hello, Mikaila. Why are you here? How do I know you?" I asked.

"A friend of yours sent me. It's funny... This was actually the last place he expected you to be."

"Which friend? How did I know him?"

"I'm not supposed to say his name. He told me not to. He said you'd understand if I told you that you two grew up together."

"Well, that's great because I can't remember growing up. I'm sorry to say, but I have retrograde amnesia. I don't have any memories of my past."

"He said that as well, but he said you would still understand."

Apparently, whoever had sent this woman had no idea how amnesia worked. There was no way I could remember growing up with this person. Why did the woman not understand this either?

"I don't know who you are talking about," I responded.

"He said to tell you that. He said that was how you would know who he is."

"Why did he send you here?"

"He wanted to tell you to go to Alemande and visit somebody. Here's the address: 238 Paterson Street. You have to remember it. He said to go there as soon as possible. He has information you need."

"Well, then I'm not going to get that information. I am currently serving a life sentence here. If I need the information so badly, he'll have to come here and give it to me himself."

"Well... That's not possible," she said, a tear forming in her eye.

I was too embarrassed by the tear to speak momentarily. I glanced around the room. I noticed a clock on the wall. The time was 1:54 pm. I noticed a calendar also. The date was January 4th. My vision then returned to the woman on the other side of the glass. I had to speak.

"Why is that?" I asked awkwardly.

She was crying softly as she said, "He's dead."

"I'm sorry. I...I didn't know. What happened?"

Mikaila looked up into my eyes and then back down.

"I'd rather not say."

"I'm really sorry. I...I know that must have been hard on you," I said, not knowing how to comfort anyone after having been locked up for so long.

"Don't...worry about it. Just remember: 238 Paterson Street. Come as soon as possible."

"I already told you. I can't. I'm stuck here," I said, shaking my head apologetically. "I'm sorry."

A guard on the other side of the glass came up behind Mikaila.

"Your time is up, Mrs. Lamb," he said.

She sighed and looked back up to me.

"Goodbye, Martin," she said, raising her hand to wave goodbye.

"Goodbye, Mikaila," I said and mimicked the gesture.

The guard guided her out of the room and away from my sight. My guard arrived behind me and guided me out as well. When I left the room, my thought remained there. I was returned to my cell, and the door slammed as always, but I was still thinking about what had happened.

This was my very first visitor. It was nice to think that there was someone on the outside that cared about my status. Although I did not understand what she was trying to tell me, it was good to see that someone outside these walls was thinking about me. It had been a strange visit, but it was a visit.

I wondered about who this person was to whom Mikaila had referred. What kind of information would be so important that I had to come to that address to get it? Many questions came to mind when thinking about this mystery man. How did he die? How did this woman know him? I did not know any answers yet, but perhaps I could ask Brandon about this. He usually had answers for me.

Dinnertime of that day, I did speak to Brandon. I met him with a tray of the ever-present beans. We sat where we always sat, row number two and column number six.

"I have another question for you," I said as I took my seat.

"What is it you need to know this time, Boss?" he asked, looking up from the table.

"I had a visitor today and..."

"A visitor? That's great! Even I haven't had a visitor my whole stay here and I had, like, fifteen people I knew at my trial. But continue, Boss. I apologize for my interruption. That was rude."

"It's okay, Brandon. I can understand your excitement. The visitor was a woman named Mikaila Lamb. I just wanted to ask you if that name seemed familiar."

"Nope. Not at all. Only other Lamb I know is that Jack Lamb guy who beat you up. Probably not related. That would be a bit of a stretch."

Jack Lamb, the man who had defeated me in a fight when no one else could. Could he be related to this woman who had just contacted me. If so, he was most likely the one who was trying to get me that information. Also, that would mean that Jack Lamb was dead.

"I don't know. I think she may have been related," I said.

"Really? I guess it's possible. But you didn't really know Jack Lamb. You only met him once...that I know of. I don't think he's related."

"Just a thought. I'm the one who knows the least here. Amnesia and all."

"True, but you're a smart guy, Boss. You have some pretty good detective skills."

"Let's just settle on the opinion of the guy without the debilitating brain condition."

"I'm all right with that!" he laughed.

We dropped the topic and continued eating. As slimy as the beans were, I needed the sustenance. Besides, I had become accustomed to their rather unique taste. A meal is a meal.

Buzz, return to cell, door slams, lie on bed. Back in my cell, I contemplated my relationship with Jack Lamb. Was this man related to Mikaila? Mikaila was in her twenties, so was he her father, brother, or uncle? She was Mrs. Lamb, so was it possible that this man was her husband. She told me that he and I had grown up together. This meant that we were the same age, ruling out father and uncle. Given that she seemed to be there alone, the most likely relationship seemed to be that he was her husband.

Now that I had determined Jack Lamb to possibly be Mikaila's husband, I had to make a guess as to how he could have died. She refused to tell me how, so I had good reason to conclude that it was no ordinary death. Next, I had to figure out if the information was withheld because it would disgrace his memory, such as drinking oneself to death, or because it was horrific, such as a fire in which he burnt to death. Knowing that I had grown up with this man, I would have understanding of his habits. Nothing he could do would really surprise me, so I could now conclude that it was not a disgraceful death. Jack Lamb had died in some horrific way.

Even without complete sureness that Jack Lamb was to whom Mikaila referred, I had deduced that he was her husband and that he had died in a horrific accident. What could I do with this information? Not much. There really was nothing I could do with this information. It had only been an exercise to keep my mind active.

It was nice to speculate and deduce in a place where there are so few occasions to solve such problems. I enjoyed these mind games. I felt intelligent solving something that appeared to be difficult. It was an escape that I appreciated in the confines of the concrete and barbwire that kept me here.

Whoever it had been of whom she spoke, I would not get the information that they wished to give. I was stuck. It was that simple. My destination was so far away that I could not even dream of ever reaching it. Thinking about what I could learn if I was able to go there was pleasant, though. Another escape for me to utilize. Dreams are what can keep you living.

Chapter 8
Prison Pirates

Many mundane months passed. No one to help, nothing to discuss with Brandon, Blood Tooth's antics growing old. Was the mind-numbing routine part of the punishment for my crimes? It had to be. With a schedule so uninteresting, I felt as if a threat was exactly what I needed. That was a foolish thought, and I would soon realize it.

It was noon of my 324th day in the prison. The buzz ordered me into place, and I complied. I was off to the cafeteria as I was forced to do three times every day. Entering the familiar swinging doors, I entered the line and got my food. I began to look for one of my daily eating companions. Not able to find Brandon, I went to go sit with Blood Tooth.

"Hey, Slippy, just leave your tray here. Mr. Finder told me he wanted a word with you," Blood Tooth said just as I set my tray down.

"Really? Why? What was the reason?"

"Said he had to show you something. That's all he said."

I left my tray with Blood Tooth and made my way to the doors that would release me into the yard. I passed through the first set of doors into a long hallway that led to the doors that opened to the yard. Just as I opened the last door and was stepping out, Brandon's big hand hit my chest and held me from exiting. As this happened, everything went blank.

When light returned to my mind, it was quite unfamiliar to me. Without any control, I was walking down an unfamiliar hall. I was nearing a door when a family with four obviously upset children passed me. Reaching the door at the end of the hall, I opened it. Suddenly, a hand was shoved into my chest accompanied by a voice saying, "Whoa, Whoa, Whoa!"

"Show me your ring," said the man I now recognized to be Brandon.

Behind him was splashing and laughter. Was that a pool behind Brandon?

Brandon looked up at me and, with sudden realization, said, "Boss?"

Everything went blank again. What had happened? What was this strange vision? Why was Brandon there? Why did it seem so unfamiliar and familiar at the same time? Nothing made sense.

Light returned. There was Brandon before me, blocking my path, the same as in the vision. I flew back in alarm. I fell to the ground in my shock. My breathing quickened, and I could not speak.

"Boss, what's wrong?" Brandon said, obviously surprised by my reaction.

"What...happened?" I asked, breathing heavily.

"Nothing! What's wrong?" he said, looking over his shoulder nervously.

"I just saw...something."

He closed the door and ran to me. Giving me his hand, he helped me up. He looked at me in bewilderment. This was something completely unexpected from me.

"What did you see?" he asked in a hushed tone.

I fell back against the wall and caught my breath. I thought about what I had seen. There was only one way of which I could think to sum it all up for Brandon.

"I saw you," I said. "I was walking down a hall that I didn't recognize, and then, when I opened the door at the end of the hall, you stopped me."

"Well, what else did I do? What did I say?" he asked, deeply interested.

"You asked to see my ring. You were also looking down...as you always do, but, when you looked up, you immediately recognized me."

"What? That sounds like... Where were you? Did you see anything out of the ordinary?" Brandon asked, grabbing me by the shoulders and looking into my eyes.

"I thought there was a pool behind you. That is all that I remember that was out of the ordinary."

Brandon stepped back from me. He did not seem to believe what I was saying. He leaned against the opposite wall. He shook his head in disbelief. He could not find the words to reply to me.

"That sounds just like a time when you and I were in the mafia," he finally spoke. "Don Sanzano had told me to control who went in and out of the pool in the Vaillancourt. So I was playing bouncer that night. Well, you came down right after I turned down this family with a bunch of kids and you opened the door and I asked to see your ring and I looked up and I saw my boss. I...was so embarrassed."

"You said you turned down a family with a bunch of kids right before me, right? In that vision thing I just had, I saw a family with a bunch of kids going the other way!"

"Then, it must be true! That's exactly what happened that night! My god, you're getting your memory back!" Brandon exclaimed quietly.

"Is that what's happening? Is there any other explanation?"

"Not one I can see. Does this sort of thing happen? I mean, do people recover memories like that?"

"I have no clue. I'm not well-educated on amnesia."

"I guess it doesn't really matter right now. We've got to go. Come on, Boss. Let's..." Brandon started to say, grabbing my arm.

"That'll teach him, eh?" he was interrupted by a group of men who had entered the hall from the yard.

"No one messes with us! We're da Pirates!" the second member of the group said, and the rest of the group responded in a cheer.

"Let's go," Brandon said again as he started to move to the other door.

I was still in a shock and could not move. I stood there, staring at him.

"Come on," he said, but it was too late.

The group of self-named Pirates had reached us. Since I was standing in the middle of the hallway, I blocked their path entirely. They were not the type to ask me politely to move.

"Hey! Move it, pal!" the first one said, shoving me to the ground in front of them.

"What's your problem, buddy?" the second one said.

I stood, now shaken free of my trance. After reaching my feet, I backed away.

"Where you going? We just wanna talk," the first said.

"What's there to talk about? I'm sorry I was in your way," I said.

"Oh, are you? What's your name, pal?" the first one asked me.

Before answering, I took a moment to analyze my enemies who stood before me. The first speaker was a bald-headed, tattooed, ugly man. He was a good deal shorter than I, but his cocky attitude looked right past that. He wore a sneer now, but I felt that this was a common accessory to his face. His overall appearance was disconcerting.

The second man was about as tall as I was and a bit more muscular. He was a big guy and he knew it. Everything about him was aimed towards intimidation. His eyes were filled to the brim with rage and they were locked solidly on me. He thought he could break your bones just by looking at you.

The third man in the party was much like the first, but facial features gave away that they were not the same. He wore a sneer, but it was evident it was not the same sneer. His posture was similar, but he could not pull it off. I noticed that the third man was even trying to blink at the same time as the first. He was in every way trying to imitate the appearance of the first, but he was not very good at it.

The fourth and final man was the runt of the pack. He was very short. His eyes pierced through me as if he could tell I was judging him for his height. I could see that the weight of teasing from his youth had worn him thin. He looked very angry, and his mental state could definitely be in question. He seemed to be a sufferer of Napoleon-syndrome.

Finished with my evaluation, I answered the first. "I am Martin Yellog."

"Well, we are the Pirates. We don't take too kindly to morons who stand in our way. You got that?"

"I've got it."

"I don't want to ever see you again."

"No need to worry. I don't really want to ever see you again."

Anger was quite easy to detect when this man was in a normal mood. Now, it was impossible to see anything but anger. His sneer inflated suddenly, and his fingers twitched. I could see the insult in his eyes. I had made a mistake with my previous comment.

"You dirty, rotten, piece of shit! How dare you! You're going to pay..." he yelled, coming closer as I backed away.

His screaming was cut off by the guards who had entered the hall on alert. He stopped approaching me and shut his mouth. His glare burned through me into my soul. If I understood anything about how he looked at me, it was that he was going to take vengeance on me.

"What's going on here?" asked one of the guards.

"Nothing," breathed the enraged Pirate.

"We were just leaving," Brandon told them as we moved past them and out the door.

Brandon and I returned to the cafeteria and sat at the usual spot. We were both slightly shaken up and neither of us spoke. This was a danger that was all too serious to us. He broke the silence first.

"I was going to show them to you. I was going to show you how bad they can be. That's why I told Blood Tooth to send you. I'm sorry for what happened."

"What did happen? What were those guys doing?"

"They're an alpha prison gang from another prison. They just got transferred here. People call them the Pirates. They just finished inflicting punishment on a prisoner they don't like."

"I thought I heard them say that they were the Pirates. They have the same name..."

"They're the same people. They were arrested before we ever attacked them. Before the mafia had any hold on the city. They have no clue that their gang was totally wiped out by you, luckily. You'd be dead if they knew that."

"So now, I have the strongest force in this prison out for me. Great."

"Isn't it? I should have never tried to show you what they were doing."

"It's okay, Brandon. What happened wasn't your fault. You couldn't have known I was going to freak out like I did. It probably was a good idea to show me what I'm up against. How do they get away with something like that, anyway?"

"The yard isn't completely open. The west wall bends in a way that, when anyone is there, the guards can't see them very well. They take the person there when punishment needs to be given."

"Am I safe as long as I don't go there?"

"Not at all. Any of them will take solitary if it means killing you. I don't think they will try that because you haven't offended that badly. But I don't know. Todd was a bit more pissed than usual."

I assumed by Todd he meant the leader of the gang whom I had insulted. I could get by with nicknames for the rest. There were Giant, Copycat, and Napoleon. Those were fitting titles for all of them. The Pirates consisted of Todd, Giant, Copycat, and Napoleon.

"How did they all get transferred here together? And how have they already come to prominence in this prison?" I asked.

"I believe they have some connections...much like I do. But their connections get them power...not just stuff. I think that some of the guards are on their side."

These were dangerous men. I had been terrified of who Mr. Finder was, and he was only a guy who could get stuff. These Pirates had real power behind them. They had corrupt guards at their disposal. Most likely, they had even more following them than what I knew. I would be in big trouble if I ever had to deal with the Pirates again.

"I've heard enough about them. What about what I saw? You said it matched the actual event perfectly," I said to Brandon.

"It did! Everything you said was exactly as I remembered it. Every last detail."

"I'm actually recovering. That's amazing!"

"Soon, you'll remember all of our glory days! I'll actually have someone to reminisce about the good old days with! That's a lot better than having to tell you about them."

To think that I could get all my memories back, it was crazy. I wondered what had brought this on. I guessed that having such a similar event occur caused me to remember the corresponding event from my past. Did this mean I had to experience a moment like this every time to recover more memories? It was a theory, but a loose one.

"You'll have to tell me more about the good old days if you want me to remember them. That is probably how it works," I told him.

"Oh! I can tell you..." Brandon started, but the bell buzz finished.

"We'll finish this later. Shall I see you for dinner?" I asked Brandon.

"Of course, Boss. Expect me here."

After returning to the cell, all I could do was think. I remembered every second of the flash. The royal red walls, the crying child, whining kids, aggravated adults, and Brandon's large hand in my face were all plastered deep in my memories. I felt as if I had always known this part of my life, but this was not true. That glass door, laughter, splashing, and that shiny ring on Brandon's finger. It was all so clear.

I remembered the ring. It was the same ring with which I had woken up from my amnesia. Silver with gold surrounding a ruby in the center. Beauty was easily seen in this mark of villainy. I had enjoyed the feel of it on my finger. It had carried a weight that I missed all too much these days.

I knew what to discuss with Brandon next. I wanted that ring back, and he could get it for me. He had people working on the inside. How would anyone notice one tiny item missing from a box? Perhaps Brandon could also get me the picture of Tyler. Maybe that would help me to remember something.

When that buzz finally came, I was relieved of my residence in the cell where time stood still. I was first in line as I almost always was these days. My fellow inmates trudged to their places, and I was allowed to move forward with them. We moved to the cafeteria and to Brandon.

I sat at the table at row number two and column number six across from the man known here as Mr. Finder. Finding was his specialty. Soon, he would find an item for me.

"I have a request for you," I said to him.

"If it's a weapon, no," Brandon responded casually.

"It's not a weapon. I want my stuff back in my possession. I want my mafia ring and I want a piece of paper."

"What's on the piece of paper?" he asked, intrigued.

"It's information about Tyler. I had it on me when they found me."

"Where did they find you?"

"I've never told you? They found me in front of a government facility. It was the facility that they charged me with blowing up."

"Why did you have the information about Tyler? Where does that come in?"

"To tell you the truth, I have no clue. Tyler did help me destroy the building, but I don't know why that would cause me to have the paper."

"Strange, but that is beside the fact. Yes, give me until tomorrow if you will. I can get those to you through the Book Man."

"Perfect. Thank you, Mr. Finder."

"It's my job. No appreciation is necessary, Boss."

"If I can do anything for you, it is appreciate what you are doing for me. Thanks, Brandon."

"You insist. Well then, you're welcome."

Dinnertime concluded as did that day. Breakfast, lunch, and dinner passed just as easily, and, before I realized it, it had been a whole day. I lay in bed as such activity was my only pastime. I listened for that squeaky wheel.

It came on cue as it did every day. I munched on crackers as he cast a shadow on the bars of my confinement. My whistle sounded, but it was in redundancy. The Book Man knew to stop here.

"Here's your book...Boss," the Book Man said, handing me the book through the bars instead of tossing it to the ground.

"Thank you, sir," I said politely.

The Book Man nodded and continued down the walkway. I opened the book without hesitation and found the hollowed center. There was a folded paper with a piece of tape on it as well as my spectacular ring.

I removed the ring from its place in the book and fit it on my ring finger on my right hand. It fit perfectly. Making a fist, I examined the beauty of this chunk of precious metals adorned with a gem. It shined in the low light of my cell. I felt its power seeping back into me.

I next took the folded paper out of the book. Unfolding it, I found a note.

"Boss, thought you may want to hang it on your wall. Use the tape. Brandon."

I flattened the paper against the wall and then stuck it there. Tyler had found his place in this prison. I leaned against the concrete wall and analyzed this precious document. Again, I read every word on the paper.

Not that I had forgotten it, but a good piece of literature warrants a few rereads.

I lay back down on the bed and looked at my spoils. How great it was to have a smuggler for a friend! I set my head down on the pillow and raised my fist above my head. For the rest of the night, I would stare up at this symbol of unity and brotherhood. I fell asleep with the ring rested on my forehead.

Chapter 9
The Return of Martin

"It looks good on you, Slippy. Not really my style, but you can pull it off."

Blood Tooth sat across from me and returned to slurping up the gravy on his tray. Crumbs of the biscuits remained on his hairy face. It made me think of my own face. I lifted my hand and ran my fingers through my thick beard.

Another thing for which to ask came to my mind. Brandon might have a problem with weapons, but what if I was using one to shave? A razor was seen as impossible to get in here by the guards, but it was not. I did not have to keep the razor. I could return it right after using it.

Unfortunately, a clean shave like Brandon's would only distinguish me further. The ring was probably making me stand out enough already, but a hairless face was quite evident of a higher status. Was shaving really necessary at this time? I was in danger at the moment, and provoking the enemy is never a good idea. Maybe a clean shave could wait.

Mr. Finder was in the yard again today. Today, he had business there. Two days ago, he should have never come so close to the Pirates. It was foolish to even try to get a glimpse of their official business. Of course, there would have been no problem had I not had the flashback.

Buzzing caused me to leave the ever-slurping beast at the table. I walked to the line as I always did, but the end result would be different. Right as I was taking my place in line, a fist was thrown at my jaw. I saw it out of the corner of my eye. Reflexes kicked in, and my hand grabbed the fist, stopping it inches from my face. The owner of the fist, Todd of the Pirates, seemed shocked. Light laughter broke out from the other inmates, and I could see that Todd was not happy at all about this. He was embarrassed, and that was easy to see.

I let go of him, and he backed away, having been seen by the guards who were ready to respond. He locked eyes with me as he entered his line. He shook his head in anger and disbelief.

"You...will...pay," he mouthed.

All I could do was stare at him until our lines moved. Here it was: the end of my life. I saw that he was done messing around. I had just embarrassed him in front of almost all the prison members in the cafeteria. Now, it was known that Todd could not even punch some guy who was not even looking. He would get even with my death.

As that slamming door locked, I knew I was trapped. He would be waiting for me when I left the cell for lunch. He would find a way. It would bring my death earlier than expected. This man was serious, and, with his whole gang against me, I did not think I could fight them off. Things were looking bleak for me.

I lay on that bed, staring at the door. When would that bell buzz and send me outside the safety of these bars? When would I have to face him again? He would not mind killing me in front of everyone. It would only show them that they were wrong about him. He would redeem his illusion of power for any price, even if it meant taking my life.

It would be here soon. It had to be almost noon now. The buzzing that I had always been so eager to hear would sound and send me to my death. This death would destroy all for which I had worked. I would die an evil man. I was not ready to die. I might not have been ready, but it was coming. It would be here very soon.

How could I face it? I had vowed to become a changed man. While I had been able to save Hailie's father and make friends with a murderer, I had not gone very far on that journey. If I died now, I would die the same man who had killed so many in the past. My legacy would be all evil. I was not ready to die. It could not be time for me to die.

Just as I thought that, the buzzing came. The cell door opened, and I was forced to step out. I had no choice but to go to my death. I would face it as I must. The line moved, and I was as paranoid as ever.

Nothing seemed out of place. Everything was normal, but still I watched everywhere. From where would he come? Would he attack me while I was in this line or while we were in the cafeteria? How many would attack me? Would they be armed? Would anyone help me if I was ambushed? The only thing that was for sure was that he would come.

Walking down the two flights of stairs, I was sure he would come. This was a perfect place for an attack. He, being on the fourth level of cells, would have the higher ground. I knew he would strike here, but he never did. We went down to the bottom floor and to the swinging doors that led into the cafeteria.

As soon as I entered, I hastened my steps to the table with Brandon. I threw myself into the seat, and Brandon seemed surprised.

"You look distraught, Boss. How can I help?"

"They're coming for me. Right now. I'm not sure exactly when, but it will be very soon."

"The Pirates? Boss, how do you know they're coming for you?"

"Todd tried to punch me, and I caught his fist in front of everyone. He wants revenge. I know he does. He thinks I made him look weak and he is very willing to prove that he is not."

"Are you sure? I saw what you did, and he didn't seem too enraged about it."

"Of course, he didn't! He doesn't want the guards to know anything is up."

"Boss, please don't be offended, but you sound paranoid as hell."

"I know they are going to hit me. I know it!"

"All right, Boss. I'll do everything I can to make sure they don't."

"Thanks, Brandon. Just keep an eye on them, will you?"

"Of course. Have some faith, Boss. Everything will be all right."

I did not see a single one of them. The Pirates were as nonexistent as ever now. I had no idea where they were. How could they be so ghost-like? I needed to know their location. If I did not know where they were, then I could not escape.

That bell came later than it ever had. It felt like hours until it buzzed. I could barely stand as I moved towards the line. I was not watching as I should have been. I was beginning to think that I had escaped. The relief of it made me drop my guard. I walked in a daze to my place in line. When the line moved, I moved with it, mindless.

I was relieved. Had I escaped? All I had to do was get to my cell and I would be free of this torment. The cage would, for once, afford me an escape. I needed that safety, and my need for it became greater and greater as we became nearer and nearer. It was so close. So close.

When we had climbed the stairs to the third level and walked on the walkway to my cell, I felt very close to at ease. The doors to our cells opened, allowing entry. Did I just make it? The prisoners behind me entered their cells. I reached mine and thankfully moved towards the opening.

Without any warning, all the cell doors slammed shut. Mine closed right in front of my face. The inmates who were in front of me were pushed aside, and there I saw the Giant, blocking the path to my right. To my left there was a single inmate, Todd. Behind him, the guard closed the door behind him and locked it. I was trapped, now more than ever.

I approached my enemy. Todd grinned at me, showing his decaying teeth. He laughed in anticipation of my death. He was ready for his vengeance, so ready. He pulled out a six-inch knife from his orange jumpsuit. As he did this, everything went blank again.

When light returned, I was sitting in a subway train. To my left was a man with a grinning face. He reached into his pocket and retrieved a wallet.

"Would you like to see some pictures of my family?" he asked me.

"Sure," I replied.

His hand darted inside the wallet and pulled out a switchblade. He flipped out the blade and lunged at me. I grabbed the man and threw him to the ground. He rose to his feet and showed the knife to the other passengers on the train. I heard screams all around me.

The man thrust out the knife at me. I quickly grabbed his arm and pressed it the wrong way. His arm snapped, and he dropped the knife and screamed in pain. I then threw the man backwards.

All went blank. Light returned on the scene I had left. There was Todd, standing with that evil grin pointed at me. He seemed so confident in his victory, but I understood that his outcome was not in the possible future. I had more of a chance in this fight than I had believed previously. I had more power than I had known. I knew what I had to do.

The inmates cheering for a fight, I ran at Todd. His pupils grew huge as he pulled back the knife in preparation to thrust it forward. His hands twitched in awful anticipation. When I had entered his reach, he threw his arm forward, and the knife headed straight for my heart. I dodged to the left and let the blade sail by me. Everything slowed down as I grabbed his wrist with my right hand and pushed his elbow inwards with my left.

The snapping sound was just as I had remembered it...as was the scream. To hear it, something within me loved it, and something else hated it. Even with that feeling of joy in his pain, I felt disgusted by what I was doing to him. It was in self-defense, but I understood that such action might truly be indefensible. I had hoped that this type of interaction was gone from me. I did not want to return to the violent man I had been before.

The knife fell off the balcony and down to the first floor far below us. I heard its clattering between the gasps for air from Todd. My enemy defeated, I tossed him from me. He hit the walkway still screaming. I had victory.

The Giant, witnessing the fall of his leader, ran at me with a war cry. I flipped around and listened to the deep bellow inspired by the necessity of revenge. It was an intimidating sound, but I felt calmer than I had in a long time. He neared me, and I readied my stance for a fight. Before I could do a thing to him, the world faded away again.

Light shown on an open area where a man and I were surrounded by a cheering audience that formed a circle around us. The man was very large, and one characteristic stuck out the most: he had an eye patch. The man was bulky and only slightly shorter than I. He almost looked a little wounded as well. I assumed that this was because of my actions against the man.

I saw him wind up a punch and, with all his strength, try to knock me out. I ducked below the punch and grabbed his fist. I used his momentum to throw him into the crowd. The people gathered watching us ran for cover before this unfortunate soul hit the concrete right in front of them.

The blankness returned and it was immediately followed by the light's return. The Giant rushed at me with his fist ready to punch my head off. A quick dodge gave me a chance to replicate what I had witnessed. Using his incredible supply of momentum, I chucked him, but there was nothing to catch this unfortunate soul. Down he fell, only stopped by the hard floor two stories below.

I ran to the edge of the balcony as did many of the other inmates. There was the Giant, blood flowing from his mouth. It had already pooled all around him. His neck was twisted in that way that assures you that it would be unnecessary to even call an ambulance. I had killed again.

I turned back to my audience who looked at me in terror. I was suddenly a threat. I had killed the Giant, the strongest member of the Pirates. They had seen me as they had never imagined. I was a beast just as they were.

The door behind me unlocked, and the guard who had hidden behind it came out with his taser aimed directly at me. I now knew I could handle myself. I was stronger than I ever could have believed. With this strength, I would take back what was mine: freedom.

I ran at the guard, fueled with a fearless flame within me. Just as he fired, I rolled under his legs and was behind him. Grabbing his neck, I slammed his head against the metal bars that kept us in endless waiting. I stole his keys and ran out the door.

Making it to the stairs was the easiest part, but as guards were alerted by a siren sounding, I was found. They were armed with pistols and they aimed to kill. Bullets hit the wall behind me. I would not allow them the pleasure of hitting me. Quick punches finished my foes efficiently. I stole their weapons and continued, now on the first floor.

It was as if they had called every available guard to stop me from leaving my captivity. Now with assault rifles and shotguns, they did not risk letting a mass-murderer out on the streets. They blocked off checkpoints, only trapping those who had stayed behind to fight me. I hid behind the corner, letting my now rioting inmates charge them. With this distraction, their defeat was all too simple.

I was making alarming progress in my escape. Reaching the first checkpoint, my progress was slowed by large metal bars. Behind them were six guards armed as well as they who were before them. Was I really to be stopped so soon? I had to be only about halfway to the exit.

Then, with only the warning of the red light turning green, the bars moved out of my way. In fear, shots were fired at me. I had no choice. Rushing at them, I took many bullets, but I finished off the threat. I fell to the ground, surely finished. Everything went blank.

Light this time shown on a simple wooden door. When it opened, a gun was shoved into my face. My head moved to the side, and my fist showed no mercy to the gun owner's ribs. I kicked the man in the head, snapping his neck. I noticed a badge this man had dropped said "L.I.F.E." on it.

I was deafened by the gunfire so close to my ear, but still I knew the presence of the two to my right because of the bullets hitting me. I fell to my knees and grabbed the fallen hitman's weapon. My bullets slayed the rest of my foes.

I could hear more coming. In necessity of escape, I pulled myself into a laundry chute. Down through the darkness I went. Blood flowed from my wounds, and bullets left their positions in my body. Reaching the bottom, I hit a pile of clothes. A large red mark was left in my absence, and I lay on the cold floor. The memory began to fade.

When I awoke from the flash, Hailie stood above me.

"You have to get up, Martin. You need to go!" she told me urgently.

I forced myself up. Standing, I felt somewhat better. Hailie ran to a room adjacent to this one. I could see her through a glass window between these rooms. She pushed a button, and, in a second, the barrier through which I had entered closed, sealing off this section to the rampaging inmates. Hailie reappeared in this room.

"You're the only one I'm helping. Now, go! They are coming this way soon!" she ordered.

"Thank you. I shall never forget this!" I said, running off to pursue my freedom.

I broke bones and shot kneecaps, but never did I kill a single one of my enemies. I merely made them unable to stand in my way. Death would be an unfair punishment for those who were only doing their job. I had stepped away from my previous lifestyle and I refused to return. I had killed one today; no more should have to die.

I was quite amazed at how I fared against my foes, but I understood it to an extent. My visions showed me how genuinely powerful I used to be. Brandon had spoken of it, and now I could believe him. I was a machine, but not a killing machine. A machine for my escape and for my victory. A machine for freedom!

It was not long before another checkpoint blocked my path. Again, guards, closer to soldiers, were at the ready behind it. Hailie was not here to assist me this time. A beginning of understanding in my abilities gave me confidence that I was not yet beaten. I took my stance before the door. After preparing myself for a moment, I launched my foot at the bars in my path. They strained under the force exerted by my kick.

The guards backed away in fear at what they had just seen. This barrier was bent inwards to an extreme. Never had they been witnesses to such power. I took the stance again and prepared myself, a smirk coming across my face.

"He's going to break through! Fire!" a guard yelled in terror.

The bullets flew as my kick burst through the bars and the door flew inwards. This door, having previously been an obstacle, became a weapon. It wiped out three men, and, a roll and a jump later, I was in position. With extreme speed, the threat was neutralized.

I was so close to my freedom. There was one final gate that stood in my way. Not to mention, another twenty guards at least who would attempt to put a stop to my success. I had stopped the legion that they had already sent at me in these narrow halls, so why did they continue to fight? Their attempt was irrelevant. I could not fail now.

Arriving at the final gate on the road to freedom, I noticed the lack of guards. Not a single guard hid behind the bars prepared to fire this time. I had not gotten past all of them, had I? Not in any hurry, I grabbed onto the bars and ripped the door off its hinges. Setting the destroyed door on the floor, I walked through the barrier and neared the lobby where I would find passage to the outside. All I would face past here was a large fence topped with razor-wire.

My feet touched the tiles that marked the lobby. There trembled about fifteen armed men and women who were not about to let me stroll out that door. Their assault rifles shook in their hands, but they mostly kept aim directly at my heart.

"If you let me go, I will spare you all," I said to my audience.

"Your rampage is over, 108. Put your hands above your head and drop to your knees!" a guard who had taken the role of leader told me.

"As you wish," I responded, falling to my knees and putting my hands above my head.

Surprise was the reaction of everyone in the room besides myself. Four guards approached me with caution. They had to restrain me and lock me away in solitary now. They had to lock me away and throw away the key. That was all they had to do, and this nightmare would be over. I would not allow that.

The handcuffs having been locked onto my wrists, they stood me up and began to push me towards my detention. The four surrounded me and the others stood behind in careful watchfulness. Two were to my sides, one was behind me, and the last was in front of me. They thought I was secured. They thought.

I broke the cuffs easily and, with the same motion, hit together the heads of those beside me. I then used them temporarily as a shield to obtain my more permanent shield. I put the guard in front of me in a headlock and took his rifle, aiming it at the enemy.

Surprise was my ally as it once again was shown on their faces. My shield struggled for his unobtainable freedom, so I hit him with the butt of the rifle, knocking him out. I carried his deadweight towards the fearful gathered in front of me.

"Out of my way," I commanded.

They backed away, nothing more to say to me. I moved to the middle of the lobby where I stopped. Knowing that I could not let these guards follow me out and seeing a door that connected to a room adjacent to this one, I motioned with my gun to the guards.

"Into that room...or he gets it," I threatened.

They complied to my demands, and I found myself alone in the lobby. I quickly moved to the door, always pointing the rifle at the closed door which housed the threat. When my back touched the doors that would send me to the last leg of my escape, I dropped the comatose man and fled to the outside.

I found it was absurd to abandon my shield so soon, for liberty was not mine yet. Even more surrounded than ever, I stared down the people who understood the threat I could pose to society. Was this the end? With so many, how could I win? This was a question that needed answering very soon.

"Freeze! Down on the ground!" shouted the soldiers.

What could I do? No time remained for any contemplation. Attack or flee into the prison? Retreat was not my style, but neither was death. My pride required no test today. It was too great for my own good. I chose the path of danger.

I ran, screaming, at the enemy. Shots were almost immediately fired, and bullets raced past me. My steps carried me much faster than they had anticipated. I had reached them before a single bullet had touched me. I somersaulted through the front lines and emerged on the other side with my body still intact. Bewilderment assaulted the force as they questioned how their weapons had become so inaccurate.

To the fence I ran. The front gate was beyond my skills, and the fence was only sixteen feet tall. My choice made sense in my mind. I grabbed the chain-link and threw myself upwards with each additional grab. The guards did not shoot, for civilian houses lay beyond the grounds of the prison. They had no choice but to allow me to reach the top of the fence and throw myself down.

I hit the ground and began my sprint that would lead me to a decent hiding place. I ran across the grass of the decorative prison grounds. Reaching the road, I did not stop for even the cars. This was a mistake. As a police cruiser rushed towards me, everything faded to the blankness that was all too familiar now.

The light hit a man who I recognized as Tyler Ishler. He was running behind me. I could see that a police car was about to reach him. I then threw myself into the front of the vehicle. We collided, but it was obvious that I was the victor. The front of the car was destroyed, and the police inside were stunned by the airbags. I was a little stunned myself, but I gestured for Tyler to continue running. After that, everything went blank.

Could I do it? It seemed so impossible, but everything else I had done was on the same level of plausibility. With all I had shown myself in these previous minutes, why should I not be able to do it? It would be done. And I would be the one to do it.

I braced myself for impact and took the hit. Just as in the vision, the vehicle was totaled. I fell backwards, amazed once again. Nevertheless, I had no time to be awe-stricken. So many were in pursuit of me. I had to run. I had to run far, far away.

I flew past cars and pedestrians as my feet moved me faster than anyone could comprehend. Through alleys and across roads, I would flee for my life. I covered great distances so quickly. No one could catch me.

After I had run for what I perceived as four minutes, I fell to the ground in an alley on the outskirts of the city. I pushed myself behind a dumpster and breathed a sigh of relief. In the eyes of the law, I was a fugitive. It was terrific! My freedom had been obtained, and I would no longer be burdened by imprisonment. I was free and I would stay free. Every threat made against my life was now forgotten with my time in prison. I was safe and I was happy.

Having caught my breath, I stood. Reaching the height of my being, I had strange feelings. Suddenly, I was knocked down by a terrible pain. I clutched my head in agony. It had never hurt like this before. The world's presence betrayed me in that moment as I fell back into my memories.

Light shown on a boy holding a bow and a quiver of arrows. The boy set these items on the table in front of him and turned to me. Joyful anticipation shined in this child's deep blue eyes. I pulled off the ring on my finger and handed it to the boy. "Happy Birthday, Cody."

Those joyful eyes inflated, and I could see the wonderment on his face. He stared at it, really taking it in. Then, his gaze returned to me. Even though I was only a mere three feet away, the boy ran to me and practically tackled me with a hug.

"Thanks, Martin!"

The memory faded, but I could not yet return to the real world. Again, I was thrust into the past and light reappeared to guide me.

The light now shined on the kind face of a woman who had to be in her thirties. She stood above me and looked at a paper laid on the desk in which I sat. My hand moved a pencil across the page, drawing graphs of quadratic equations. My hand set down the pencil, finished with the drawing.

"That's perfect. You drew it exactly as I would have. Martin, you've

learned so quickly. I just taught you this! Your grasp on it is astounding!" the woman said to me.

"You're just a good teacher, Mrs. Taylen," I responded.

She smiled down on me and shook her head. She walked back to a board at the front of the room about five feet from me. The woman began writing as the memory started to fade.

Again, I could not escape. It was similar to the last time, but something was different. I was remembering so much faster now. Voices flew at me nonstop from the deepest corners of my mind.

"Mission complete!"

"Are you shipwrecked?"

"Wow, nice job...uh...kid."

"Me being taken down by a...14-year-old, maybe. I think not!"

"God has a plan for everyone, Martin."

"You cling to L.I.F.E. and then you cling to death!"

"I'm really, really excited! Are you ready for this?"

"I said drop the gun, Shepard!"

The voices were split apart and silenced by a loud boom. Momentarily blinded, I could not see what had caused this explosion. I lowered my hand, and there stood my greatest friend.

"They can't take us down, kid!"

Tyler saluted me and flashed a toothy grin. He then ran off, and the memory began to fade.

I returned from my past and found myself clinging to the ground. Here, I was exactly as I had left, but one major detail differed. I now possessed that which was previously unobtainable. I remembered. I remembered everything. Truly, Martin Shepard was back! I remembered. I remembered!

I stood, now with full strength. I reminisced in my past, which I now had at my disposal. I remembered my family by the sea, my parents and siblings, the fishermen who gave their lives for a good cause, the officers who sought justice with all they were, everyone else I had met on that journey, and I remembered Tyler.

In the next second, I remembered their fates. Collapsing to my knees, I saw the pavement dampen with my sorrow. I wept for them, everyone who had fallen in my faults. They were gone. Terrible guilt laid its hands on me. My tears fell silently for them all.

I would not let it be that way this time. I would not let the enemy take the lives of so many. It was all because of me that they died. I was going to change. I would not allow myself to fail as I had in the past. Never again would I allow my actions to doom others.

After I had knelt there for an unperceived amount of time, I returned to my feet. I was back to my old self once again. Even better, now, I could see back all the way to my own birth. I had become the new and improved Super Soldier. I had been remolded for a better life. I was ready to live.

Chapter 10
Compassion of Strangers

It was time to move on, but to where? I was in a very dangerous situation. The police would be searching the whole city for me. I had to leave, but even showing myself outside this alley would have me almost immediately sighted. Was there no option of safety left for me?

I had to get a change of clothes, and that needed to be done quickly. The police had not been very far behind me when the visions had brought me to my knees in this alley. Disguise was my number one concern right now. Where would I find new clothes?

I dropped back to the ground behind the dumpster. I could not wait here any longer. Leaving this place was essential to my survival, but I could not risk being spotted. Even though I was outside the prison, I still felt trapped. Orange was my enemy now. Nothing could be accomplished while this was on me.

Suddenly, I heard a squeaking sound that was nearing me terrifyingly quickly. It was coming into the alley from the street. I pushed myself further behind the dumpster, but I could not escape the inevitable. I was about to be found.

A pink bike tire came to a halt right next to me, barely peeking out from behind the corner of the dumpster. There was noise of dismounting and the kickstand hitting the pavement. Small footsteps tapped, approaching even closer. I heard the creaking of the dumpster's lid being opened and then closed. The kickstand returned to its origin, and the tire edged forward. Not a second had passed when the child on the bike looked over and down at my face.

"Who are you?" said the little girl.

She, perhaps only 4 feet tall and about 80 pounds, was a startling sight for me. Her green eyes were glued to me as she awaited a response to her question. Her shoulder-length black hair, shifted by the breeze, was the only thing about her that moved. I finally opened my mouth to answer her question.

"Martin Shepard. Who are you?" I responded.

"I'm Liz. What are you doing here? What are you wearing?"

However frightening I appeared with the orange suit and my hardened look from almost a year in prison, Liz was unaffected by it. She showed no fear for the dangerous man behind the dumpster. I believed myself to be more afraid of her than she was of me!

"I'm hiding, and trust me...if I had other clothing options, I would take them."

"I can get you some different clothes. My dad is out of town for a while, so you could borrow some. He wouldn't care," Liz spoke joyfully.

"Actually, I am going to take you up on that one. Do you think you can bring some of your dad's clothes back here? And quickly?" I said with excited anticipation.

"Sure! I'll be back in a few minutes!" she said, quickly mounting the bike once more and pedaling off.

This girl would be my salvation. With her father's clothes, I would be permitted to leave this alley and to pursue my next location. What would be my next location? Usually in this situation, I went to someplace familiar, but this time that did not seem to be an option. Almost everyone from my past was dead. I had no close friends who would allow me to stay with them, let alone harbor a fugitive. There was no place for me.

Then, I realized that I was looking too far back for the answer. Mikaila Lamb, who I now guessed was Jack Lamb's mother and not wife, had visited me about ten months ago. The address she gave me was 238 Paterson Street. I was sure this was correct because, with my memories' return, I noticed that everything was very clear in my head, even recent memories. That was where I would go and perhaps that would lead me to Tyler.

After another minute, the girl returned, carrying a complete business suit in her arms. She no longer rode the bike, so I assumed that she must live near here.

"Here you go!" Liz said cheerfully.

"Thank you so much, Liz! But you didn't have to get me such nice clothes. Anything would have done. Anything besides an orange jumpsuit..."

"It's all right. Dad's been gone for a while now, so I don't think he will be using them."

"Gone for a while? How long has he been gone?"

"Two years. He didn't take much with him, so I think you could borrow his suit until he gets back."

"Uh... Thank you. I have to change into these right now, so..."

"Okay. I live right over in that house," she told me, pointing at a single-story, tan building directly opposite the alley. "You should come over after you change."

"Um... That's okay. I have to go soon or I will be really late."

"My sister can drive you if you need. She drives a lot, and it'd be no trouble."

"No, that's okay. I can get there by myself. Anyway, it is really out of your way."

"Nowhere's out of our way! Just stop by really quick and tell her about it. Please?"

I was very hesitant about this offer. If the police had released a warning about my escape, her sister could recognize me. Should I take the risk only to possibly get a ride to Alemande? I was not even sure exactly where I was and how to get to Alemande. Maybe it was worth it.

"If you insist. I will join you in a couple minutes."

"Yay! I'll tell Melody. See you soon!" she said and ran out of the alley.

Now alone in the alley with a change of clothes, I ditched the orange. I donned instead the suit of highest quality. It was a little small on me, but I was very pleased with it, anyway. It was so great wearing this outfit of prestige. I looked official and, not to mention, just a little like the agents who had stolen my life from me. That did not put me off this suit too much, but it did affect me. I hated resembling them, but I did look good!

Having obtained my disguise, I walked out of the alley. There stood the house where I would soon be a guest. Was I ready to meet somebody new? After being forced into meeting so many people in prison, it would be strange to meet a person whom I chose to meet. At least, I was dressed for the occasion.

Walking across the street after checking for the police, I arrived on the doorstep. Knocking resulted in the door being flung open. Liz stood in the open doorway smiling up at me.

"Melody! He's here!" she called to her sister.

I did not hear a response from the sister, but Liz motioned for me to enter. My feet hit the tile of the floor. Here I was, not to be detained but to be welcomed. Liz guided me to the dining room, where a single expansive table took up all available space. She pulled out a chair for me and pushed away an empty box of cereal that was on the table in front of it.

Sitting, I was then devoid of the presence of the little girl. She had gone to find her sister. I sat in silence and analyzed the room. The light fixture above me had only half its intended amount of two light bulbs. All around the room, empty boxes of cereal lay about. Among the boxes were a single hat and apron that both had "Cluck Bucket" stitched on them. The wallpaper peeled off the wall, and its original color was impossible to guess due to extreme fading.

Supplying me with more to analyze just as I had run out, Liz emerged with the leader of what I assumed was a two-person family. Her appearance was shocking. While Liz had looked happy and healthy, her sister appeared to be deteriorating on the spot. Her skin clung to her bones and her eyes were red as if she had been crying. Even though I was pretty sure she was only in her teens, she looked aged way past that. It was clear that she had suffered much.

"Hello. Wow... Man, you look like him," the sister spoke.

"Yes, hello," I said, standing. "My name is Martin Shepard."

"I am Melody Pluth. Nice to meet you," she said, shaking my hand which I had stuck out for her.

"Liz insisted that I come to meet you. She wouldn't leave me alone until I agreed!" I laughed.

"Heh, heh. That is Liz, all right. But she mentioned to me that you needed some help. Um... What is it you need?" she asked me, wiping her red eyes.

"It's nothing. I really don't..."

"He needs a ride to Alemande. He has an important meeting there that he doesn't want to be late for. Isn't that right, Martin?" Liz interrupted.

"Uh...yeah. That is correct. I do need a ride, but it is not urgent," I answered, speaking mostly to Melody.

"It's okay, man. You look like you're in a bit of a pinch right now. I would be glad to help you out," Melody said to me.

I was about to interrupt and comment about my ability to get there myself, but then I remembered that I still had no idea where I was. Should I really put any more burden on this family that I could see was already struggling. It reminded me of when Jonah and Mia wanted to help me so badly. That circumstance worked out very well for them. Maybe this could work well for this family, too.

"Thank you. You are being so helpful. I hope that I can repay you somehow."

"Unnecessary. Just let us help you," Melody said.

"Yay! Let's go, Martin!" Liz shouted, trying to pull me back out of the house.

"Okay. Are you ready to leave?" I questioned.

"We don't want you to be late, do we?" Melody asked.

"Of course not. Thank you," I said as Liz pulled me out the door.

We piled into the car, and Melody started the engine. Pulling out of the driveway, we were on our way to 238 Paterson Street, where I would find information that was supposed to be given by Jack Lamb. I assumed that Mikaila would now present the info to me. Anyway, I would learn something that could be very helpful in my search to find Tyler.

Melody, now driving towards the city limits, let out a sigh. I glanced at her and saw that tears were forming in her eyes. I said nothing about it, not wanting to embarrass her by bringing attention to it. I was curious why she was sad, but I let it go. It was none of my business.

As we passed a road sign announcing our departure, I learned the name of the city where I had been trapped for so long. This place was known as Hiltavare. I also learned that West City was only about twenty miles from here. It would not be as long as I thought to get to where I needed to be. Fortunately, I would be there even sooner because of this family's generosity.

"You doing okay, man? You need anything?" Melody asked me.

"I'm doing fine. Thanks," I answered.

She seemed to have some doubt about what she was doing. Was there regret in her for helping me? She looked worried. I wondered if I really should address this problem. Perhaps I could help her as she was now helping me.

"Is anything wrong?" I asked her.

She immediately wiped the tears from her eyes and responded, "No, nothing's wrong, man. It's just allergies. I'm okay."

I looked away and back out the window. I did not believe that nothing was wrong with her, but I guessed that I would have to take her word for it. Even still, many things could be going wrong. Judging by the state of her house, she and Liz were living in destitution.

Despite the state of their living quarters, Liz seemed to be in great shape. Could it be that the older sister was fully devoted to supporting her younger sister? If this was the case, then Melody would be living with immense stress. She looked to be only about eighteen years old. She had to struggle through more than any kid should.

Liz had mentioned that their father had been gone for about two years. I guessed that the mother had been gone for even longer or never was present at all in their lives. This meant everything fell on Melody. Even worse was the emotional pain caused by losing both of their parents.

I remembered the hat and apron that I had seen on the table. Judging by how the uniform was just thrown onto the table with little regard and by the red eyes with which the sister first saw me, I guessed that she had been fired from her job. A place like the "Cluck Bucket" did not sound as if it paid its employees well, but it was all she had. They were barely afloat before that, and now it was all over. No wonder she cried as she drove with what was most likely her last tank of gas.

Hours passed in this car, and they were silent. It was as if they were afraid to talk to me. Maybe it was the fact that I was dressed in their father's clothes. If these two girls were living without their father, that meant he left them or he died. I was not sure which it was, but Liz had alluded to the father taking some of his things with him. It seemed as if their father had left them, and now here I was, dressed the same as he had dressed. This must have made them quite uneasy.

When I saw that all too familiar name of Alemande on a road sign right outside of it, I rejoiced. Soon, I would be there and I could learn more and more. I craved learning. My mind could handle such complex ideas, and I wanted to test it as much as possible. More information awaited me.

The tires hitting that pavement which was so precious to me, I smiled. Melody and Liz noticed my happiness.

"What's with the face, man?" Melody questioned me.

"I have some information that I'm ready to receive ahead of me. I can't wait."

"Opportunity awaits you, huh? Well, you're dressed for it. You look professional."

"Thanks. And thank you for letting me borrow this. It has been more helpful than you can imagine."

"It's no problem. You wear it better than him. That deadbeat would never miss it, anyways."

There was no denying it. There was tension in this car. It was now evident that her father had left her. For two years, he had left her to fend for herself and her sister, too. They were forced to live in a barely habitable house. This man had taken so much from them. I knew what this was like and I could sympathize with them. Though, with her resentment filling this small space, it was getting harder for me to stay in the car.

"You can just drop me off here," I told her.

"Is this where you need to go? If you need to get somewhere else, I will drive you there. I am not going to let you walk there. You asked for my help and you've got it," she returned.

"Actually, if you could take me to Paterson Street, that would be very helpful."

"Of course, man. I'll take you wherever you need."

She kept calling me "man". I did not take this as a sign of disrespect, but as a sign of disconnection. I guessed that she most likely called many people by this, and it had become quite generalized to fit all people. She saw everyone as the same and she feared to get close to anyone. Betrayal was a risk she was not willing to take for friendship. It was only she and Liz in her life. That was all she needed. Everyone else was just some "man" that could hurt her.

Coming to this conclusion, I could not understand why she was helping me. If she really feared betrayal, then why did she so freely offer me assistance? She owed me nothing, and all she could gain would be a friend, something of which she had no need. What brought about this compassionate nature? I did not know her, but I could tell that this was out of character for her.

We arrived on Paterson Street, and my eyes searched for the blessed numbers two, three, and eight. I was ready to begin my next mission, and the atmosphere in this vehicle had grown thick. As much as I was curious of Melody and Liz, I was prepared to continue my own journey. I was grateful for her mysterious surge of kindness, but I still had someone to rescue. Where were those numbers?

Still, I wondered what would become of my two heroes after they dropped me off. Their lives were headed towards rock-bottom. Could I do nothing to help them? Did they not deserve a reward for helping me? How freely they gave away their time for me! I did not want to walk away from such a sacrifice. They deserved better, and I wished the best for them.

There they were! 238 graced the side of a particularly nice looking home. The structure had interesting architecture and generally looked very pleasing. It was a nice place to spend one's life. Doubling on the fact that it resided in Alemande, I wished this was my home.

"Here it is!" I shouted, my anticipation relieved. I unbuckled myself and threw open the car door. The vehicle stopped, and I stepped out onto the sidewalk. I turned back to my heroes and said, "You have helped me in my time of need. Thank you so much! If there is anything I can do for you, please tell me."

Melody seemed to be thinking about what she wanted, but then she stopped. It looked as if she was struggling to believe that her choice was right. She wanted something so badly.

"No, we have no requests. I wish you the best of luck," she said, the tears showing just barely.

"What about...?" Liz spoke up from the backseat.

"Liz! Quiet!" the older sister scolded. "We need nothing. Good luck."

"Thank you once again. I won't forget this," I said, closing the door.

I saw her nod her head before she returned her gaze downward. She shifted the car into drive and lifted her eyes to the road. With one last look at me, she put her foot on the accelerator. Off they went, my heroes were gone to a destiny unknown to me.

I left the sidewalk and went to the door of Mikaila's home. Standing on the welcome mat, I rung the doorbell. I looked back down the road just in case I could wave goodbye to the two sisters who saved me, but they were already gone. They were out of my life. I only wished that she would have asked something of me. I would not have to feel guilty for leaving them the same as I found them.

My call to the house was answered, and Mikaila was right in doorway behind me. I turned to her and smiled. Astonishment was immediately present on her face. She could not speak because she knew how unlikely it was that I would ever make it here. She shook her head and regained her senses.

"Get inside. They might be looking for you here," she said, grabbing my arm and jerking me into her home.

Chapter 11
True Allies

While I reclined on her couch in the living room, Mikaila was preparing some tea. I could see her in the kitchen from my seat as she poured the hot water into two cups. She then reentered the living room and set my tea on a coaster on the small table that was equidistant to the couches on either side. Mikaila sat on the couch opposite mine and sipped her tea.

"Why have you asked me to come here?" I asked.

Setting down the cup, she said, "I am speaking on behalf of Jack Lamb. But...you don't remember him, do you?"

"I do remember him. My memory has recovered. How, I don't know, but it is back."

"It's...back? You remember everything? Well, I cannot understand how something like that happens, but it is good. You can fully understand everything I'm about to tell you then." She sighed, "Where do I begin?"

"Is Jack Lamb your son?" I interrupted with a question.

"Yes, he...was," she answered, her eyes beginning to fill with tears.

I felt immediately guilty. She was mourning the loss of her son, and I was the one who had taken his life. I had killed Jack and I had taken him from her. I had not known what I was doing at the time, but I now fully regretted what I had done. I was sorry.

"I'm so sorry. I did not know what I was doing. I never wanted to kill him," I said with guilt.

"I forgive you. You cannot be held responsible for what happened to him. L.I.F.E. is to blame for what they did to him. I just wish he could have lived a normal life."

"I understand that completely. Never have I been normal. L.I.F.E. is the plague that has ruined me."

She nodded. Her gaze was downward and no longer on me. She could not bear to look at her son's killer. Guilt was a major factor in my life now. With my memory's return, I could no longer escape the gravity of my past deeds. How I had ruined so many lives!

"Jack wanted to tell you this on his own, but things did not go as he expected. L.I.F.E. stole you from him and used you against him. I just want you to know, Martin, he always wanted the best for you. He cared about you so much."

"I remember. He protected me from them whenever possible in their labs. He wanted us to escape together. But when they tried to kill me, I left first. After that, he found me at the Vaillancourt and taught me that I was not as strong as I thought, that there were forces greater than I. He put me on the path to become stronger so that we could go together and defeat L.I.F.E. as a team. But I failed him," I spoke, remembering it all so clearly.

"Your amnesia was something he never expected. All this would have been a hundred times easier without it. But he accepted the fact that you wouldn't remember him and he chose to guide you to where you needed to be."

"I had been so wrong about him. I was a fool."

"All that is irrelevant. It doesn't matter anymore. Martin, have you ever heard of Santidigo Island?" Mikaila asked me, taking a sip of her tea.

"Yes, I believe that is another L.I.F.E. base and also where they are holding someone very important to me. The Commander mentioned it before I blew up the facility."

"I am going to take you there. You are going to finish off L.I.F.E. and avenge Jack."

"You know where it is?! How do you know? How are we going to get there?" I asked with excitement, accidentally bumping the table and spilling a small amount of my tea.

"Jack found out about it and he told me. I have a private landing strip and a plane in a hangar. I will fly you to the outside of the island where you will leave the plane and swim to the shore. From there, everything else is up to you."

Here was my chance! I would stop L.I.F.E. and save Tyler. Evil would be brought to an end, and Tyler and I would be reunited. All I had to do was get there, and that would happen very soon.

"When do we leave?" I asked urgently.

"We will leave shortly. First, you have to be ready to take down an entire organization. I have an armory in the basement. Anything there is yours, Martin."

A whole armory was at my disposal. I would have to be suited to the max if I wanted to have a chance to complete the mission. That is, if I was to kill everyone there, I would need an armory. I did not intend to kill the agents. My plans only involved stopping them. I had stepped away from the death that had led me here. I did not want to kill anymore.

"This is a stealth mission. I'm not going in there guns blazing, trying to kill everyone in sight. I'm going to sneak in and convince their leader that what they're doing is wrong. I shall stop them that way. There is no need for anything in your armory."

"What?! Don't you want revenge? Have you forgotten what they've done?" she asked me, confounded by my change of heart.

"You know I have not forgotten. Even after everything they have done, I shall not kill them. Everyone deserves a chance at redemption."

"You're crazy if you think that they should be allowed to live! They are monsters! You should have no doubt that, given the chance, every single one of them would happily kill you. You will go there and you will kill them!"

"No, I cannot do it. You cannot force me to kill."

She scowled at me from the other side of the table. Mercy was not due for these people is what she thought. They deserved death. I was a fool because I could not see that. We held opposite views on the subject. In my obstinate stance, I knew I was right. I did not need to prove myself to her.

"Fine," she gave in. "If it's a stealth mission you want, then a stealth mission you will get. There's a whole lot of silenced weaponry down there, too. I guess that will be all you have to take."

"Thank you. If it comes to it, death will be their punishment. But until it comes to that, I shall not kill them. I hope you understand that."

"I understand. Let's go," Mikaila yielded.

Descending into the basement, we were blinded by darkness until Mikaila flipped the light switch. The bulbs gave light to the thousands of weapons stored in this huge subsurface room. I felt as I did when I saw the weapons that would lead to the destruction of the first L.I.F.E. facility. There were so many.

"My son collected these over the years, but he never used them. He preferred to kill in more creative ways than just shooting down the enemy," Mikaila told me.

"That explains the flamethrower machines he built. He was no ordinary killer."

"He would never have been a killer if it weren't for the L.I.F.E. Organization."

I nodded solemnly and approached the wall of weapons. Here were both semi-automatics and automatics. They all could be fitted with suppressors, and that was what I needed. I would be required to be unseen and unheard during my time there. Silence was key. The loud bang of a gunshot would only spell failure.

"Here. Take this," Mikaila said, tossing armor at me.

I caught it and inspected it. The color was black as night. It was made completely of Kevlar, the whole suit. Along with the suit, a belt with harnesses was provided as well as a black mask. For an ordinary person, this would be insanely heavy, but I was not ordinary.

"Where did Jack get this?" I questioned Mikaila.

"He made it. It's crafted especially for you. He said it would be your size when you were about five years old and that your size shouldn't change too much after that."

Jack Lamb had made this for me. Ignoring the fact that his intelligence had to be off the charts to predict the size of someone's body years in the future, his compassion towards me was stronger than I had ever seen. He made this to protect me. His heart might have been darkened by L.I.F.E., but it shined brightly with the love that was inside it.

"He was preparing for a long time, wasn't he?" I asked, looking up from the armor.

"Ever since I've known him, he was preparing. He understood that you weren't as strong as he was, so he put all his energy into making it so you could be that strong."

Jack Lamb was a true ally. He taught me and guided me. He worked endlessly to assure my victory. Jack only desired justice and he wanted me to be right there with him as justice was served. He probably could have done it himself, but he thought I deserved to be part of his plan. As much as Jack was my ally, I was never his.

"Change into that and meet me upstairs. Grab two pistols and two suppressors as well," Mikaila told me, ascending the stairs.

I removed the business suit and slipped into the advanced armor. I could feel the weight of protection on my shoulders. Powerful was how I felt. I believed I was indestructible in this. I was an unstoppable force for good. If anyone could stop L.I.F.E., it would be I.

I took two pistols and two suppressors from the wall. Screwing the suppressors onto the weapons, I was ready. I was ready to fight L.I.F.E. and to bring justice. I was ready to save Tyler. Now that I was ready, I harnessed the weapons and moved upstairs.

"Are you ready to leave?" I asked Mikaila, reaching the top step of the stairs.

Sitting on the couch in the living room, she told me, "We have some time before we have to leave. It needs to be night when you get there. Go ahead and shave off that bushy beard first. Then, we can leave."

I took her advice, and she led me to the bathroom and showed me Jack's razor and shaving cream. I went to work on the beard that had formed on my face after so many months in prison. I removed large chunks with every slice. My hair fell from my face as my past had fallen from me. I finished my shaving and splashed water over my newly clean face. Yes, Martin was back.

I exited the bathroom and yelled out to Mikaila. "Now, can we leave'?"

She turned back to me from her position in the kitchen. Grabbing a key from a hook on the wall, she nodded her head. She turned around and opened a door in the kitchen.

"Follow me, Martin."

I followed her into the garage, and we both entered the vehicle. She turned her head to me and smiled. I smiled back, and she started the car. Her hand reached over and grabbed a remote on the dash. Pushing the button, she made the garage door open. We drove out into the light, and she hit the button again, closing the door. Off we went to her private landing strip and hangar.

On the road again, I had time to think. What progress I had made today! This accelerated rate of progress was as it used to be. Just this morning, I was fearing for my life, but I had escaped and made it all the way to Alemande. Now, I was on the way to Santidigo Island and to save Tyler. I was on the right track again.

I wondered if L.I.F.E. would be ready for my attack. Had they heard of my escape from prison? They most likely had, but did they think I could make it all the way to their base? They probably would be taken unaware, which would cause them to surrender more easily. They would realize that they had no way of killing me and they would yield to my power. L.I.F.E. would be over. My mission would be completed.

Closing in on the strip, I turned to Mikaila and said, "Is this something Jack prepared as well?"

"Um... Not exactly. You'll see when we get there."

Instead of pulling into the driveway to the house that was adjacent to the hangar, we parked along side the road. Mikaila left the vehicle as did I. She then jumped the fence and started jogging towards the hangar. I followed, confused, and we approached the hangar.

When we were at the door to the hangar, Mikaila pulled out a key and put it in the lock. Correction: she tried to put it in the lock. After several attempts at sticking the key in the lock, she threw down the key in frustration. Sighing, she reached down and grabbed a rock on the ground.

"He changed the locks," she said before shattering the glass with the rock.

Mikaila reached around and unlocked the door. Opening it, she allowed me to enter first. In the hangar, a Cessna sat in the center of the open building. "Something tells me that is not yours," I said to Mikaila uneasily.

"Nope, it's my ex's. But I know how to fly it...kinda."

"Are you sure this is the best plan?"

"Martin, have some faith in me. I've got this, okay?"

She moved to the opposite wall and flipped a switch there, lifting the hangar door. I saw the runway that led towards the ocean. It was the path to Santidigo Island.

"Get in," she commanded, pointing to the plane.

We boarded the plane, and she turned the key in the ignition.

"He never takes the key out of this thing," Mikaila said with memories on her mind.

She taxied it out to the runway. Lining up the plane for takeoff, she looked around, searching for the man who owned the plane.

"I don't think he's here right now. That's lucky," she told me with a smirk on her face.

"Is it really smart to steal a plane before going to destroy a government organization?" I asked with a nervous smile.

"No, of course not. But we only have this one option. I'm taking it."

Mikaila adjusted the flaps and played with the instruments. She then took the thrust and pushed it forward slowly. We accelerated towards the sea which was at the end of the landing strip.

"Let's do this," she said with a chuckle.

The thrust was pushed even further. Our speed increased as we approached the end of the strip. When we had reached the appropriate velocity, Mikaila pulled back on the yoke, and up we went. The ground was left behind as we soared to our destination.

The view out my window was fantastic. There was that beautiful sea that I had always admired. It glimmered in the soft sunlight of this May evening. The plane raced towards that same sunlight as it attempted retreat behind the waves in the distance.

"Crap! I just realized we forgot something," Mikaila said.

"What?"

"Your shoes. They're not really cut out for this type of attack."

I looked down at my fine dress shoes that had come with the suit Liz had allowed me to borrow. Lucky for me, they were not uncomfortable. I felt as if they had been worn quite frequently before being left behind with the girls. They were not perfect, but I felt they would do the job.

"I'll be fine. I have dealt with more difficult circumstances."

"If you say so. I'm only looking out for you, but if you can do it, I won't doubt you. Whoever heard of someone storming an island with dress shoes?"

"I wouldn't worry about me at all. I've got this. I've defeated them before, I can do it again. Even in dress shoes."

She nodded in confirmation and returned her focus to piloting the plane. We would be there soon. Night would also be here soon. I could not wait. My life was filled with anticipation, and it was all for this moment. I could end L.I.F.E. right here, right now. The moment was so close.

As we flew into the sinking sun towards my destiny, I was ready.

Chapter 12
Santidigo Island

Just as the sun set, I could see the outline of the new L.I.F.E. facility. This small island was covered in their structures. The silhouettes of their labs, armories, training facilities, and dorms were only slightly visible as we approached. All variations of evil occurred down there. Tyler was down there, too. This was a place that any sane person would avoid, but I had a mission to complete.

"You ready for your leap of faith?" Mikaila said to me.

"Of course, I am. I could do with a little fresh air."

"Yeah, maybe the air will be nice, but the water's a completely different story. You could do without any of that. But I'm almost as far as I can go. You gotta jump here pretty soon."

I peered down at the icy waters below. I could withstand the cold, but that did not mean it was not painful. I had to drop hundreds of feet into the waves only to then swim all the way to the island where I would have to wear the soaked armor for the duration of the mission. It would not be pleasant, but I would endure it.

"Okay, it's time. Jump now!" Mikaila commanded suddenly.

"Goodbye and thank you for everything," I said before I opened the door and fell downwards into the black ocean so far below.

Down and down I fell, away from that plane. The mission had begun. I was the only one who could reach the finish and now I was here. The time to take action was now. Down into the icy waters I went.

The splash instantly woke me. I resurfaced and looked around. The shore was a couple hundred yards away. Above me, the plane circled back and then returned to the mainland. I was now alone. I began the arduous swim to Santidigo Island.

The time, though it may have only been minutes, felt like hours. My arms and legs became sore with the repetition that was swimming. On top of that, the icy cold of the water was making my whole body stiff. But I had to keep going. Now that it was night, I was on the clock. I had to clear up this whole ordeal by morning.

When at last I touched the sandy shores, my stamina was gone. I collapsed there in the sand, barely awake. I was tired, but I had a job to do. I forced my arms to push me from the ground and I rose to my feet. I was up and I could continue.

I marched through the sand and up a hill that was just before the first building. This first building looked uninhabited, so I passed it quickly, not wanting to waste time. There was another building to the east and that was my next destination. Hiding in its shadow, I believed this one to also be empty.

Was this place really this empty? The previous L.I.F.E. facility bustled at all hours of the day. It was only minutes after sunset, and no one even came near these buildings. They were on the outset, but that was no excuse for no agents. Where were they?

I moved through the shadows unseen. Often, I would see guards patrolling an area in the distance and I avoided detection. The difficulty of this mission had been overestimated by me. Barely even trying, I was safe. With little effort, I moved without raising alarm.

I noticed something else that starkly contrasted their previous base. There were no cameras anywhere. I did not have to worry about being detected by their security system because there was not one in place. How easy could this be?! What had happened to L.I.F.E.?

After navigating the shadows for tens of minutes, I came to a building that was very well-lit and loud noises could be heard from quite a ways away from it. Was this where everyone was? I would have to investigate. I climbed up a ladder on the outside of the structure and reached the roof. Light emanated from skylights up here. I made my way to one and peered inside.

About thirty feet from where I watched, a single man stood in the middle of an open room. All around the walls of this room were scientists, watching from behind barriers. It was a strange scene to say the least. It reminded me of my days in the Fight Arena.

The man himself was strange. He wore a suit that looked similar to mine. This armor covered all of his body besides his forearms, his feet, and his head. Metal boots covered his feet and metal gauntlets covered his hands to his forearms. On his head, a high-tech helmet with a heads-up-display system rested. The man was even more armored than I. He just stood there, unmoving, in the center of the room.

Suddenly, turrets rose from the floor and took aim at the man. He took action and bent his arms upwards. Shields emerged from the gauntlets and blocked the spray of bullets. The man raced forward and jumped onto one of the turrets. Hiding behind it, the other turret destroyed the first. His shields emerged again, and he ran at terrifying speeds towards the next. Just as he reached it, he jumped. He then brought down his huge metal fist into the turret and decimated it.

What power! This man was obviously a Super Soldier. He commanded such strength and speed. Even his armor amazed me! L.I.F.E. had created another superior power. This being was magnificent!

An SUV then rose from the floor on the opposite side of the room. He faced it and stared it down. The car sped towards him, and all he did was stare. When it was just about to collide with him, he threw an uppercut. The car flipped backwards into the air and then came crashing back down to the floor.

This giant car was flipped as if it were a bicycle. If only I could do that! This being's power was so much that he appeared invincible. He looked as strong as The One! The experiment had given him such strength. He was incredible.

He hit the car again and knocked it out of the way. Behind him, a wall rose from the floor. He turned and greeted the threat. Metal balls the size of grapefruits shot out at him at terrific velocities. Each one he either elected to catch or to knock to the ground.

After every one had been accounted for, another turret came up from the floor. This turret was equipped with different weaponry than the previous ones. I noted the laser rifle mounted on the turret. It was also armed with a machine gun and a flamethrower. The gun opened fire first. All he did was stand there as the machine guns blazed at his chest. He took the pain.

I knew how it felt to be hit with so many bullets. Even with armor on, it hurt like hell. It had sapped all my energy just trying to keep moving after being hit. There he was, allowing them to hit him. He never faltered.

The machine gun stopped firing and retreated. Out came the flamethrower. The flames encompassed him. Again, he stood, resilient. Even though I knew he was my enemy, I was rooting for him to make it through these trials. He was so strong.

The flames retreated as well, and the final weapon emerged. The laser aimed right at the center of the man's body. I saw him shudder right before the laser fired. The blast connecting with his torso instantly, he was flung backwards to the ground. Beyond the glass, I could hear his scream of agony. His fists clenched. The laser rifle was the bane of all Super Soldiers. It was a weakness that could not be beaten. I knew that pain as well, and it was excruciating.

The scream stopped. His fists unclenched, and he placed them on the ground. He heaved himself up. There in the middle of that room, he stood once more. A huge hole was blown in the armor covering his chest, but he did not care. He stood perfectly straight and perfectly still. What a soldier!

The scientists gathered behind the barriers applauded loudly. They saw what they had created. This being was beyond anything anyone on the mainland could ever imagine. This Super Soldier with his advanced armor could destroy anything to which he set his mind. That was exactly for what they were looking, and they had him.

I had certain admiration for the Super Soldier. His embodiment of power was one to be admired. Another thought ran through my head as I watched him take his bow down there. Who could this Super Soldier be? The answer was clearly one of two options for me. It was either Tyler or it was not Tyler.

Remembering Commander Zak's words before Tyler was taken away almost confirmed that this had to be Tyler. He had told me that they were taking him to Santidigo Island to be experimented on in the project that could turn a grown man into a Super Soldier. Was this really Tyler? He was cooperating with them, and that was something Tyler would never do. I did not want my friend to have to suffer the consequences of experimentation by these monsters. Was this Tyler?

A scientist was telling the Super Soldier something. The Super Soldier nodded and turned to leave this testing facility. This was my chance. I could follow him to his quarters and possibly I could speak to him alone. If it was Tyler, we could take down L.I.F.E. together. If it was not Tyler, I would have to assume that he was dead. Perhaps this man would assist me in avenging Tyler's death.

Below me, the scientists left the building and scattered among the many other buildings, chattering about the spectacle in which they had taken part. Looking back through my skylight, I saw that the Super Soldier was still in this building. He clenched his fists and trembled slightly. He appeared past anger and into rage, but, in the next second, it subsided, and he shook his head. He slammed open the door and walked outside.

I snuck to the edge of the roof to see him leaving. He walked the path that connected this structure to another close to the southern shore. He was trudging, and his head was down. This gave me the opportunity to follow him without being noticed. I at least hoped that he would not notice me.

After he had gone down the path quite a ways, I jumped down to the ground about thirty feet below. Rolling when I hit, I sustained no damage to my frame. This was good because a fight with this Super Soldier was still in play. Except, in that case, it would not matter if I was injured or not. I would lose. I doubted there was anything I could do in a situation such as that.

Now, I did not fear being noticed by the agents, even though that would end up just as badly for me. I was terrified of the beast in front of me turning around and spotting me. I had accounted for his advanced hearing on top of the heads-up-display that he still had activated in his helmet, but was the distance I had put between us enough? I followed, frightened.

This march was as slow and nerve-wracking as my first marches to and from the cafeteria in the prison had been. His trudging steps were mind-numbingly small, especially for his long legs that should have yielded a stride that was many times longer. Instead, we listened to the sound of his metal feet tapping the dirt, creating a tune that can get stuck in your head for the longest time. How could he walk this slowly?

I was about fifty feet from him when my foot struck a rock, sending it flinging down the path. Immediately, I tossed myself behind the corner of the nearest building. Sitting there and trying not to breathe, I felt his powerful eyes watching. My heart pounding in my chest, I noticed that I could no longer listen to the rhythmic stomping of his feet. There was no doubt that he had heard the rock and turned around, but nothing confirmed if he knew I was following him. All I could do was not move.

After an eternity, the feet began their trudging down the path. I would have sighed in such relief, but I feared his ears' hearing. I sat, motionless, basking in the release of terror on me. When my legs once again could operate, I used them to continue the pursuit.

At last, we were nearing the building to which the Super Soldier was directed. This structure varied greatly from the others on the island. Its shape was only a simple square much like the others, but its size was so much smaller. It was also grouped with a bunch of other structures, all the same. It looked as if these were only there to house one person each. Those people were Super Soldiers.

At least, I would not have to fear guards when I approached him. The building likely had only four rooms at the most, and that would allow me enough room to discuss my past with him as well as affording me a place to stay if he was to be friendly with me. This house was in my favor.

Grabbing the doorknob and turning it, the man revealed the entrance to his home. He entered, never checking behind himself. I crept to the door just as it was closing and flattened myself against the wall. I was about to address a Super Soldier. I needed to be prepared for this.

I breathed in and breathed out. For the first time in this slow pursuit, I could fill my lungs with air. With my lungs full, I touched the doorknob. Turning it as slowly as possible to avoid any noise, I managed to open the door. The door failed to squeak upon being pushed open, and this pleased me.

I crawled inside and pulled the door to its closed position. I scanned the hall for any sign of the Super Soldier. There was a door that was closed to my immediate right, but I could hear nothing behind it. From what I could hear, he was in the living room. I got to my feet and, staying crouched, moved to confront him.

Walking on this carpeted floor, any sound from my steps was suppressed. I passed the bathroom and glanced inside. He was nowhere within the bathroom. Further I went until I passed a closet. Not wanting to alert the man, I elected to leave it closed. I continued forth.

Just as I was about to round that corner and confront the man, I heard a door open behind me. Turning back, I was too late. The closet door was open and the Super Soldier stood above me. Before I could make a single move, he grabbed me by my throat and lifted me high into the air. My head touching the ceiling, I grabbed my pistols and took aim at the weak part in the armor covering his neck, but it was futile. With his other hand, he slapped the guns out of my hands as if it were nothing. I was caught and close to my death now.

His big metal hand landed on my head. I flinched when he tore off the mask that covered my face. I looked into the screen on his helmet and tried to bring about compassion in this mighty being. It was unnecessary. He dropped me, and I fell on my back before him.

"Martin? You are... They lied to me. I lacked judgment to believe them, for here you are, alive and in my home," said the Super Soldier, his voice muffled by the helmet.

"Yes, I am Martin! Tyler, is that you?" I imposed excitedly.

"You are incorrect," he said, pressing a button on his helmet.

The helmet hissed and released its hold on his head. His metal digits maneuvered the helmet from his head. The helmet now off his head and in his hands, I bore witness to the face of a new Super Soldier. My gaze sunk into his endlessly deep blue eyes that showed a curiosity for everything they saw. His head was close to baldness, having been shaved recently, but brown hair built up a short layer regardless. His face reflected such strength and independence. It was as nothing I had ever seen before.

"Who are you?" I asked.

"You cannot tell? I have changed greatly, but still I believed that I was recognizable as my past form," said the Super Soldier.

"I cannot recognize you, but why should I be able to? I ask again, who are you?"

"Martin, my friend, your eyes refuse to interpret me as you used to be able to see me. So much has changed within me, and I do not blame you for your inability to embrace your friend."

"Tell me your name. Please!"

"Martin, my greatest ally, shake the hand of one whom you have lost to misfortune. Come greet the one who has admired your existence and followed your every step. Bid a euphoric embrace to one who has suffered in the loss of all his heroes. From the dead, revive the life of the one who died in your absence: Cody Callison."

Chapter 13
Sorrow Revisited

Blinking did not change the scene before me. Cody Callison, the son of Jonah and Mia, was standing above me in a suit of advanced armor designed by L.I.F.E. scientists. He held his high-tech helmet at his waist and smiled down on me. I had believed him dead, but he was so much the opposite. My friend was alive!

"Cody! How are you alive?" I said, launching myself off the floor and hugging him.

Laughing in joy, he said, "I am not dead because I was such a perfect candidate. I am not dead because they thought higher of me. I am not dead because I proved their suspicions about me."

"What were their suspicions? Why did they pick you?" I questioned, full of curiosity for the one who I thought was dead.

He showed me to the couch in the living room and sat across from me in a recliner. His face turned away from me, and the smile left him. His eyelids fell over those deep blue circles, and tears formed. Shaking his head did not make them leave.

"It is so hard for me to speak of it. It is the single most horrific moment of my life. Yet...it is the single most defining moment as well. Please, allow me to weep as I try to speak," Cody told me.

"Take your time. I wish for you not to suffer more than you must over it."

"Much gratitude is yours for granting compassion to me. I have longed for that very compassion for an incomprehensible amount of time. Its presence in you warms my soul. Thank you, my friend. I shall speak as informatively as possible..." he paused, "...My unceasing nightmare begins in your absence."

"When Tyler and I left to hide from L.I.F.E.?"

"Correct. They came that very night. The knock on that front door still haunts me in my slumber. Only a mere hour had passed on your exit out of my life. My father...he...let them in. But what choice did he have?! What choice..."

Cody's face flooded with soft tears. He buried his face in his hands and cried silently. I pitied him. It was apparent that he had suffered through much. L.I.F.E. had cursed him with this trauma. His tears almost brought me to my own.

"My apologies to you, my friend," Cody said, wiping away the tears. "Permit me to continue. As I said, my father allowed them entrance into the house. That was all they needed. Within a minute, Alyssa and I were on our knees beside our parents and Donovan. Oh, Donovan! How unjust this life is! Why?! Why did... Why did... How could..."

His emotional state was in shambles. His trauma was too much for even this Super Soldier to bare. All I could do was stare. I had no words of comfort for him. I had left him in that house. I knew they would go there. Foolish mistakes only result in never-ceasing guilt.

"Those damned agents along with their pet, that Super Soldier named The One, were taking us one by one and interrogating us in my mother and father's room. Maybe we could have tricked them into thinking we did not know you, if only I had not been wearing that ring," he said, motioning to my hand.

I had given the ring as a gift to young Cody. I had thought it would help him remember me even when I was not there. It was true that the ring brought back memories of me, but ever so more important was the fact that it condemned the family to suffer. If only he had not worn it that night!

"Each violent punch and horrifying scream sent an icy chill down my spine. How I cried! I had not known that my parents were as weak as any other human being. I had thought of them as special. They returned after only minutes, but they were only half of what had entered that room. Before that day, fortune had shined and granted me the favor of never seeing true agony. Fortune has never shined on me ever again after that day... Please excuse me."

He removed the gauntlets and the boots. Leaving his chair, he walked to the closet which he then opened. After setting the equipment in there, he removed the top of the armor. After placing that in the closet, he removed the pants. Everything in its place, he closed the closet. Now, he only wore a thin spandex suit that covered all of his body excluding the head.

Cody crossed my vision, moving to the part of the house I had not seen, and I heard him closing the door to what I assumed was his room. I waited patiently for his return, desiring the end of the story he was telling. I needed the closure that would come at the end. I truly missed them. I needed to know. What had happened to the ones I had loved and who had loved me?

The door's opening was apparent, being the only sound in the whole house. He emerged, wearing a common green T-shirt and blue jeans. He sat softly into the chair across from me and looked into my eyes. After a deep sigh, he began again.

"Chosen last before my sister, I was shoved into that room. After all to which I had been forced to listen, I understood exactly what I had to do. The room empty of all but one agent and myself, I made haste to the closet when his back was turned. Opening the door alerted him, but not as much as the shotgun blast. It almost knocked me from my feet as well. When he fell, two more took his place. My finger was just touching the trigger when that true masterpiece, The One, grabbed me. I unloaded the weapon into his chest, but that was irrelevant."

The One had spoken of this encounter. He quite clearly intended to make me believe that they had all perished, but that was obviously untrue. He said that someone else had killed them for him. What he had told me was, at least, partially untrue.

"The One only laughed at me. He held me in the air and replaced me right before my family. He told the agents that he had a fantastic idea. Procuring another two shells, he loaded Mrs. T. Shoving it into my chest, he said, 'The fight within you is evidently much more than any of us suspected, Cody Callison. If you wish to live so badly, then show us you are committed to that life. Show us by sacrificing that which is highest in your heart. Do it, and I assure you that your life will be yours.'"

Cody's breathing intensified as if reliving the moment. His face was drenched in his grief. This was no ordinary infamous moment of sorrow, this was pure torment. The deepest depression mixed so perfectly with the fiercest rage. His grotesquely contorting body made me tremble.

"I told them I would never do it. I told them they were crazy to think I could do such a thing. That is exactly what I told them, but they...persisted...like...demons. Never did The One move from my ear. His whispers drove me to insanity. What could I do? What could I do?! They drilled themselves into the core of my soul! How could I fight it?! How?! I could not! I could not fight! So...there was only a single option. I raised that shotgun...I pointed it right at Donovan's head...and I blew his brains out! What choice did I have?!"

If I ever experienced terror in that prison, I could not recall it now. Fear filled every nook and cranny of my being as I gazed into this form that I had once known as Cody Callison. There was nothing left of him. He was gone. This creature before me was one I had never known. I sat, frozen in all-consuming fear.

"Next in the line was my own mother." Cody jerked up and aimed his fiery eyes at me, saying, "I see that look on your face! You fail to believe that anyone could be driven to kill their own mother! Well, my friend, you are wrong! The One pushed the gun's barrel so that it pointed directly at her. 'Next,' he said. She did not beg for her life as one might expect. 'Cody, if it means you live, then kill me. I want you to live,' she said. My father instructed Alyssa to turn away as I steadied the gun. I squeezed...then...my mom was dead!"

He fell uncontrollably into his chair. As he cried in his agony, I wept. I knew how this story ended. They would all die at the hands of one whom they loved so much. It was so disgusting. How could I not weep at such extreme sadness?

"The One loaded the shotgun again and then returned it to my grasp. My father knew his fate and turned to my sister. 'Alyssa, look away. It'll be okay. Just look away.' He shut his eyes and sat there on his knees, still as death. As I had done previously, I pointed and I fired. It was just that simple. Killing was just that simple. It did not matter that it was my dad. It did not matter that I loved him. Every moment I had spent with him...did...not...matter. It was just that simple!"

My face dug into my hands. There was no action that I could take that would stop the tears. The reality was sinking into my head. All the death was so clear in my mind. This story refreshed all their deaths, and there was nothing I could do to combat my grief.

"The last one was Alyssa. All I had to do was pull that trigger one more time. If I did not, I would die, and she would die. Was there really any other option? This one...made me hesitate. Unlike the others, she begged for her life. She reminded me of all through which we had been. She would not let me forget that I was her little brother. She truly did not think I would kill her. But I tell you, it was easy. Simple. The action was so basic! Anyone could have done it. All it required was the ability to hold up the weapon and to squeeze that trigger. So...easy. So...easy! 'I love you,' I told her. Then...I squeezed, and Mrs. T did all the rest. The deed was done. I had slaughtered them all. I fell to my knees into the flowing pool of blood. I could say nothing. It was done."

Cody was calm now. His eyes were locked on the floor. He said nothing for a long time. He just stared. He was a mess. Tears from his face had dampened his shirt. There was nothing I could say. Staring at him was what I did. I awaited more from Cody.

"The One grabbed my arm and lifted me from the floor. 'Throw him in the truck. We are taking him to Santidigo Island,' he said. I remained limp the entire time. My body shut down due to the absence of my mind. I do not know what happened after that, but I do know how my conscience aimed to kill me for what I had done. I believed myself evil and I still do. Is it not true? Could there not be a more accurate description of what I am? Evil, purely evil."

"You're not evil, Cody," I said, and his red eyes met mine. "That's not in your heart. They put that there. They made you do it. Do not blame yourself. I know you."

He chuckled at my naivety and said, "If you believe that, then it is quite apparent that you have never known me. That has always been in me. Never have I had a sensitivity to death. I loved that shotgun and I loved that bow and those arrows because they were weapons. I loved their killing potential."

"That's not true! All little boys think guns are cool, but they would never dream of killing somebody in real life. You have never been evil!"

He shook his head in disbelief, "Again, I tell you that you have never known me. All you knew was a boy you thought kindhearted. You thought! You never cared enough to ask me who I really was. A faithful admirer was all you needed. That is what you saw in me."

I could not speak against him, for he was correct. Though I cared deeply for him as a boy, did I really care enough to investigate into his life? The simple answer was that I did not. If only I cared, maybe I could have combated this evil dwelling in my friend.

"My friend, I do not mean to attack you. I apologize for what you have seen of me today. I am a monstrosity, and you should not be drawn into my failings. Just count yourself fortunate, Martin, for you have not suffered as I have. Do not take the beauty that is your life for granted."

"I don't. Never do I forget that I am blessed, Cody. I hope your story can help to remind me when I stray from that understanding."

"Thank you, my friend. It plagues me every waking moment, but I have no doubt that it will work towards your good. Now, it is time for me to retire, and I suppose you as well need sleep. You may sleep on the couch in my room. I shall close the curtains and lock the doors. There is no need to fear them. They are only feeble humans. Have faith in the fact that we are much greater than they. Come with me, my friend."

He stood from the recliner and motioned towards his room in the back of the house. I followed obediently and, when we had entered his room, I sat on the couch.

"It is yours. Use it as you wish," he said, closing the curtains.

This room was about the size of Cody's previous room at his old house. The walls were bare, unless you count the gaping holes in the drywall. Cody had punched this wall many times, and it was starkly evident. However, aside from the holes, there was nothing but his bed, a table beside, and this couch in the room. Perhaps the holes were for decoration.

Cody threw me a blanket from his bed and a pillow also. Setting the pillow at one end of the couch, I made a makeshift bed. I kicked off my dirty shoes and lay on the couch. I wrapped myself in the blanket, and Cody switched off the lights.

"Goodnight, my friend. Tomorrow brings us many an opportunity. I shall guide you through a tour of the island. We shall remain unseen, of course. But...until then, I bid you sleep well," Cody said softly.

"Goodnight to you as well, Cody. It will definitely be a journey. I do wish to see what L.I.F.E. has been up to. Until then, I hope you sleep well, too."

Cody fell into silence, and I mimicked the silence in fear of aggravating him. Cody Callison, he had changed, and I knew it. He believed that, even as a little eight-year-old boy, he was evil incarnate. I could not accept this. Even now with the L.I.F.E. experiment corrupting his mind, I was very confident that I could save him from this evil. I had to save him. Knowing everything I now did, I could not let him suffer with it for the rest of his life.

Speaking of saving, I began to think about the mission that brought me here. Cody had not said a word about him and left me wondering about my greatest friend. Was he here? Was he alive? I did not know the answers to these questions, but those would come tomorrow.

My eyes adjusting to the dark, I glanced towards Cody's bed. One, no, two things I noticed instantly. His eyes were locked on me. While I was attempting slumber, this maniac was staring me down. I only looked back. Was I safe in here with him? I did not doubt Cody's loyalty to me, but still I remained cowardly in his presence. He was the scariest thing I had ever seen.

All I had learned today was beyond belief. Fortunately, it all had not fully sunk in. Numb to the horror of which I had learned, I was not yet plagued by the suffering that Cody endured every day. I would continue to hope that it never would sink in. I could not take a hit that heavy without losing my sanity. Cody had taken that hit and now he was a different creature. This news hopefully would not be my downfall.

However, tomorrow was a new day. It could be left behind me. I did not have to let it affect me. After all the losses I had endured, why should I let this get to me? I was a new man and I would not let the past weaken me. My strength would overcome my weakness. With that very strength, I would save Cody Callison from the evil brewing inside his heart.

Chapter 14
Evil Shows Its Face

"Wake up, my friend. They will become curious if I stay in my house for such periods of time. It is unusual for me to not venture outside at this hour of the day," said Cody from above me.

I knocked the blanket off me and sat up. "Give me a second, Cody. What time is it?"

"6 o'clock. We have to go soon, my friend. How much time do you need?"

"Um... Just give me a minute here," I responded, wiping the sleep from my eyes.

Standing, I stretched. Did Cody really get up this early every morning? Never had I been forced to wake so early. Even in prison, the bells did not buzz until 9 o'clock. I was obedient anyway and I wrapped my belt around my waist. I was about to retrieve my pistols from the living room, but Cody stopped me.

"Leave the belt and weapons here, my friend. This is a simple tour and nothing else. You wish to survey the facility; I shall afford you that opportunity. I ask that you refrain from attack until the time is right," he instructed.

I nodded my head and removed the belt. "I understand. No need for weapons if I'm not going to use them." Cody left the room, and I followed.

"You will not be wearing that armor when we go, either. You are to wear a suit of the enemy. I have one you can borrow. Previously, I had worn it, but I rebelled against its presence. We are similar in size, and I believe it will fit you."

Cody led me to a smaller room near the door to the house. It was a storage room and it held the suit for which we were looking. He took it off the hangar and analyzed it for a moment. He appeared to be reliving the times when he had worn it. Looking back to me, he held out the suit for me.

"Thank you, Cody. It should work fine."

"Good. It will protect you from their eyes. With that said, I shall let you dress yourself in it."

Cody left the room so that I could change without his presence. I appreciated this because his presence made me rather uncomfortable. I removed the armor and felt the weightlessness of freedom anew. Feeling the heavy armor on my shoulders for so many hours had acclimated me to its weight. With it gone, I felt much more agile and free. This feeling was good.

I then had to stuff myself into the attire of evil. Though the suit had an overall appealing appearance, it tired my soul. I had worn a mock copy of these suits just yesterday, and that had been enough for me. If I had to wear this symbol of villainy all day, I would burst from the polar opposition in my heart.

Completing the final steps of tying my tie, I stood prepared. I straightened the suit on my body, analyzing its fit. Black and white made up the color wheel for this apparel. Its audacity was difficult to ignore. Ironic that these were the clothes that would camouflage me.

Stepping outside the small room, I greeted Cody with a nod.

"Let us move. I have already informed you of my tardiness. Leaving in the near future could get us noticed leaving at the same time from the same place. We must go," Cody commanded.

"All right then. I am ready. Show me this facility," I said, throwing on the shades that accompanied the attire. The door was opened, but I stopped Cody before we left. "Wait! First, tell me. Am I going to see Tyler today?"

"Of course, my friend. Why would we not?"

"I just feared..."

"He was dead? He is alive and...in stable condition. He is one of our last stops. I shall save my explanation and simply allow you to see him."

"I want to go there first. Why is that stop last?"

"I have carefully crafted a foolproof path for us. If you are looking to get caught, deviating from it would be a great way to accomplish that."

"Fine. I get it. Let's just go."

Out the door and into the morning light we ventured. The sun was just beginning its ascension, and the sky was beautiful. The orange glow illuminated the soft clouds high above. I enjoyed the sight, but Cody refused to acknowledge it. He walked with his vision always pointed at the objective. He was blind to this beauty.

We were moving eastward, having left his house at the southwestern corner of the island. There was much of this island I had not yet seen. That would be resolved today. I could study my enemy and form a plan to see their destruction and defeat. This tour was essential to that.

"First, these are the Super Soldier boarding domiciles. All of the ten are left empty, excluding mine. L.I.F.E. has been low on funds after you demolished their main base. The American government is hesitant in ceding more funds to an organization that keeps its business secret from its benefactor. As a result, Super Soldier experimentation has almost been fully ceased. Now, they work on improving the armor and weaponry in which they have been outfitting me. They have made progress, but it is a creeping progress compared to what they desire," remarked Cody as we passed the two rows of five houses in which his house was a part.

We moved towards two larger buildings that stood right outside the rows of the boarding domiciles. Cody glanced at them, but to such a slight extent it was barely worth noting. He said nothing about the structures, but I read signs on the buildings that stated their purpose. These were agent and scientist quarters. This area must be the residential side of the island.

It was pleasant to not have to sneak around and to be able to take a leisurely stroll in broad daylight. Worries were scarce during our walk down the simple paths that were the bloodlines of Santidigo Island. The songs of small birds echoed in the idyllic emptiness. After all I had put on myself yesterday, I enjoyed this environment.

Coming upon another complex that rose about two stories, Cody said, "That structure to the south is the optics research and development lab. They have been working to improve the L-series laser rifles as well as the heads-up-display in my helmet. To give them fair credit, they have done quite well this past year. Laser rifles are being produced in high quantities and they are deadlier than ever. It actually is an accomplishment worthy of some praise."

Along with making deadlier Super Soldiers, they were making deadlier Super Soldier killers. I hypothesized that this was in fear of Cody's betrayal. Although the weapons would be astoundingly effective against a rival military, they were better used to assure cooperation with the Super Soldiers.

"These next buildings to your left and right are simply a waste of space. They lie vacant as L.I.F.E. has not the funds to make anything of them. I have gone into them before and found nothing of interest. They would not be a bad spot to trap an enemy, of course, but still I find them quite worthless," Cody said as we took the path north.

I had thought the buildings empty when I first arrived here and I was correct. L.I.F.E. truly was in a weakened state after I had dealt a terrific blow against them with the destruction of their main base. I had hoped to finish the organization that day, but now here I was. I would finish them this time. That much was assured.

Upon further trek to the north, we approached a humungous hangar. Cody said nothing, but his feet carried him straight towards it. My feet did as well, and we walked together in silence, nearing a mystery that I hoped would be soon explained.

"This," said Cody finally, "is L.I.F.E.'s special hangar. Inside its walls, you could find maybe one or two helicopters. The absence is not caused by lack of funds. Quite the opposite, actually. A multitude of funds filled the hangar and caused a lack of funds. With what, you wonder? Come within and see for yourself."

He opened one of the side doors for me, and I entered. Inside, it would have been completely black if it had not been for the numerous glowing panels I could see in the distance. Cody, entering, flipped a number of light switches. The dark retreated and revealed its secrets.

Before me, stretching for what felt like a mile, were hundreds of huge metal spheres. This infamous threat had returned exactly as L.I.F.E. had. The flying, fiery spheres of death lay in their designated spots, idle. If activated, nothing but horrid chaos and mass death would occur.

"What are these doing here?" I asked, stunned.

"L.I.F.E. recovered them from the confrontations with Jack Lamb. They then researched the inertial-propulsion devices and replicated them. They added more devices to stabilize and speed up flight. They improved targeting by adding a secondary heartbeat sensor with every thermal camera. The flamethrowers are now fueled by a stickier and more flammable tar-based fuel. The shells are made of a denser and more resistant metal. A layer of insulation nullifies electrical weaponry. These machines are the LIFE Spheres. Ultimate killing machines that show mercy only to those whose body-signatures have been programmed into their mainframe. Death in a thousand spheres. You ask what these are doing here? They are here to conquer an old world and bring about a new one."

With these, L.I.F.E. could have whatever they wanted. The new and improved spheres were nearly impossible to destroy and could kill hundreds each. Release them in a city, and they would burn it to the ground by the end of the day. L.I.F.E. always possessed such immense power. It was unbelievable.

"There are one thousand machines lined up in here with an additional five that are to be piloted. Each pilot sphere has a control panel that can change the attack patterns of the other spheres. Utterly destructive. It is beautiful," Cody remarked.

Beautiful was not the word I would have used to describe it. Impressive, maybe, but not beautiful. I was not sure what Cody saw in these that I did not. His mind was clearly much different from mine. That much was obvious.

"We have no need to remain here, my friend. Let us continue," Cody said, moving to the light switches.

"What is so beautiful about it, Cody?" I asked just before he flipped them.

He paused and dropped his hand from where it rested on the light switches.

"You wish to know why I see beauty in these metal spheres but not in the sunrise? Is that your question?" Cody asked, turning to face me.

I had not said anything about the sunrise and how I saw beauty in it to Cody. My only explanation for this was that he was doing something I had witnessed from The One. He deduced my thoughts based on the environment surrounding me and what had happened. Using what he knew about me, he could accurately guess what I was thinking.

"What's your multiplier? I mean, how many times stronger than the average human are you?" I asked.

"Another question? Do you not wish that I answer the previous first?"

"Answer this question first."

"If you insist, I shall. I am 15 times more than the average human being. The experiment could not yet handle higher multiplication on those who were past their infancy. I thought you would have already guessed that due to my perceived age of approximately 23 when I was given the experiment not long after my eighth birthday and the fact that it has been a year. It was a simple puzzle, so why do you ask? Did the solution truly escape you?" Cody said, verbally spitting on me from atop his higher IQ.

"I only wanted to be sure. Your 'mind-reading' is just about as advanced as The One's. He had a 30 multiplier. I was only curious of how you had perfected this technique."

"The truth of this matter is that I am not as good as The One. I can read you well only because I understand your nature. That is why I can deduce your thoughts so effortlessly. Now, shall I answer your first question?"

"Yes, how do you see beauty in this army of metal?"

"I see beauty because I see my conquest. I see my revenge. I see justice, and it is beautiful."

"Justice? How could these be used for justice? They are merciless killing machines! They are incapable of justice!"

"You are incorrect, my friend. They are the perfect vehicle to justice. Under my command, they will slay every evil soul on this damned planet. That is justice and that is beauty," he explained to me as if I were a foolish child.

"What are you talking about?! You want to kill everybody on the planet?! Why?"

"These humans are incapable of anything but malfeasance. You know that. Their deaths will cleanse the planet of wickedness. Life without evil. Pure beauty. Undeniable, pure beauty."

"You seek to take the life of every human on the planet, but you forget yourself. Why is that?"

"You and I are no longer humans, my friend. We are above the humans. We would never steal a baby from his parents out of nothing but curiosity. We would never kill innocents merely to weaken our adversaries. We would never command a little boy to gun down his entire family. That is why we are different from the humans. That is why we are allowed to escape demise. We are different. We are better."

"You believe that we are better than everyone else because of an experiment?" I asked Cody, shocked by the confidence with which he spoke such evil words.

"I believe that we are better because our minds have been advanced past evil. The humans' minds can only comprehend the ways of evil. That is why every one of them must perish. They have wounded me enough with their evil ways! I shall not permit this evil to reside on my planet any longer! They all will burn. All of them!"

"You are mad! Not all humans are as evil as L.I.F.E.! You would take billions of innocent lives in the pursuit of revenge?"

"They are *not* innocent! All of them are so capable of being that very evil that brought me to my knees before my family! They *all* would paint their filthy paws red given the chance! That is why I am going to kill every single one of them! Do you not understand yet? I can never be the same after what they did to me! I shall have my revenge!"

My advanced mind raced to come up with a resolution to this raging lunatic's wrath. Hate had twisted his perspective. He would not listen to any attempt to stop his killing spree. I had to divert his anger. I needed to have him feel as if he was accomplishing something against his enemy.

"You can be better than that! Forget your revenge! End this organization with me! The evil will be finished, and there will be no need to kill so many! Please!"

Cody stopped entirely and just stared at me. I dared not move while those deep blue circles were piercing through me. He looked so angry, yet...he was thinking. After exhaling loudly, he moved his eyes to the ground. He unclenched his fists and exhaled once more.

"Then, let us go...Martin. Their leader is in the Central Control building at the heart of the island. Let us go and stop all their evil. Together, we shall end this," Cody said, keeping his gaze on the floor.

"Yes, let's go. End this with me, Cody. There is no need for all that death."

He nodded, looked up, and grinned at me. He had tears in his eyes. He turned back again and opened the door. Switching the lights off, he and I left the hangar.

Our steps now moved us westward, straight to the center of Santidigo Island. This was my chance to end L.I.F.E. once and for all. With such a powerful ally by my side, there was no place for failure. I was worried about Cody and his overreactions, mostly because of his outburst only a minute ago, but I felt that he would listen to me if any issue arose.

Then again, this being with whom I had partnered had shown me that he was not the same boy I had met in that shack by the sea. He was clearly different. His mind had been infected by malice, and his thoughts were poisoned with odium. In his deep blue eyes, I could still see the little boy I loved, but the rest of his being was distorted. The contents of his heart were rising to the surface. Evil had shown its face.

My heart beat fiercely at the thought of ending it all. In only seconds, we would reach those steps that would carry us up to the door. Through that door, their leader sat in his comfortable office, suspecting nothing. Together, we would end his organization. Would this all really be over?

In the same instant that we arrived on the steps leading up to the entrance of the Central Command building, Cody put his hand on my chest, stopping all my motion.

"Stop," he commanded.

"What's wrong?" I asked, concerned with what might follow.

"The time is not right. However strong you and I are together, it is not enough. Let us prepare ourselves for this moment. Haste will waste us. Tomorrow is another day."

The main issue, Cody's hatred of humanity, seemingly disappeared, I had no problem with ending L.I.F.E. tomorrow. A feat such as this should involve further preparation. As long as Cody was not preparing to kill off all humans on the planet, I would do as he said.

"You are right. We can come back tomorrow. I want to make sure we are completely ready for this," I said, showing a smile that was full of loyalty and trust.

"I am glad you understand, Martin. Come with me. I have more to show you," he said, turning from the mission with a grin on his face.

Chapter 15
The Friend and the Foe

We continued the tour of Santidigo Island. Cody led me around the Central Control building and towards the north coast of the island. I had a good view of the ocean and I enjoyed the scenery. It calmed my nerves that Cody had stirred up only minutes ago. Fortunately, it seemed as if whatever was stirred up in Cody had calmed down as well. To the east, not far from the hangar, there was another structure that had not yet been identified. I saw Cody turn his attention to it and I turned my own attention to him in anticipation of an explanation.

"That building next to the hangar is where the LIFE Spheres are developed. Much work has been put into those machines, and the result, as you have seen, is tremendous success. There is no need for us to enter that building either. Follow me now to the west, Martin."

It was strange to think that so many machines had been made in that building next to the hangar. The building was only several times larger than Cody's house. It was difficult to comprehend working for hours in that cramped space. Still, work could be done in there, and that was proven by what I had seen in the hangar. There is no place that work cannot be done.

As we walked to the west, approaching the place where I had witnessed Cody's skill last night, Cody was silent. He looked as if in thought, but not deeply. He was keenly aware of what was around him, yet I could tell his mind was active at the same time. I could not know what he was thinking, but I feared the worst of him.

With a slight motion towards the building, Cody said, "I am sure your memory has not discarded this place. This is a battle simulator through which I am put every week. They must test my abilities as well as their suit. It is an entertaining, albeit painful, experience. I love smashing those turrets and flipping their cars. I feel powerful, and that is exactly what I am."

Power in the hands of my dear friend Cody. Never would I have even contemplated the thought of Cody being this strong. Never did I believe that L.I.F.E. would curse him with their presence. Never did I think they would take everything from him.

"Look south, Martin. You can see those two buildings just north of my house. The one on the left is utilized for agent training. The second is where the scientists design my armor. Both are necessary to this island, but I have interest in neither. Where I take you next, my interest lies."

I now knew the purpose of every building on this island excluding one. That last one I already could guess the purpose. This final destination had to be where Tyler was. It had to be the Super Soldier Research Department. Finally, I would be reunited with Tyler, and, together with Cody, we would finish what we started so long ago.

"It's the Super Soldier Lab, isn't it?" I asked.

"What else would it be, Martin? Inside, you will be able to see your good friend Tyler Ishler. Rescue will not be an option yet, but we shall return. First, an introduction to the lab."

My steps sounding on the cement paving that surrounded the lab, I gazed upwards at the rest of the structure. This building was a rectangle, the same as all the others before, but it stood above all the others with an astounding elegance. It had an air of superiority that came with its expensive design and modified exterior. This lab, being of greatest importance to L.I.F.E., was showered in funds. Its elegance separated it from the common-looking buildings that covered the rest of the island.

We walked right in the front door. Not one of them even glanced at us. Through the front door and down the hall. Scientists merely passed with no regard for two Super Soldiers taking a stroll through their precious lab. I thought this was going to be difficult. Not one spared us even a single word.

The halls looked to be emulating the perfection that those within strove to create. They were pure white and gleamed with the fluorescent lighting above. White as snow and void of any fault. These walls boxed in those with creation as their occupation, but true creation could not be found here. Alteration and modification were the tools of those who thought they were so original. No one can create true perfection.

"We are almost there. Remember, we are only viewing. Ask no questions and make eye contact with no one. I do not want to fix any of your problems," Cody said condescendingly.

"I've got it. Don't worry, I won't forget."

What was with Cody? This attitude was both unnecessary and unlike him. Why did he treat me as if I were so far beneath him? He was three times more than I, but it was unfair to make such a comparison between us. Surely, something had changed between us.

I pondered angrily as the glass window came into sight. I barely noticed it, for I was consumed with my own inadequacy. I scarcely noticed Cody's head nod when we were close. I snapped out of my thoughts and turned towards the window.

Without thinking, I flew to the glass and looked desperately inside. Cody's powerful hand slammed down onto my shoulder and pulled me back. I apologetically turned my eyes to meet Cody's. He gave no remorse in his harsh correction. What had caused me to lose my favor with my friend?

Forgetting my mistake, I returned to the window and peered through. This window was high on the wall of the room with which it was connected. The room was dark, but I could see the glow of computer light. Downwards, a single female scientist analyzed the readings of digital flashing displays. She darted from panel to panel, checking off items from her list. Having filled the list within a minute, she walked to the far side of the room.

Laying her hand on a noticeably blue button, she pushed. Activated, shutters moved from their original positions and uncovered a chamber full of strange liquids...but not all liquids. My greatest friend, Tyler Ishler, floated, seemingly lifeless. He was only supported by tubes and wires. His naked and hairless body looked strange compared to his former glory, but it was quite clear. This was definitely he for whom I had searched so desperately.

"It's really him. That's Tyler! He is okay!" I said quietly to Cody.

"Calm yourself. Do not make me regret taking you here."

Here was the same type of response from my supposed friend. He had been so happy to see me before. What had changed? Almost every response was hurtful. Had I done something wrong?

The scientist wrote her observations on a clipboard she carried. After scribbling for a moment, she slapped the blue button and the metal shutters closed over my friend. Just as easily as he had appeared, he disappeared. Now, I knew he was alive. I could save him and I would save him.

"You can now rest assured of his condition. They keep him in homeostasis only because they wish to use him in the future. Without money, operations cannot commence. So...they wait. That is all they can do for now. Rest assured; he is safe," Cody whispered to me.

"Thank you for taking me here," I whispered back.

"I knew you needed to see this. But...shall we not linger here? Come, an exit is necessary at this time."

"Of course. It is time to leave."

Moving through the pure white halls, I left the company of my greatest friend. I knew it was not the right time, but how I wanted to stay! Why could we not bring down this organization today and save him? Why could the right time not be now? I was ready. Just give me that chance.

Conflicting emotions hit me as the cool air of the island did. I was angry to have to leave Tyler, but I was relieved to leave that lab. Something about it...made me sick. The knowledge of L.I.F.E.'s villainous activities drove me from their presence. I hated their crimes. How evil these deeds were! That was the origin of my sickness.

"I know how you feel about Tyler's well-being. You feel obligated to save him for all he has done for you. I never knew him well, but it was easy for even the blind to see his heart. He is a good man even still, Martin. He will be rewarded for it with his rescue. That will be your job."

"Are you saying that he is a truly good man, unlike every other human on this planet?" I questioned Cody.

"No, of course not. He is as evil as the rest, but I shall not be the one to put up with his filth. You are to rescue him and you are to deal with him. I know what it is to have what you love taken from you. This man has shown great merit. For that, I shall allow you to keep him," he answered.

I breathed a sigh of relief. While Cody sounded as if he was holding on to his hatred of humanity, he did not plan to kill Tyler. This was one thing about which I could be happy. Still, things were not going very well for me, but I believed that I could change the mind of the murderer with whom I partnered.

"His loyalty was something that I wouldn't trade for anything on this Earth. He was like family to me when I had none. We needed each other and, together, we could conquer all."

"There is no need for you to explain your bond to me. I may be one to have none, but truly I say that I understand this friendship has made you so many times stronger than any force against which you have come. It has done more for you than L.I.F.E. ever did. If only I could have such stability."

"Am I not your friend?" I asked, finally cornering him into answering my thoughts. "You and I have had a similar bond, have we not? We rescued each other, did we not?"

"Do not fool yourself, Martin. There is no bond between us besides the forced bondage of the experiment. We are the same, yet I feel no compassion towards you. Such allegiance as you hold with Tyler is not possible with me. One who attempts to show compassion to many will surely fail. Withhold your compassion from me. Is one good friend not enough for you?"

"Why would you shrug off an invitation to my friendship? I have had so many friends in the past, but they have fallen dead before me. Each death stings me, for every life is so precious to me. Yes, I aim to save Tyler for everything he has done for me, but that does not mean I wouldn't do the same for you...or anyone else for that matter."

"You say you show compassion to all? How do you justify your murderous rampages, Martin? You hypocrite! If life is so precious to you, why do you seek to take it from them? If all killing is wrong, how can you possibly justify yourself to me?"

I clenched my fists and turned from my accuser. Again, my past was thrown back into my face. This transition was more difficult than I could have imagined. Changing my life would not be so simple. I aimed to leave the past behind me, but I was going to have to fight for it.

"I am not that man anymore!" I confronted Cody, stepping forward again. "I avoid death at all costs now! The truth is...there is no way I can justify what I have done. I am a killer and, thus, I am evil. I do not fool myself in that fact. But don't let my point escape you just because of my hypocrisy. I am saying that your life is precious to me and that I would prefer us as friends. That is what I am saying."

Cody and I stood in the emptiness of the pathway that connected the lab to Cody's house to the south. He stared at me, his intelligence shining through those eyes. Could he see any value in what I was saying? Could he not believe that I aimed to spare lives now? Could he not see the importance of human life I held in my heart? Silence was the only answer I was given for what felt like forever.

"We have digressed," he said finally. "Understand that I do not hold your values for human life. I aim to send them all to an early grave, but you aim for the antithetic outcome. You asked if I was your friend. With two people so different, how can a friendship flourish? That is my answer to your question."

"You are my friend," I said as he turned his back.

Facing me, he said, "And you are not mine. Let us return to the house. Such discussion should not proceed in the wide openness of these simple dirt pathways."

Again, he turned away and now continued his trajectory towards the house. I followed, feeling quite beaten. I had poured the contents of my heart out to convince Cody of my loyalty. It worked, but he did not grant the same loyalty to me. In his mind, we were enemies with a similar goal in the near future. When that goal was accomplished, he would turn on me. It was no secret.

As Cody had trudged last night, I now trudged this morning. Demoralized by whom I had considered one of my greatest supporters, I held my head low. Did he really think I was going to help him exterminate all human life on the planet? How could he believe such a ridiculous notion?

Was his mind that twisted? Cody had changed in totality after he had been forced to kill his family. I remembered how I felt after the deaths of my family, and their deaths were not by my hands. Even thinking about it brought tears to my eyes. What had that incident done to Cody?

When we were at his house, Cody opened the door and motioned for me to enter.

"Go inside and wait. I have to pick up something of importance. I shall return shortly."

I did so and took a seat on the couch. I realized that I had not had the chance to analyze this room the previous times I had been here. Now, I saw a shotgun mounted on the wall. Yes, this was Mrs. T, the beloved weapon of Mr. T. There it was, high on the wall to my left. I knew it had not been cleaned since moving to Cody's hands, due to the blood splatter dotting its surface.

A T.V. was past the recliner and against the far wall. Simple, cheap paintings adorned the white walls randomly. Low-budget wooden tables were covered with neatly stacked papers and books. The carpet was a dull blue color and seemed to cover every bit of the floor of this house, excluding the floor of the bathroom, which had a mixture of white and blue tiles covering it. All in all, L.I.F.E. did not throw much money at this construction project.

Having covered the entirety of the room rather quickly, I awaited the return of my supposed enemy. I laid my back against the soft couch. Sitting here, I relaxed for the first time in so long. Never did I relax when I was in prison, driving with Melody and Liz, preparing an invasion with Mikaila, or in the presence of Cody. Here I was alone on this comfortable couch. Peaceful relaxation met me at last.

I thought back to my days of relaxation in the past. Joy filled the days I spent with my family by the sea. I could never forget the kindness shown to me by them. Never would the memory of those whom I had saved and who had saved me fade. Now, only one of the family remained and he was not the same as I had remembered. He was different in entirety.

My memories also contained the brotherhood found in my place in the mob. How I had loved every one of them! They were my brothers and a family when I needed one. Their genuine support and admiration of me was always a motivator for me. They kept me going when I thought I had lost everything. Now, only two remained, and they were trapped away from me. One was jailed in justice, and I felt I had no right to free him, but the other was mine to free. There would be no stopping Tyler's salvation.

And how could I forget the love of those who shared my last name? I never could, and that is the truth. Their love and acceptance of me made me a better man and planted a seed within me. They gave my life value and direction. They showed me forgiveness and how to obtain it. They helped me to see that there was something above me. They gave me hope, faith, and love. They supplied me with all I would need for my life.

Even all the others in my life meant so much to me. While many had attacked me, I could forgive them, for I knew that they only wanted the best. The fishermen who had aided me in my attempt to end injustice, the officers who had pursued me for my crimes, and the agents who had wished to misdirect me, they all had purpose in my life. Yes, we quarreled, but, in the end, they led me to where I was now. I was thankful for their work in my life.

So many had touched my life. I would not forget their sacrifices, making me better and better. My life might have been difficult, but these difficulties were what had made me stronger. Every difficulty was an opportunity to become a better man. When they put me through the fire, I was not burned, but refined. I was glad that these opportunities had not been missed.

Leaning back in the couch, I was thankful. I hoped that I would never again take my life for granted. Whatever I faced, I hoped that I would be able to see the good in it. I needed a new outlook on life if I was to win all my battles. A new outlook was exactly what I had just gained.

I relaxed even more so now. I felt new peace hit me. I could not place from where this peace came, but I was glad it did. I had accepted that my life was not perfect, but that I could make it through with a little help. When adversity came, I would be ready. I had peace and I could relax.

My relaxation ended with the slamming door and the heavy footsteps of my adversary. He threw another version of his armor onto the couch beside me. He then added the new gauntlets, new boots, and new helmet to the pile.

"Give me some of your time so that I can change, Martin. I need to show you this."

Chapter 16
The Power of the Beast

After he had changed into the black compression suit, he jumped into the armored pants. Fitting perfectly into the pants, he threw on the armored shirt. Having the armor covering all but his head, feet, forearms, and hands, he put his feet into the big metal boots. Cody adjusted something at the top of the boots, tightening them firmly to his leg. Next were the gauntlets, into which he stuck an arm and then tightened with the other hand. With the gauntlets and boots on, he placed the helmet on his head. He pressed a button which secured the high-tech headgear. It was complete. Cody was prepared for battle.

"Let me demonstrate my true power, Martin," said Cody.

He flexed his arms and shields emerged from the backs of his forearms. Thin strips of metal fanned out from a compartment and combined to form a metal semicircle. This semicircle had a radius of the length of his forearm. They looked incredibly resistant and strong.

"I can see you are impressed. They are triggered by my muscles contracting in a specific pattern. This pattern is only achieved by a single action. That prevents them from popping out when I flex my muscles for such reason as punching someone's brains out of their head, which I could easily do with these gauntlets," Cody said, letting the shields retract when he finished his last sentence. "These are made of a tungsten alloy that is astoundingly strong and heavy. With my strength behind them, I could punch through a wall of concrete a foot thick!"

"Seriously? They are that resistant? But are they not too heavy for your arms?"

"Ha! Too heavy for my arms? What are you saying? I am a Super Soldier! I can do almost anything, and you are concerned about the weight on my arms? Martin, I am not assured that you understand of what you are capable," Cody answered, his smirk mocking me for my question.

"It was only a question. I'm just curious about their weight. I wanted to know how effective they really are," I responded, shrugging off the insult.

"I shall tell you one thing. They are more effective than you know. They are the perfect weapon for any Super Soldier. The same is true for the boots. They, too, are made from a tungsten alloy and, with my force behind them, have terrifying momentum."

"But what of the helmet? Anything special with that?"

"Of course! The heads-up-display alone is terrific! It has thermal vision as well as night vision. It finds targets based on their heartbeats. Basically, it is much like the targeting systems of the LIFE Spheres. But besides that, it has voice control that is directly connected to the LIFE Sphere control system. I can control their attacks with my voice! How great is that?"

There was no argument against Cody's excitement. This was the single most powerful suit of armor for which a Super Soldier could hope. His abilities were not at all restricted by this suit, only amplified. He was safer from any kind of attack as well as many times more deadly. There was only one thing that could stand in his path of destruction: the laser rifle.

"What is the rest of the armor made of?" I asked.

"It is composed of layers of a protein that is similar to that found in the brain during Alzheimer's. L.I.F.E. calls it 'Compound 23'. Many times stronger and lighter than Kevlar. Bullets would have a hell of a time getting through this! It is ridiculously resilient! The best ever made!"

All of his composure had faded with the introduction of the suit. The enigma of his calm and mysterious aura was gone. Now, he acted more like the nine-year-old he truly was. He no longer was composing himself as he had.

"What about lasers? What effect do they have on the armor?" I questioned, knowing the answer.

His faced dropped when he said, "Lasers? What do you think? They tear right through it."

"So...you aren't really as unstoppable as you put on?"

"Ha! Haha! What are you trying to say, Martin? You think you can beat me if only you have access to a laser rifle? That is foolish, and you know it. I could kill you before you put a single blast in me. Do not forget how powerful I am without the suit."

However strong I was, he was unmistakably better than I. Even if I was armed with a laser rifle, I would have such low chances of beating him. Only the lasers could pierce those fantastic materials. With his intellect and technology, he would already be impossible to hit. Cody Callison had become the most powerful being on the planet.

"That is not what I was saying," I responded.

"Martin, I am not the fool that you are. I know, and let me emphasize that, *know* when you are lying to me. You aim to fight me to the death after we finish off the L.I.F.E. Organization. Let it be made known to you now. You are the one who shall meet death."

Cody had been calling me a fool for quite some time now. Why did he choose that word? What was so foolish about my actions? Who was he to belittle my intelligence only because he had amassed so much? Cody called me a fool, but I knew I was not.

"I do intend to fight you. As foolish as that is, is it not the right choice? Should I not stand up against you even though it is so obvious that you will win? Answer that question, my friend," I said, my face twisting with the lack of patience I had for him.

"My friend? Why do you keep referring to me as an ally? Do you have the trust I had in you originally? Martin, I am not your friend. Learn that if you ever learn anything. To answer your question, no. It is so stupid that you would hand over your life for something so meaningless as the death of those who mean nothing to you. Why would you ever willingly end your life? That is why you are a fool."

"I would end my life in the low hopes of ending yours. Your evil intentions boil my blood. If I could just get that chance to stop you, I would take it."

He said nothing to this remark. He turned away from me and shook his helmeted head. Cody would never listen to a second of my logic. While I always had good intentions, his intentions only led back to himself. All was for him, and, if someone wanted to fight for the greater good, they were a fool. This was Cody's mentality.

"Fine. Stand by me now. That is what is important, the present. But understand, thought was meant to dwell on the future. If you refuse to plan for such a crucial moment, you will have no chance of killing me. I shall let that sit in your mind, Martin."

"What difference do my thoughts have on the situation? You say I cannot win, so why should I worry about it?"

He turned back to me and stopped. I could see his eyes within the helmet, searching me. They met mine and looked deeply. He looked away and shook his head again. He then scoffed slightly and returned his attention to me.

"I only jest when I say you cannot win. At your full potential, you could kill me so quickly, even you would fear yourself. You are not yet there, but if you truly were to hone your skills and place your thoughts in order, there is no way I could escape death. That is what I mean when I say you must prepare for the moment of our betrayals. You can win, and that is the very reason you must never stop worrying about it. You can win; I never meant you could not," Cody said.

Was what he was saying true? Could I really become so many times stronger than he? It seemed impossible, but perhaps the numbers that the scientists had given us were not as meaningful as I had thought. Maybe I could ascend higher than five times the average. That was what Cody was telling me, and I was told he knew better than I. I could become greater. I could be as powerful as he.

"Do you believe in me again?" I asked, hopeful of an affirmation. He paused and stood the same as a statue. I felt every second pass as I awaited response.

"No...you are no longer my hero. I do not believe you can accomplish this feat. It would be for my own good that you do not," he responded, looking to the floor.

"What have I done to fail your expectations?"

His eyes swung back to me. They were full of disappointment and disgust.

"You do not focus on yourself. Your gaze is perpetually on others now. You fail to protect yourself. I do not understand this transformation in you, but it has weakened you. Keep that in mind when you finally realize you cannot save them all."

"Them?" I asked him, taking a step closer.

"The humans, Martin. You can never save everyone. You will fail if that is your mission. Set a realistic goal, and your chances of completing it skyrocket. No man has the power to bring the salvation of which you speak. You will fail and then you burn along with them."

The words he spoke were intelligent, but I would not believe what he was saying. He was incapable of seeing a future in which I was the winner. He had no idea what true strength was. Cody only saw strength coming from inside himself and not being given by others. He would fight alone because he thought himself so strong. If only I did not have to fight him alone, I could be a thousand times stronger than he and I would win. None would have to perish.

Sadly, I was fighting alone. All of my allies had fallen into the grave because of me. They could no longer stand by my side in this fight. Tyler was the only one surviving and he was unable to save me now. I was alone and I knew that people would die, but I could not give up hope.

"With the rate at which you can kill, I understand that saving everyone is impossible. But it remains my goal! I won't stop until you are put to a stop. Whether it ends in your death or my death, that is when I shall stop. Understand that."

I could see the rage building under that helmet of his. Cody Callison saw my obstinance, and it made him angry. He was so frustrated by my unwillingness to accept what was so obvious to him. He felt like I was purposefully denying all of his grand intelligence. He thought himself so smart and I so foolish.

"I understand everything. I understand your goal is unachievable. I understand that I shall kill billions. I understand that you will die. And I understand that you are a fool. Do not tell me what I should understand because I have it figured out already. Do you think you know better than I? If so, you are *so* wrong. You will always lack the understanding that I have. I understand, Martin. Do you?"

"I understand that you are the true fool and I understand that you will fail," I stubbornly answered.

I could hear the grinding of his gauntlets as his fists once again clenched with such fury. A sneer formed on his face. My insolence and foolishness were too much for him. He was so angry. Truly, his heart was filled with only two things: wrath and hatred. If there was only one thing he loved, it was revenge. Revenge on me would be so sweet.

"Then...you really do not understand. It is a shame that my company is wasted on a fool such as yourself. I have been wasted on you, Martin. Allow me to not waste my time further. I could not possibly spend another day with the likes of you."

He paused and stared me down. Cody was making an important decision, and I knew I would have no choice in what he decided. From here on out, his word was law. He would not permit my opinion to be spoken and he would not let me deviate from his plan. It was all his way. I was not going to be able to defy him any longer.

"It is time," he growled.

Cody immediately made his way to the front door. What choice did I have but to follow? As he thrust his giant metal hand through the door, I watched. As we left the house where I had witnessed his resurrection, I said nothing. I knew where we were going, but I could do nothing. It was about to begin. The end of L.I.F.E. was coming.

Chapter 17
The End Begins

Cody, having lived on Santidigo Island for almost a year, understood exactly how the island functioned. It was about ten o'clock, and he was assured that very few people would be out walking the simple pathways. He also was assured that no one would see us due to the fact that no one had ever walked the same route we now took at the same time as we were taking it. I had thought that this was spontaneous, but was it really?

"Let me do all the heavy lifting. You will stand back and watch," ordered Cody, not expecting anything but obedience from me.

I obeyed the command without rebellion. With how he was right now, I dared not mess with his plan. At this time, taking any other action would set him off. There was no option but to comply. I did not want to be a spectator to his mayhem, but to intervene now would be a death wish.

We two Super Soldiers marched right up to the Central Control building and right through the front door. Only about two hours ago, Cody had abandoned this place for tomorrow. We were far ahead of schedule. Now, I felt it was absurd to have been so eager to get here.

Pillars from floor to ceiling stood along the sides of a carpet that led to the far end of the room. Between each set of pillars on each side of the room were doors that opened to rooms inside which I had no idea what might be. The carpet ended with two guards standing in front of a pair of fine wooden doors that stretched far above our heads. I assumed that this must be the leader's office. Just as with Zak Kurien, the Commander would have the fanciest room in the facility.

Cody and I walked this carpet, nearing the guards. I did not know what to do other than watch. That, of course, was exactly what I had been commanded to do.

"What is your business, Callison?" asked a guard.

We stopped only feet from the two suspicious guards and the door that opened to the Commander's office. Cody took another step closer to the guard who had spoken. He looked down into the nervous face of the one who had so rudely addressed him.

"My business is your boss's head," said Cody, thrusting his gauntlet into the man's gut.

Blood poured from his mouth. He fell, dead. Was death that simple? The adjacent guard raised a pistol, but was hit unmercifully by my partner. The same as the last, he hit the floor, blood flowing on the white floor. These gut punches had taken lives. Precious lives. How easy it was! For the first time, Cody's power truly disgusted me.

Cody flung open the huge doors and walked into the office of his adversary. After I had entered, he slammed them closed. I was in a room where bookcases lined the walls to my left and right and a large window supplied light behind the desk of the Commander. Monitors flashed with information all around the room. A startled leader looked up from papers scattered over his desk.

"W-what are you doing in here, Callison?" he stammered.

Cody disregarded him and locked the door. Not finding this sufficient, he tipped over one of the numerous bookcases in the room and blocked the entrance and exit with it. His work done, he shoved me to the side and moved to confront the man in charge. The Commander and I were trapped with the beast.

The man in charge had to be almost as old as Zak had been. In fact, I knew I was not mistaken in assuming that this man was his brother. It was overly clear when I looked at his face. This was a Kurien. This was of the same seed that ruined my life and destined me to my place here. Looking at his face, anger swelled within me, but I would not let it control me. I would not be like Cody.

"Well, I suppose this is the end, Kent. The end of L.I.F.E., is it not glorious?!" Cody remarked with a joyful laugh.

"Callison, what are you talking about? The end of L.I.F.E.? We thought you were part of us. Callison, you are family to the whole organization. We are all working to make you bigger and better. Is that not what you wanted?" said Kent Kurien.

I did not suspect this. I was mistaken in believing that L.I.F.E. was controlling Cody. It was much the opposite. This leader looked terrified of the monster above whom he was supposed to be. He said they were family. This was not the L.I.F.E. I remembered.

"This you did for yourself. I may be benefited by your efforts, but your main clientele is the L.I.F.E. Organization. It is all about which you think. It is your only concern. You never cared about me," Cody said, his words carefully thought out.

"What about all the services we have offered to you? We want to include you in this operation, but you refuse us at every turn. What can I do to help you through this? What do you want?" Kent said, his fear becoming more and more obvious.

"You could return my family. That is what I want. But never will you be able. What you forced me to do was permanent. It can never be taken back."

"What I forced you to do? Callison, it was my brother that ordered those agents to your house, not me! I would never have killed your family just to find a lost Super Soldier! Our organization here is different from the one you knew. The one you faced that day is a forgotten remnant of our past. We no longer claim it! Callison, please listen to me!"

I was wrong about this L.I.F.E. and its followers. They were much different than the ones I had defeated. This commander saw the errors of the last and refused to be as his brother was. I, too, was this way. I did not want to fall into my old ways. We had both turned away from the past to seek a more prosperous future. I had falsely condemned them. They were not who I thought they were.

"You fail to understand me. I did not mean you when speaking of the fault brought down on me. I spoke of all humans. All of you despicable creatures brought down a fate that no person on this planet should face. I have suffered due to your deeds as a human. And...you will suffer the same as I. All humans will understand my agony."

"Callison, you group our organization with the scum of the Earth. Such comparison is false. We are not like my brother's organization. We don't experiment on babies like he did. We don't take innocent lives like he did. We certainly don't force a child to shoot down his entire family. Do not group us with them!" Kent shouted, his anxiety not covered up by his insult.

Cody stood, looking down on the leader of L.I.F.E., and suddenly he was silent. His body slowly swelled and shrunk with his breathing. Kent, in his desk, looked up in desperation, pleading to the immortal being before him. Cody was trapped in that silence to which I had listened on few occasions. He said nothing but meant everything.

"False," he spoke at last. "All humans are evil. They start off evil and they end up evil. All are the same. Only the powerful mind of a Super Soldier can distinguish and eliminate evil, making us the pure beings of this world. Super Soldiers like Martin and myself, brought up away from your influence, are the only ones who should be allowed residence on Earth. You humans are filthy rats beneath my boots. I shall squash all of you vermin."

"Cody, let me speak to your heart. I will end the experiments. I will stop the research. I will stop production. I will stop training agents. Everything will stop if you choose to spare us. That is what I offer you. Please, is this what an evil man would do?"

Cody let out deep laughter, and I knew that no mercy would be given here. He was going to end it very soon. What could I do to stop it? My legs failed me as I tried to move forward to confront Cody about what he was going to say and do. I had to watch what was about to happen.

"An evil man would fight for his own preservation for as long as he could. He would sacrifice anything to live just a little longer. Anything would be worth the price of another opportunity to do his evil deeds. You think you can surrender it all now? You trick yourself into believing such lies and, thus, do not deserve what you so long to protect. No deal."

Cody unfastened the gauntlets, and they fell to the floor. With his spandex covered hands, he reached up and pushed the button on his helmet. After a short hissing, the helmet released its hold on his head. He removed it and let it fall as well. Cody stared down his prey.

"I want to savor this kill. This one kill... I shall enjoy it as much as possible," said Cody, moving slowly towards the leader.

I found my strength at last and I spoke out at this encroachment on Kent Kurien. "Cody! Don't be so heartless! He said he will end L.I.F.E.! You don't have to kill him! Cody, the mission is over!"

I noticed first his clenching fists, and then his face. It was so flooded with rage that Cody could not possibly be in there anymore. Before I could notice anything else, he punched me in the center of my chest, right where my heart was. The force was so immense, I crashed into the bookshelves that lined the walls. Hundreds of volumes covered me as I lay in terrible agony. All I did was lie there. The pain was so much that I could not move. Motionless, I was forced to watch what came next.

Cody regained his composure and turned back to the prey. In fear, Kent raised a pistol to the head of my partner. Cody effortlessly grabbed the weapon and, with a bare hand, crushed it. Tossing it away, Cody's right hand latched onto the skull of the leader. He pulled him across the desk and lifted him high. His other hand now joining its pair, Cody had Kent Kurien, new commander of L.I.F.E., screaming for help.

Next, Cody's thumbs drove themselves through Kent's glasses and into his sockets. The screaming refused to cease as Cody squeezed his skull and drove his thumbs deeper. Cody's teeth gritted between his grinning lips as the leader screamed in excruciation. The hands surrounding Kent's head pushed mightily inward, and all he could do was scream and flail without rescue.

Here I sat in the office of the one whom I had come to stop. I was a simple spectator in the horror unfolding in this room. I could not intervene. I could do nothing to save the man whom I would have shown my mercy had I come here alone, but I had not come alone. In my place, a psychopath was brutally murdering him. I wished that things could have turned out differently.

Sitting in silence, I felt as if I had always been here on the floor. It felt as if I had never moved from this one place in this one moment. Had this been all to which my life could amount? Was I to fail in stopping the end of the human race by an enemy I had believed friend for so long? My goal was as unachievable as I had been told. Failure was finally mine.

I had almost become deaf to the screams of suffering by the time I heard that dreadful cracking. Cody's hands collapsed inward on the skull, decimating any recognizable trait of Kent Kurien's face. Blood exploded from this epicenter of horror and painted the walls crimson. Kent's body lingered in the air as Cody admired what he had done. Satisfied, he dropped the inanimate cadaver to the floor. Blood, even more, flooded out over the hardwood floors. The deed was finished.

Cody, his red-painted paws covering his face, chuckled. This chuckle was then followed by a deep laugh. This laugh was soon abandoned for a gut-retching laughter that more than filled this open office. As he gripped his skull as he had Kent's, a psychotic, screaming laughter emitted from his gaping mouth. His body convulsed with exuberance that I could barely watch.

I looked down at the body of the former owner of this island. I could no longer make out his mouth, but his scream echoed in my mind. Overlapping were the maniacal emissions of the monster. These two horrid sounds almost drove me to my own insanity. I closed my eyes tightly and gritted my teeth, for I could take it no longer.

All at once, he stopped. Silence filled this void. I opened my eyes again and saw the beast as still as death. He dropped his hands to his sides. Again, a soft chuckle could be heard. Cody looked down on me, his face now as red as his rage. He grinned and shook his head at me.

"It...felt...*so*...good. How could you turn your back on this feeling? Taking a life...the *best* feeling in this world. I shall not discard it," said the monster, still laughing.

"You are...sick. Do you not understand what you've done?" I asked, already knowing his response.

"Of course! Was it never clear to you that I thirst for these unmeritorious humans' blood? More of an idiot than a fool, I suppose."

"I knew of your thirst, but I did not believe you were evil enough to act on it."

"You accuse those doing justice of evil? Martin, you are confused. If you fight on their side, you surrender any claim to that justice-seeker I knew before you took his place. The old Martin would kill off evil and he would enjoy it. He would risk the lives of many only for the pleasure of seeing evil dead. Hypocrite, I shall not have you any longer."

Before I could respond to this insult, banging was heard at the blocked door.

"Sir! Are you all right in there? SSX-16 cannot be found anywhere. Two men are dead! We are locking down the facility!" said a voice behind the door.

"I have begun. Oh, have I only begun!" said Cody as he took up his helmet and secured it to his head.

He then inserted his red-painted paws into the gauntlets. Tightening them, he moved to the door. When his suit of armor was once again whole, he grabbed the bookshelf and tossed it to the other side of the room. Then, with his enormous foot, he knocked down the locked doors.

The guards on the other side, having been quite near the doors when they were toppled, were half crushed. Immediately, the other half stepped back and aimed their rifles at the menace. The menace only stood in his place, surveying his future murders.

"SSX-16, stand down!" shouted a guard.

"Why do you call me by my forced title? Have I not asked before that I be called Callison? But you might as well anger me. Perhaps, in my rage, I shall end you sooner," said Cody, addressing the insolent guard and stepping forward.

"Callison, please! Stand down!" shouted the guard, the last words he ever spoke.

Cody launched himself without warning at his prey. His tungsten gauntlets and boots tore through his opponents, if they could even be called that. Not even one bullet hit his impenetrable armor. They all died after a single blow.

Having just killed a dozen heavily-armed men, Cody laughed in his euphoria. He then desecrated the corpses by ripping limbs and heads from their lifeless bodies. How could this possibly be that little boy to whom I had given my ring last year?

"Not even one laser rifle, Martin," said the monster, standing right outside the office. "I am disappointed to say the least. But I am sure that they will step up the challenge somewhat when I make more progress. I have no doubt that they have more to offer."

I rose from under the books where I had lain for so long, watching. I walked out of that defiled place where I had been trapped for a seemingly infinite amount of time. I came right up to the monster. I looked him in his deep blue circles through the glass as he grinned at my approach.

"I shall be the one who ends your life. Do not think this will go without punishment," I told him.

"And you are the one to supply that punishment? Do not think that you could ever lay a hand on me, Martin. It would be ever so...foolish of you to think so."

"You will die at my own hands. I shall kill only once more in my life. And for that one life, I have chosen yours. I shall forget my stance, and you will die. Understand me?"

"I understand all too well. Now, I believe you have somewhere to be. A great friend is awaiting salvation at your hands. Perhaps you should concentrate on that first. As for me, I have obligations to fulfill as well. If you truly are convinced you can stop me, then make sure to catch me before I leave the hangar. I have no doubt you will miss this last chance to say goodbye. Farewell for now, Martin."

He walked out of the building. I had no way to make him listen to me. Whatever I could say meant nothing to him. He understood that he knew so much more than I, and, thus, any information with which I could supply him was already of such low value. It was true that I was lesser than he in knowledge, but I would always take insult in it.

My enemy gone to end more lives, I was left in solitude. Alone in the midst of the death, I fell to my knees. What a failure I had become! I did not even attempt to stop the monster. Where was my courage when I needed it most? My cowardice had just ended all life on this planet. Every death would be more weight on my shoulders, forcing me down into my own repugnance. Why could I not act?

Not able to dwell among the corpses any longer, I stood and walked slowly to the door. Out I went, to save the only life I could.

Chapter 18
Reunion

My mind was starting to clear up this issue. I had to get to Tyler first and secure his safety. It sounded as if Cody did not intend to kill him. I hoped that this was the truth. With Tyler safe, maybe I could contemplate further action in this atrocity. First, I had to save my friend.

My strong legs took me swiftly to the west side of the island. I had to get there fast. If I could not, perhaps the scientists might terminate his stasis. This would most likely kill him slowly and painfully. If I could just get there in time, I could demand their assistance in this problem.

Although my mind was focused on the task at hand, I could not block out the faint screams coming from somewhere on the island. The monster had begun to take his vengeance. They screamed for help and for mercy, but none was given to them. The destruction of L.I.F.E. and its followers was taking place, and I was no longer a part of it. It was all Cody's doing now. I ignored the pleas for rescue and quickly ran to the entrance of the Super Soldier lab.

Bursting through the lab's main doors, I remembered my path. I sprinted down the white halls towards my destination. Such little time was given to me to complete these tasks. Saving Tyler was first on the list, and Cody was second. I had to be fast enough. I had to be.

Arriving at the viewing window, I threw a punch at the glass. It shattered into thousands of pieces and fell to the floor far below. I tossed myself in and collided with the hard floor. Not at all interested in my condition, I ran up to the chamber and slapped the blue button that opened the shutters of the chamber.

As the shutters opened slowly, I stared intently forward. Just as I was able to steal a glance of my friend, the same scientist that had been in here this morning came through the door. She dropped her clipboard, and her eyes locked on me in terror.

I lifted my hands in a non-threatening manner and took a step away from her. "I need your help," I said, but she refused to respond or to even move. "Please! This man is my friend. Take him out of stasis safely so that we can be reunited!"

Realizing that I was not threatening her, she took cautious steps forward. She was trembling, but seemed rather stable for having a Super Soldier before her. I could see that she did not want to turn her eyes from me. Doing so could result in my attacking. She knew how Super Soldiers were.

"It's okay. I am not like he is," I said, and she stopped all movement. "Cody is violent beyond belief, and I can see that. I do not wish to be the monster he has made himself. You do not have to fear me," I reassured her.

"I...I can't get him out of stasis quickly. It is going to take about half an hour if I'm going to do it safely. Please, forgive me," she said, shaking uncontrollably.

"There is nothing to fear here. Do what is necessary."

Turning from me and to the console, her fingers danced rapidly over the keys. Then, she moved left, turning knobs and flipping switches. Further left, she punched in a code and hit a button. Back and forth she moved, working urgently.

Hoping to calm her nerves, I sat at a stool that was behind one of the desks about fifteen feet from the chamber. Here, I sat and watched. It did not seem as if she noticed, though. She was too far into her work to notice anything going on around herself. My effort proved unnecessary, but, at least, now I was sitting.

This scientist looked pretty young to be working here. Of course, most of the agents of L.I.F.E. were only about twenty years old, but I understood why that was. Many of the agents had been failed experiments that had somehow survived. They had grown up in the facility as I had, only much earlier than I had. L.I.F.E. must have abducted hundreds of babies from all over the country to create such an army. It made me quite angry just thinking about it.

This woman was young not because of L.I.F.E.'s abduction of her, but because she was talented for her age. It was very obvious that she was more skilled than most, with her fingers dancing away on the keyboards of the stasis chamber. I was glad to have her working to save Tyler's life.

I analyzed the scientist who was going to save my greatest friend's life. She had a face that suggested that she did not rest very often. Her long blonde hair was put into a ponytail to keep it away from her work. She was tall, thin, and she wore glasses. I was not sure if it was only because I was here, but she also seemed quite timid. These features made up the woman before me.

Hissing and sucking sounds came from the chamber. Bubbles released from the tubes connected to Tyler's body. Still, he was motionless. I wished dearly to see him move. I wanted to be sure he was okay. His well-being was very important to me.

Minutes passed, and still she worked. I became more impatient with each stroke of the clock's hands. My fingers tapped continuously on the desk due to anxiety. I could not wait in this silence. It was not until 15 minutes had passed that I decided to speak again to my assistant.

"What is your name?" I asked her.

She jumped at the sound of my voice. She, now having a slight bit of rest due to the machine's work not being finished, turned to me and, for the first time, looked me in the eyes.

"My name is Delani Hanley," she told me.

"My name is Martin Shepard," I returned.

"*The* Martin Shepard?! We were told that you were dead. What happened to you?" she asked, astounded to be in my presence.

"I destroyed the L.I.F.E. facility outside of Alemande, and the blast threw me outside. The police soon showed up, and I was arrested. I had been in jail up until yesterday afternoon."

"You were arrested? Why did you let them take you?" she asked, resuming her work.

"Your previous leader, Zak Kurien, shot me in the head right as I set off the charges. The bullet wiped my memories. I did not know that I could have escaped them had I chosen to do so."

"But...how do you remember losing your memories?" she questioned, confused.

"After a long time in the prison, I started to have flashes. They only occurred when something familiar happened to me. After I had undergone many of these flashes, my memory was restored."

She dropped everything and faced me. I could see her mind racing. She seemed mystified yet so afraid. It was as if she was witnessing a pride of lions surrounding her, preparing to devour her. It was something terrifying yet strangely beautiful.

"You...just recovered...everything? Do you understand what that means?"

"It means that my mind became advanced enough to repair the fragments of memories I had once lost. What is so surprising about that?"

"Well, it means that your mind is always advancing...like we predicted it could. But in your case, you are only a five multiplier. While that means that you have lesser power than Cody does, it also means that you will live longer. You can live to an age of about twenty when he will only be able to live another five years. With that extra lifespan, you will be learning, and your mind will continue to advance. But see, the longer the mind is active, the more easily it advances. In the long run, you can become so much more than he can. Isn't that incredible, Martin?!"

This was a surprising bit of information I had received. With my many more years of life than the rest of the Super Soldiers, I could advance my mind even more than theirs. That was amazing! Truly, I would become stronger, if only I could live long enough.

A beeping sound summoned Delani back to the chamber. She adjusted dials and typed more gibberish into the computers. More beeping and hissing sounded. Yet, Tyler remained trapped in the chamber. How much longer would this take?

Unexpectedly, the door to the right of the chamber was flung open, and in stepped another scientist.

"Delani! What are you doing in here? We have to evacuate! SSX-16 has gone rogue!" shouted the scientist in fear.

He looked my way and then saw me. His eyes grew huge, and he let a gasp escape his mouth. He backed away, feeling his way back to the door.

"Sir, it's okay! This is Martin Shepard...and I am helping him," said Delani.

"I shall not harm you. All I want is my friend back," I said.

He had his back against the wall, staring at me. He was completely unsure of his situation. Why was this Super Soldier not attacking? That was what they were made to do, kill. Could this all be some trick? What is he going to do?

"You're not going to kill me? Why?" asked the scientist.

"I wish to kill no more. You deserve my mercy," I responded.

"A merciful Super Soldier? You especially should understand that that is a contradiction," said the scientist.

"I am a special case. Circumstance has saved me. Mercy is now my greatest weapon."

The scientist plopped to the floor and heaved a sigh of relief. He looked up at the one whom he no longer feared. He chuckled slightly and then, stopped by his thoughts, went silent. The only sounds in the room came from Delani's diligent work.

His eyes were wide, and that made it easy to see their color. His brown eyes were unable to move from one spot on the floor. This man appeared to be in his mid-twenties, as I thought Delani was. He lifted his hand to his head and ran it through his thick brown hair. He then pulled on the long beard hairs growing from the end of his chin. He sighed as if imagining something fantastic and then he lifted his gaze to me.

"What is it like? I mean, how does it feel being a Super Soldier?" asked the scientist, studying me as he would a specimen in his lab.

I shifted my body on the stool so that I was facing him. I paused and pondered the question. I was a Super Soldier almost from birth. I did not know what it was like to be normal. This man was normal from birth. He did not know what it was like to be super. Perhaps our differing perspectives could help each other.

"It is hard for me to describe the differences between being normal and being super because I have never been normal, but let me try. You have infinitely more potential than ever. More strength, knowledge, speed, and talent are within you than you could ever imagine. You feel powerful. You feel intelligent. You feel fast. You feel skilled. You feel limitless."

The man marveled at these words. Being a Super Soldier was everything he had imagined. I could see that desperation to achieve his dream in this man. He looked determined to become what I was and, perhaps, even further. This man desired advancement.

"But...it isn't all perfect in my case," I continued, wishing to discourage any ideas going through this man's head. "Your organization has chased me my whole life. I never had the opportunity to live a normal life. And trust me, a normal life is something that I have longed for the entirety of this life."

"Is an abnormal life not worth the power you control? Don't you know how lucky you are?" he said, becoming slightly aggravated.

"I shall always know that I am blessed with this life, but that is not to say the experiment hasn't plagued me with much sorrow. Your organization, in attempts to capture and kill me, killed everyone I loved. The only one remaining now floats in that chamber. All of that did not have to happen...but it did. I can live with the fact that it happened, but I will never believe that so much death was worth my power."

He turned away, seemingly unaffected by my statement. Was he so heartless that he could be blind to the horror of death? It was as if I was looking at the mirror image of Cody. A lack of compassion made them seem so similar.

"I'm done!" said Delani from the machine.

"You have completed the rehab procedures?" said the now interested scientist.

"Yes, of course, Dr. Giffin! He is ready to return from his stasis!" said Delani excitedly.

"Then, free him from his prison! Let him and me be reunited at last!" I shouted, aflutter.

She typed in something on the control panel, and a sucking sound commenced. The strange fluids in which Tyler was suspended drained away from him. In a matter of ten seconds, he was no longer submerged. Now, he was held up by wires and tubes.

Another code she input moved away the glass barrier between us. I ran forward, ready to assist Delani in this step. We entered together, while Dr. Giffin, the scientist, remained back to watch. I held up Tyler while she removed all the protrusions from his body. Once he was free, I carried him out of the chamber and set him on a chair. Removing my jacket, I covered the naked and shivering Tyler.

Delani then began a number of observations to check his condition. They were basic tests, but still I watched, mystified. I wanted to be assured of his health. Would he be okay? Was this desperate journey to end L.I.F.E. and save my friend finally over?

As she went to check his eyes, Tyler awoke and stared with wide eyes at those gathered above him.

"What?" barely escaped Tyler's gaping mouth.

"Tyler!" I said, overjoyed by his response. "It's me! It's Martin!"

"Martin?" he said, slowly. "Where are we this time, kid? What's going on?"

"We're in a L.I.F.E. laboratory. They were going to experiment on you."

"On me? Ha, but no one could do that to me, kid. No one."

I smiled down on the glorious return of my greatest friend. He was exactly as he always was. I had missed him so much. Now, here we were. The biggest threat L.I.F.E. had ever faced. We had a new mission and, together, we could complete it.

"You know it. No one can beat us, Tyler. That is...if you are still with me?" I said, recalling those historied words once more.

He looked briefly around the room before answering, "No offense, guys, but I don't see anyone I would rather be on a team with but you, kid."

Chapter 19
The Commencement of Terror

Tyler was given a robe and he sat up on a stool, surrounded by the three of us. His color was returning and his cocky attitude returned faster than I could even perceive. He rubbed his bald head with a look of disdain. This Tyler did not look the same as the last, but was indeed the same Tyler.

"We have a team here that can help to get your friend to his best condition as quickly as possible, Shepard," said Dr. Giffin.

"His best condition? Doctor, I hope you don't mean..." I began.

"Of course not! I only want to make sure he is rehabilitated fully before you send him out to try to kill a Super Soldier. That would be foolish, and you know it," he responded.

"You know that that was not what I planned to do. I was going to leave him here. I just did not want you experimenting on him," I retorted.

"Fine. I will only check his condition. He will be at full health in no time, Shepard. No need to worry," the doctor said.

This man had displayed behavior that was not indicative of trustworthiness. His lack of compassion and his thirst for power made me wary to leave Tyler with him. Yet, I knew Tyler could handle himself in even the most dire of situations. He had proved that on many occasions. I would leave Tyler in his care, not because I trusted the doctor, but because I trusted my greatest friend.

"Good. Then, I should go. Your previous experiment is off murdering every single person on this island. With any luck, he won't come here. I'll come back when..."

"Kid," Tyler interrupted. "Don't die without me, all right? That would sure make saving me at all just a waste of time. You're not dying without me."

I approached his stool and put my hand on his shoulder. "And why would I do that? You know that no one could kill me. No way I'm dying out there."

He laughed, looking up at me.

"You know, kid, I don't remember you being older than me. You're all grown up now, aren't you? Ha, well, go then. You can take care of yourself. I will be there when you need me. Whenever there is trouble, I will always be coming shortly to end it. Remember that, kid."

I smiled and said, "I shall. Now, I have to go. Take care of him, Doctor. And you as well, Delani. This is my greatest friend, and I intend to see him again."

Delani and Giffin nodded in confirmation of their duty. Tyler only smiled at me. He remembered the past so well. We fought and we won. That was just what we did. Together, we were downright powerful. I was going alone this time, but he would be with me in time.

I walked out the door and found my way through the identical white halls. Out into the dreary world I went. Clouds now covered the once beautiful sun and its partner the blue sky. Now, all was gray and sorrowful. Why should it not be? Death had descended upon Santidigo Island.

Unlike what I expected, I heard no cries for help. I heard no screams of terror. No gunfire sounded. How long had I been in that lab? Had I given him enough time to slay the majority of the population on this island? With no idea where he was now, I ran toward the hangar, fearing that he might have already left for the mainland.

As I ran, I passed bodies of those slain by the monster. The corpses were missing limbs, and many were soaked in their own blood as well as the blood of others. It was a disgusting sight and it only encouraged me more to do what I had to do. I had to stop the monster who was doing such evil. This was my mission. I would complete it.

How my legs moved so quickly towards their destination! If he had already left, then he could already be anywhere, killing so many. I had to get to the hangar. I looked, panicked, over the horizon to the east. I could not see the storm of metal moving easterly, so, perhaps, he had not yet left. I could possibly still stop him.

When at last I had covered the large distance from the lab to the hangar, I heard gunshots ring out. I increased speed until I hit the door and I flung it open. I entered, only to watch that monster punch the head off a terrified soldier. Another came up behind him, close enough to end Cody's life with the laser rifle he held in his hands. Cody, with his immense speed, flipped around and knocked the weapon from his hands. Cody laughed as he put his large metal hand on the soldier's head and twisted. The soldier fell like so many hundreds of others, dead.

The humungous space was empty besides me, the monster, and a thousand metal spheres that read LIFE but brought death. Cody looked through the glorified windshield blocking his face and met my eyes. I saw his shoulders jump lightly with a chuckle.

"You came. And...not a minute too late. I was about to leave, Martin," he said.

"How could I let my friend leave without saying goodbye?" I said, approaching with my arms open to him, but he was not going to embrace me.

"Your friend is grateful for your thoughtfulness. But now, I must be leaving."

"No, you mustn't. Stay a while, will you?"

"You ask if I shall stay? Martin, you have to assert yourself if you want to see any results! You cannot simply ask the villain to please stop his rampage. What has happened to you? Where is the hero I once knew?" Cody asked me, becoming frustrated with my difference from the old Martin.

"Your hero now has learned that killing isn't the only way to solve problems. I don't want to kill you, Cody, but I shall if it comes to that."

He only laughed again. Was there no way to make him take me seriously? Would I really have to fight him to gain his respect? If that was what it took, then I would have no choice. Here, we would meet in battle, and the winner would have the world to do whatever they pleased with it.

In an unanticipated move, I sprinted at my adversary. Jumping into the air, I had the advantage of height, but, alas, what good did a single advantage do against this foe who held so many others? As I came down, he snatched me out of the air and flung me down to the hard concrete far below. My bones strained and sustained the blow, but my pride did not.

He now heartily laughed at me. What a fool I was, he thought. Was there even a chance I could win in this fight? Yes, there was. With the bane of all Super Soldiers, perhaps I had a chance.

Searching urgently, I found for what I looked. Down on this lowest level, there lay a single laser rifle, coated with blood from a victim of the monster above. I ran to it just as Cody jumped from the platform above. His boots drove themselves into the floor, fortunately slowing him. I grabbed the weapon and aimed at my target. I pulled that trigger, and the blast flew towards the monster.

It is important to remember that these lasers fire at the speed of light. If an individual aims correctly, then there is absolutely no way to miss their target. No one can dodge a beam of light. I do not know why this is important to remember, because it certainly did not apply to Cody.

At the same moment I fired and the blast whizzed past his helmet, Cody threw a chunk of the concrete at me. I, not as quick as he, failed to dodge. The chunk hit my weapon and knocked it from my hands and to the floor. There was no getting it back in time. In that same second, he had me in his hands again.

"Martin, I could not be more disappointed in your choice. Do you not trust me? I am a vast magnitude smarter than you. Why doubt the morality of my calling? I alone know what is right. I am sad that you could not see that."

As his right hand crushed my shoulder blade into many pieces, his left fist plunged into my gut and blood was propelled from my mouth. I collapsed on the cold ground. Intense pain overtook me, and I could not defend myself further. Even with my vulnerability, he ceased his attack. He let me look up, searching for his face.

"How sad, indeed! What a pity that you had to fall so far! Why could it not be Tyler who lost his edge? Why not someone who was not the infamous murderer named Martin? You yourself are, in fact, sad. So...I refuse to be near you a moment longer. Please accept this mercy. I shall not come back for you or Tyler. Remove yourselves from this island and go somewhere I shall not go. I shall leave two of the machines for you two to pilot off this island. This is my advice and my kindness for you, Martin. Run and never look back."

He almost escaped my presence before I was able to yell, "Stop!"

"What? What more do you have to say to me?" he shouted at me, aggravated that I would not let him get the last word and leave.

I breathed deeply, trying to find the air with which to fill my lungs. My body was shutting down, and I found difficulty in doing anything. When at last I was able to breathe a little air, I answered the monster. "You are making a mistake.... What you are doing...cannot be undone.... Think about that...before you go."

"You are persistent...and I am so damn tired of that. What will it take to make you learn? They say that fools will never learn from their mistakes; it is true. I shall repeat myself once more in the unlikely case it is false. Run and never look back. Goodbye forever, Martin."

He escaped. I watched helplessly as the machines rose from their slots and the huge hangar doors opened and revealed the barely visible sun in the far east. They flew away, and then I could not see that beautiful sun. It hid behind millions of potential deaths. Behind millions of soon-to-be orphans. Behind millions of sorrow filled nights. Behind millions upon millions of tears that could not be wiped away. They had scared away the sun.

Finally able to stand, I moved slowly to the stairs. I had to prepare myself for what I was about to face. I needed first my armor, still stored in my enemy's closet. That meant a trek all the way across the island just to be equipped to begin a resistance against this monster. Full of doubt, that was how I felt about this situation.

The clanking of my feet hitting the metal stairs was the only thing keeping me awake in this nightmare. I felt so heavy. My body was not in the mood to walk but, instead, to reconstruct what Cody had destroyed within me. Fatigue was quick to hit, but still I walked up those stairs. To the door I went, determined never to stop.

Through the door and down the path, my legs barely cooperated. As I moved so incredibly slowly, all of which I could think was the death that could be taking place in only a matter of minutes. Santidigo Island was not very far from the coast at all. Alemande sat so close to this place of infamy. This city would be the first to burn.

However long it took, I do not know. I only knew that I would get there and that I had to get there. Opening the door to the monster's house, I fell against the carpet in my exhaustion. There, I could have lain for hours, resting, but I understood the cost. I forced myself up and to the closet door. I flung it open and retrieved the Kevlar suit I had worn when I had journeyed here.

My item acquired, I fell into Cody's recliner that sat in front of his wide-screen television. Touching the button on the remote, the screen lit up. The channel already set on the local news provider, I watched as I made little progress in dressing myself with the armor.

As I had suspected, a news alert sounded as soon as I had myself suited up. Alemande News Center's Michael Wolfe was on the scene. In the sky floated a thousand steel spheres. They just floated, not at all provoked. It was a calm but unsettling picture.

Out of the sky floated one of the spheres, down to the crowded streets. Wolfe ran to greet this strange object at its landing place. When the sphere touched down, it was apparent that one man rode on the back of this fascinating machine. Wolfe looked mystified as he described the object as "extraterrestrial".

The figure on the back of the machine stepped off. In his left hand was a weapon like no other. Yes, I knew it as the laser rifle, but these spectators might as well have taken if for a toy. His metal feet slapping the pavement, the figure approached the approaching reporter. It was an odd scene, but I preferred it to the one I knew was coming.

"Sir! Sir, what are these machines that accompany you? They look much like the ones that were seen in West City and Wallace only last year. What do you have to say?" asked the overconfident reporter.

Why in the world everyone was so nonchalantly approaching this heavily armored man with a spectacular weapon at his side I did not know. All I was permitted to do was watch, something of which I was doing a lot recently. Anxiety filled me as the scene unfolded on the T.V. screen.

Cody stopped right in front of Michael Wolfe and looked into his eyes. He leaned forward to get closer to the microphone that Wolfe held for him. He took a fast glance around before speaking.

"Attention, every resident of this planet. I am Cody Callison. I am a Super Soldier and the only pure one among all life on this planet. Only I know what is best. You derisory humans must be taught of your worthlessness. I shall be your teacher."

There was a commotion throughout the crowd. What was this fantastical man talking about? Was he really to be their teacher? They did not know what he meant, but, surely, they would soon.

"Quiet, fools. You understand not what I say. It only proves my point further. Stupid humans, it is time to meet your ends," Cody announced, a bitter taste on his tongue.

"Mr. Callison, what do you mean by this? You surely do not mean us any harm, correct?" asked the oblivious reporter.

"Are you deaf to my words? Can you not see what force I command? I come to purge the world of evil. I take pleasure in beginning with you."

After finishing his sentence, Cody moved his left hand at the speed of lightning onto Wolfe's head. Here, he stopped as the crowd realized his intentions and all took a gasp in unison. When Cody was assured that his threat was understood, he ripped the head of the poor reporter clean off. So much blood splattered on the onlookers. A thousand screams rang out at this very moment. It had begun.

One of the last things I heard before the connection was lost was the sound of Cody's voice.

"Activate," he said, commencing the terror.

The camera dropped and fell to the feet of him who had warranted its presence. The fire of the laser rifle was clear to my ear by now, as was the scream of its victim.

Now, recovered from my injuries, I stood and turned away from the television. I understood the threat which I had to face. It was time for me to confront the enemy. There was no time to waste, for I had lost enough already. Lives decreased as the seconds were counted on the clock. It was past time for me to fight.

I ran out the door, strength renewed by the demand of my duty. I ran to the hangar, hoping that Cody kept his word and left me a Pilot Sphere. There was not a single second I let go by without consent. I ran as fast as I possibly could.

I burst through the door which I had pushed so lightly previously. Down the stairs I flew, in search of the machine that would take me to my foe. It was easy to spot, since it was alone in this huge room alongside one more of its kind. Only these two machines and a helicopter, considered worthless with the technology we had available, remained for me to use. I retrieved the laser rifle I had held for such a short time in my last fight. With it, I boarded one of the Pilot Spheres.

The controls were complex, but, even knowing that, they were simple for me. Flipping switches and pushing buttons yielded the result I desired. It started up seamlessly. Pushing forward a lever, the machine rose. Grabbing the yoke, I adjusted the direction I was to fly. Another lever led me out of the hangar and off the dreaded island.

As I flew away from my friends and towards almost impossible odds, I readied myself. I needed preparation if I was to ever defeat the monster. Even with it, I understood that I would not be coming back from this. I had said goodbye to Tyler for the final time in that lab. This was the end of my life and it was coming so quickly.

I knew that I could not win this fight on my own. To fight alone was death. Then, I understood. I was not alone now or had I ever been. One was with me always and had brought me success in the horror that was my life. I did not have to fight alone.

Finally understanding, I cried out to the heavens. I felt truly foolish to have forgotten something so important to me. All that was important now was that I knew who was with me. I sobbed when I begged, "Lord, may I not fail this day."

Chapter 20
Alone in Weakness

Alemande looked like an erupting volcano when I approached. The whole city was on fire. Even with my distance of a mile, I could hear horrible screams of anguish and fear. The smell of smoke had traveled this far as well. Why did it have to be like this?

I flew at speeds around 60 miles per hour, and the ride was smooth. I was amazed at how L.I.F.E. had modified these machines. With Jack Lamb's limited supplies, he was not able to construct something as powerful as these. Even with his lack, he had designed a whole new way to distribute death. Now, here they were, even more deadly. It both amazed and disgusted me.

As I came within a quarter mile of the city, I descended quickly. I reached the docks and set the LIFE Sphere down. I jumped off and clutched my laser rifle. This weapon could change things. It could end all the chaos and save so many lives. If only I could wield it correctly, many could be spared.

Once a bustling place of work, the docks now were devoid of life. Smoldering wood was beneath my feet as I surveyed the scene. Cries for help replaced the casual profanity that had filled this place before. The smell of fish was replaced by the smell of burning flesh. I felt no sense of familiarity here. How the docks had changed!

Many fled around me as I walked into the fray. Machines chased them, and I attempted to save as many as I could. The laser blew apart the LIFE Spheres instantly, making salvation easier to supply. Yet, I never allowed myself to be satisfied with the destruction of a single machine. I had to end them all. I had to save my city, my people. It was my duty to bring down the fire-breathing mayhem. This was the easy part; another threat still remained and it was many times more deadly.

Suddenly, there was a thud only feet from me. The shock of it made me flee momentarily, but then I saw what had almost hit me. The pancaked body of one who had jumped to avoid burning to death had caused the thud. I was frozen by this disturbing image when even more hit the ground all around me. What a horrible snapping and a brutal thud they all made! I fled the scene in my revolt.

This was not the only revolting thing I was forced to witness all around me. Blazing children sprinted silently by me, having the oxygen sucked out of their lungs by the flames. Corpses blown apart by an overpowered gun wielded by my enemy. People, still alive in many cases, trampled by their fellow man, all out of intense panic. These and many others were the scenes within which I fought.

Sirens, crackling fires, screaming, and the hum of those infernal machines became the soundtrack of my fight. I could not help but think that it was all music meant for me. I had failed to stop this atrocity, and now it was out of my control. If only I had taught Cody that killing was wrong from the very start! If only I could have influenced him for the better and not the worse! If only I had understood the error of my actions and the effect they had on a young boy! If only.

How mistaken I had been! I had actually justified murder! How many had I killed with no remorse? How many had I threatened with no cause but my own in mind? What was the purpose of all the pain I had caused? The only purpose was to make myself greater and greater and greater. Why could I not understand how wrong I was? Did I truly not have any compassion at all?

Lost in my regret, a LIFE Sphere locked onto me from afar. It raced towards me at alarming speeds. Instincts kicking in, I rolled away from its flames. Unfortunately, I was so lost in my regret that I rolled into the path of a speeding police car. Upon impact, I was tossed into the air, my spine as well as my ego sore.

I collided with the hard ground, but then managed to get up to my knees. I watched the car speed away with no regard for a citizen it had injured. This was of little importance, of course, because the flames hurt so much more. The Sphere blasted me with the flaming tar, and I hurt so badly that I could not move. Had I lost all competence in my fighting? I was letting myself get beaten at every turn.

I threw myself along the pavement to get away from the portable inferno. I rolled after each time I tossed myself to extinguish the flames. I tossed and rolled for a whole block before I was safe from the consuming heat, but my fight was not over.

I had dropped the laser rifle when the car hit me, and that left me with my fists. They might not have had as much power behind them or have been covered in tungsten, but they were mighty all the same. I threw them with precision at my target. The shells of these Spheres had been modified, and I could only knock the thing around, but I persisted. My punches forced it to the ground over and over again until both my fists and the machine's shell were coated in my blood.

This Sphere was a trial that I was going to have to pass. I would never give up and I needed to have that solidified in my mind. Again and again, I hit the brutally resistant steel. Never did I hold back. I put everything into every punch. I had to be stronger to be able to complete this mission.

After many minutes of battle with this single Sphere, my fist dented that impenetrable shell. A smile formed on my face when the machine crashed to the ground and wobbled back to its place. With the encouragement of this first victory, all the subsequent victories would be much easier. Again, my fists flew, and, within minutes, the machine had fallen for good.

I reclaimed my laser rifle and blasted the machine from afar. Seeing its disabled body blown to bits was satisfying, and I knew I was a force with which to be reckoned. I continued the fight, ready to bring down this menace.

Never had I seen this side of war. In my conflicts, I was always the victor. I did not know this type of suffering. I could have never imagined the mass death in which I was now a part. So many died all around me and they did not die peacefully. The Spheres were meant to kill the enemy, but that was not what they did. These evil machines tortured innocent people to death.

The advancement that L.I.F.E. desired was clearly exhibited in the LIFE Spheres. Every component within them had been modified. They were so many times above the Spheres that Jack Lamb had made. This was what L.I.F.E. wanted to do with everything. They wanted an advanced world, but they only succeeded in plunging it into darkness.

Were the lives of the common people advanced? No, they were eradicated. It was so unjust! L.I.F.E. was supposed to be about improving and enhancing everyone's lives for the better. They were supposed to help those in need and make us all better people. They could have done so much good! This organization had doomed the human race instead.

My mind and body grew weaker and weaker as I gave everything I was to the fight. This was when I started to see that I was not enough. I started to see that my strength alone was never going to be enough. I knew that God was at my side, but I still believed that my strength would determine the fate of the world. I started to see, but I had not yet come to accept that I was not enough.

As the machines surrounded me and my will was beginning to waiver, I fired my laser rifle with ferocity. I gave everything. When at last the metal hit the pavement, I was exhausted. I was running out of strength, and still so many remained. I had to continue. I had to keep fighting.

I had destroyed possibly a hundred of the machines before I finally saw him. Two blocks from me, crowds ran in futility as the beast slaughtered them with repugnant speed. He moved at the velocity of a freight train and with the same force. I knew not how many were dead, for he killed another eight before I could count four. So many lives were lost to him, and I would not stand for it any longer.

I ran to the aid of the people who stood no chance against Cody. Ignoring all other threats, I put all my focus on Cody Callison. LIFE Spheres swooped down at me and spat flame, but I paid no attention to them. I had to get to the monster and stop him.

Nearing Cody, I slowed myself down and readied myself for attack. Every time I had tried to stand against him earlier, he had beaten me effortlessly. This fight would require all I had. I would have to give all I was to kill this monster and save the city.

I began my assault with the laser rifle, but it, of course, proved futile. Simple dodges that defied physics spared him over and over. I could not hit him at all. It was impossible to even hit within feet of him. All I had accomplished with my attack was a distraction that cut his kill count by half.

I could hear the muffled laughter from inside his helmet. He allowed the worthless humans to escape him and he turned his attention to me. I stopped firing and stared down my adversary. He shook his head and began to approach me.

"What did I tell you, Martin? Did I not inform you of the consequences? You have made an irreparable mistake," Cody spoke at last.

"My mistakes only lead to more chances to fail and to succeed. The way I look at it, my chances of success are 50 percent and my chances of failure are also 50 percent. There is no third option...and I like that. My odds are perfect right where they are."

"Martin, you have gone insane!" he laughed.

"Not as insane as you are."

"Ha! I am insane to you? I have such logic, and yet you believe my mind has been corrupted? Truly, you have gone insane."

"Are you so far gone that you can't even comprehend what you are doing anymore? I know that you understand your actions, but do you understand the consequence? Where has your conscience disappeared to, my friend?"

"I never had one, Martin. Why do you use the same interrogation on me every time you speak to me? It seems to me that you actually have taken up insanity. It was Albert Einstein who stated that the definition of insanity is 'doing the same thing over and over again and expecting different results.' Insanity fits you perfectly," Cody replied, mocking me with his laughter.

"I am only giving you multiple chances to do the right thing, to denounce your stance. All I want is for you to surrender this attempt to wipe the Earth of all you hate, my friend. Understand that there is good in everyone, no matter how evil they may seem," I said, wishing that he would see the value of my words.

"You cannot change my mind, Martin. I listen to the more intelligent of the two of us...and that is I. I understand better than you. I have the better judgment between the two of us. Why should I ever spare you my ear again? You would only waste it as you waste my time now. I am done with this worthless conversation. I shall end you along with your beloved city."

His posture changed, and I could see he was going to attack me. I pointed the gun at him as he raced for me. Fired, the blast traveled by him again. He had reached me in that second. He carelessly smacked the weapon from my hands and stared me down.

"I can never wholly explicate my hatred and disappointment for you," Cody said, thrusting his metal hand into my gut.

He reached inside me and ripped out one of my kidneys. He tossed it to the ground before grabbing me and stomping down on my left femur, snapping it in two. His next move was to twist my right arm around, dislocating it horribly. It ended with a kick to my chest, collapsing my ribcage.

With my back to the pavement about 30 feet from my foe, I breathed extremely heavily. While my lungs tried to gather air, they were pushed inwards by my broken ribs. Blood flowed uncontrollably from the gaping hole in my gut. Even with all this and the pain of my arm and leg, I knew that I could not fail. Never would I allow myself to give up.

Pushing in my dislocated shoulder, I returned it to its original position. Aiding my broken leg with my now two operational arms, I stood. I pressed against the sides of my torso, aligning the ribs to where they needed to be. Blood still flowing from my abdomen, I walked towards the enemy, ever-confident.

"Seriously? Well, perhaps I can have a little more fun with you than I previously believed! You are a tough guy, Martin! Man!" Cody exclaimed.

"Stop this...now! It does not have to end like this!" I yelled in pain.

Chuckling, Cody just stood in front of me, waiting. When at last I had reached him, I threw a punch for his shielded jaw. It connected, and his head moved barely to the side with the impact. Laughing, he reciprocated my gesture. With this, my jaw broke from its place, and I collapsed. Evermore, the crimson liquid was spewed from my mouth. Cody could only find it humorous.

Again, I took up my feet and stood. I looked through his screen and into his deep blue circles. They were absent of any sympathy for my suffering. There was no mercy, no compassion, and nothing but pleasure in those eyes. He rejoiced in every bit of pain he inflicted on me. Where was my Cody?

I attempted another punch, but he grabbed my fist out of the air. All he did was squeeze...and how tortuous such a simple action can be! After turning every bone in my left hand to dust, he tossed it away. Still, I stood, but not with much strength. Riled by my persistence, he followed up with a brutal shove to my ribs, shattering them once again.

Now, I was on the solid pavement looking up at the monster. From my new position, I decided to spend the time on myself instead of on an attack that would only prove futile. I straightened out my left hand and put my jaw back where it was meant to be. I pressed on my sides to align my ribs again and I stood up. However much I had to face, I would always stand back up. He would have to kill me to make me stay down.

"From where has this come, Martin? Never could I have imagined there was so much fight in you! In most cases, it is those with the physical advantage who have the least likelihood to continue fighting knowing they will lose. They have not had to learn what it feels like to actually fight knowing they will lose. So...they do not fight. But you... Have you ever had to experience that? You have never met an adversary like I am. Even L.I.F.E. was a simple victory for you. From where has this come?"

"It...comes...from..." I could barely speak. I gasped for air in between my coughs that splattered red on my enemy's suit. "From...my...compassion."

"Compassion? Martin, compassion is not the motivator of killers like we. Tell me the truth."

146

"I care so deeply...for those you aim to kill. I shall risk everything...to stop you. I cannot live...knowing that I did not do all I could to save them. So...I shall die doing all I can for them. That is...where it comes from."

"How full of kindness your heart is! But kindness is just one of many motivators in this world. Mine is vengeance. This one comes with a pleasure that only malevolence can supply. And supply it does!"

"But you will never experience...the true satisfaction of loving others. That is...but one of your many punishments."

"Ha! Punishment? You speak backwardly as does one disabled mentally! A lack of loving others is my punishment? Martin, you are such a fool!"

"I wish that you...could understand what you are doing. That...is one thing I truly desire."

"How many times have I said it? I understand fully what I am doing!"

"No...you don't. There are consequences beyond what you know. These decisions affect you...and everyone around you. Why can't you...see what you're doing...is wrong?" I gasped, bracing myself on his shoulder.

He was done listening to me, and I could see it. Even as my vision was beginning to fade, I could see the frustration he had for having to deal with me. My mere presence was the catalyst to his rage. He was done with me.

"I have had enough of your twisted words. The real question is why I have humored you for so long. Obviously, you do not deserve the mind with which you have been gifted. It is a prize that you waste on your efforts to save those less superior than you. You do not deserve your mind and you do not deserve to waste mine."

He picked me up by my neck and slammed me down against the pavement. My head did not bounce off the ground, but, instead, cracked open with the immense force applied to it. As all breath left my lungs, I could not cry out for all my pain. Without my voice, I could not scream of the torment of excruciation that encompassed me. I was left to silently suffer.

The monster looked around him and no longer at me. Seeing none of his metallic minions, he straightened his helmet in preparation to speak.

After clearing his throat, he said, "Pilot One to Location. All units: Follow."

My vision blurring increasingly, Cody looked down on me.

"This place lacks the multitude of screams that I desire. I wish to accelerate the process. Your beloved humans in West City are next. But do not fret, Martin. Your death will surely meet you soon. Your weak body could not possibly recover from the injuries I have dealt. Embrace the end, Martin, and I shall embrace the beginning."

I could not respond as his Pilot Sphere landed and he boarded. His blurry image ascended and flew off to the northwest. Along with him, hundreds of the remaining LIFE Spheres flew, too. Nothing I could do would stop him now. My eyes closed, and I accepted my fate.

Chapter 21
Have Faith

"Wake up already! You can't die now! You're our only hope, Martin! Just wake up!"

My eyelids barely moved, but I caught a glimpse of the vehicle in which I was. Objects outside the car flew by at breakneck speeds. The dull red interior of the car captured a fragment of my interest, but still I could not hold my eyelids open. I lacked the strength to maintain consciousness. Again, I settled into my stasis.

"Martin, you have to wake up! We're almost to West City! He's there, burning down the place like he just did with Alemande. Martin! Martin!"

Although I could not look at the speaker, I recognized the voice. It was the voice of Mikaila Lamb. I inferred that she must have found me in the street after my confrontation with Cody and brought me to her car. Perhaps she bandaged me up as well, for I was still alive, even in my dilapidated state. My bones felt more in place than they did earlier. I guess I had her to thank for that.

"Martin, can you hear me? I need you to answer! You are the only one who is remotely strong enough to stand against him! No one will be able to kill him! You're the only one!"

I found it quite apparent now that she was incorrect. I was not the only one who was strong enough to stand against Cody, for there was no one alive who could stand against him. I knew I was not strong. My lack of power would only lead to death. She was counting on me, but I could only fail her. I had no strength at all.

My answer, the best I could give, was my arm falling from its perch on the armrest. Mikaila did not seem to notice it, unfortunately, because she continued driving like a maniac towards West City and screaming for me to answer her.

I could barely think of anything I could do. I had lost so much blood that my advanced brain could not even do simple problem solving. My body might have been super, but it could not run without precious blood. My body had certain precautions to avoid such loss, and they were now in effect, but it was not enough. My mind was lost, and that was what I needed the most right now.

I began to fall out of reality. I was not permitted to stay in this car, but, instead, I was sent into the depths of my brain. This place was void of any color. The darkest black surrounded me here. I was alone, dressed as I had been in reality. Nothing about me was different here, but I surely felt different. It was many times more peaceful than the outside was. Everything accounted for, I was glad I was given this escape.

"It should be known that you fought more valiantly than I would have, Martin," said a voice from behind me.

Turning to see the speaker, I was faced by the image of Jack Lamb. He looked exactly as he had before I had blown his head off, but he, too, looked so much more at peace. Instead of his greedy grin, he now wore a kind smile. I was glad to see my old rival.

"Jack, where are we?" I asked him.

"We are in the recesses of your mind. This is the one place I can speak a few words of wisdom to you. You need help, Martin. This task cannot be accomplished by you alone. You are going to need more than your own strength this time."

"I have already figured that one out. How can you help me? You are dead. Even now, you are only a delusion caused by a lack of blood. How can you tell me anything I do not already know?"

"I can help you because, even with that brain of yours, you forgot who has always been there for you. He is the only one who can truly guide you to success. I can introduce you once again."

"God has failed me as I have failed today. He has shown me that victory is impossible against such a force as the monster that is Cody. I cannot win. However much help is given to me, I cannot win."

Jack Lamb approached me with the same smile. He embraced me with a hug that seemed to ignore everything I had said to him. I hugged him back, genuinely missing him.

He whispered in my ear, "Today is not over yet."

Just like that, Jack was gone. I would have felt out of my mind had I not known that the exact opposite was true right now. I glanced around the vacancy, searching for him so that I could say goodbye this time, but he was nowhere to be found. He was gone once again.

"Searching for old enemies?" I heard from behind me.

The voice not matching Jack's, I was curious who was speaking to me now. I faced the image that addressed me. It was an enemy or, at least, of what I thought when the word "enemy" was mentioned. Zak Kurien looked at me with an expressionless face.

"Not for you," I answered.

"Naturally. Why should you be looking for the likes of me? I don't deserve your thoughts."

"What do you have to say to me? With what knowledge could you provide me?"

A smile graced his lips, and he removed his glasses. He wiped them off on his shirt and then returned them to his face. He let out a deep sigh and returned his focus to me.

"I started the L.I.F.E. Organization back in 1994. The goal was the same as I told you before...but with a different focus. We were interested in eliminating birth defects. By changing the brain, we could teach it to fight and defeat such abnormalities. That was what I had in mind at the start. It was my dream to get rid of such afflictions like nearsightedness."

"But you tackled so much more than that. And thus, me."

"Exactly. I never thought it would go so far. I just wanted people to live improved and enhanced lives without having to worry about things they could do nothing about. That was L.I.F.E.'s original goal."

L.I.F.E., like many evil things, had begun with good intentions. Misled by greed, Zak took the organization down the wrong path. From there, evil had its entrance. Things could only get worse, and turning back became harder and harder. Simple mistakes can ruin anyone and anything.

"I never knew that. And that being so, how is it possible for you to tell me this?" I questioned the image of Commander Zak.

"That is what we're trying to show you, Shepard. This isn't your subconscious speaking."

"Then, what is speaking to me right now? It sure as hell isn't God. He should have no words for a failure like me, and I should have no words for a failure like Him."

I watched the pity appear behind those spectacles of his. He believed I was wrong and that my stubbornness was hurting me. He wanted me to see my error and believe fully, but I could not. It was only a lack of blood speaking to me. Nothing else.

"Shepard, don't paint everything so black and white. You speak so definitely that there is no room for anything real. Not everything is one way or another. You can lose and be a winner. You can win and be a loser. Do you not understand?"

"Oh, I understand...but I don't believe. How could He let so many innocent people die? Is that the God I follow? One that would give so much to someone who deserves it the least? Why is He doing this? Answer that!" I yelled at the image as I turned my face from it.

"Kid! What's wrong with you? Don't you know how to follow orders?" came the voice of someone else.

I confronted the new and unsuspected image. In front of me was my old boss. Don Sanzano gave me that scowl that I had feared an eternity ago.

"You think you know better than I do, kid? No one does. I had hoped that you could have learned that during our time together," said Keir in that tone of voice that had controlled me in the days of brotherhood.

"I *always* knew better than you. You had no clue how to run the mafia! You only had success because of me! So you don't get to claim that you are better than I am!" I yelled, approaching the image with my frustration.

"Then, how about God? Do you know better than Him? In a word: No. He lets you run your life when He has always known better than you. You have no clue what you are doing! You only have success because of Him. So you don't get to claim that you are better than Him."

I had no response to this. What was said was so humbling that I was silenced on the spot. I refused to look at the image of Keir Sanzano any longer. I walked in the other direction and I was quiet. Keir said nothing more as I refused him my gaze.

It was so true. God did know better than I did, and I had no right trying to go my own path. My life would eventually end up at its own Vaillancourt if I did not cede control. Still, the path I was letting God take me made no sense to me. Was it truly the correct path?

"Why do so many have to die? That cannot be right. They are innocent. Why should they die? They cannot deserve what they are getting. Why is it this way?" I begged for an answer.

"Martin, there is more to this than you can see," came a different voice, one that I recognized too easily.

"Why do you torture me with her voice? Is that what I deserve?"

"You deserve comfort because you are in bad shape. Who better than your mother to supply that comfort?" said the image of my deceased mother.

"All this does is make me think of all the death I have caused. There is no comfort in regret."

"Learn that regret is never necessary. You only have to ask for forgiveness, and it will be given. The errors you have made do not define you, but they have guided you to this path you are on. Never forget what you have done, but do not feel plagued by it. I know your heart, my son."

"How could I possibly not feel plagued by my mistakes? My mistakes are not so simple that they could ever be ignored. My mistakes have killed so many. How could I not let that affect me?"

"This is a learning moment, Martin. And I know how capable of learning you are," said a new voice that I had not heard for such a long time.

"Mrs. Taylen?" I said, turning towards her image. "What can I learn here? You were always such an exceptional teacher. You could always make me learn."

"Well, remember, Martin, I was fired from my teaching job. I don't think it was the teacher, but the student, who was exceptional," she laughed.

I laughed as well and I could finally smile again. It was so good to see my old teacher. The days I had spent with her on the *Annabelle* had given me much. She had been so good to me. I was so sorry that she had to be caught up in my chaos, but I knew that she never blamed me. She had shown me such love.

"Still, you taught me so much. Teach me now. What can I learn here?"

"You are not alone in this fight. You can learn that. Martin, as long as you keep up the fight, He will be with you. God has never abandoned you; why should he now? You cannot fail with Him by your side."

"I have already failed, Mrs. Taylen. Did you forget the fact that I almost just died without barely touching that monster. Why should I keep fighting?"

"It will get better, Martin. Rely on His strength, not your own. And remember..." she said, but when I blinked, she was gone.

"Things will always get worse before they get better," finished Jonah from behind me. "I was forced into poverty by crippling debt caused by my lying brother-in-law. I never told you this, Martin, but, without that horrible injustice on my finances, I would have never met you. We were going to move to California. But without money, I was forced to live in that dinky little hut by the dock. When I met you, everything changed. I don't know what my life would have been like without you, Martin."

"You would still be alive," I stated bluntly.

"But I never would have found happiness. What good would being alive do me without the hope and joy you gave us? The kids would have been miserable in California. We needed someone like you. Don't you see that you were meant to save us?"

"Then, why couldn't I save you from your death? I save your life only to lose it a year later? Can you not see that injustice?"

"Martin, all I know is that my life got infinitely better after you came into it. It's not the length of life that matters; it's the quality. You gave me quality, and, for that, I am eternally grateful."

"I still failed. Now, I shall fail again. This monster is too much for me. Why can't you see that he is invincible with all that gear? Even without it, it would be all luck for me to defeat him. I am not going back to face him. I am hiding, and that is that."

My dead brother Collin took Jonah's place and spoke, "I always thought you were the seeker, not the hider. We hid, and you always found us. Why should that change here? Seek him out; he is hiding even now."

"He is not hiding! He is destroying a city in plain daylight. How is that hiding?" I yelled at my brother, frustrated by my lack of understanding.

"Not the monster you are to face, but your friend Cody. He is hiding. It will take everything you have to find him, but you can do it. Once you find him, the game is over, Martin. You always found us," Collin told me and gave me a heartwarming smile, one that I had missed infinitely.

With that last sentence, he was gone. I was left in the bowels of my mind, alone. I fell to my knees and pounded the non-existent floor. Why was it I who had to suffer this horrible task? Why me?!

"Because you are stronger," came a voice I had never heard before, but it was so familiar at the same time.

"What? Who speaks to me now? Who are you?" I said, frantically searching the void.

Nothing responded to my pleas. Did I imagine it? There was no one here to talk, so from where did the sound come? It was strange enough that people who had died at my hands were speaking to me, but it was stranger that a voice I had never heard before was speaking. From where did it come?

As I panicked and ran around the emptiness of my mind, I felt more helpless than I ever had. I felt so incredibly humbled by this occurrence. I was not in control here...and that scared me. Every time I had faced adversity in my life, I had always known there was a chance to acquire control. Here, there was no opportunity for me. Whatever was speaking dominated even my mind.

"Reveal yourself!" I commanded with fear rather than confidence. Nothing answered me. I was trapped in this infernal silence. Never had I wanted to hear someone's voice more than I did now. This silence crippled me, and I fell on my face.

"I am sorry! Please, help me! I don't have strength enough to face this enemy! He overpowers me in everything I am! There is no advantage I hold in this conflict!"

"There is one," whispered the abyss.

"What? What do I hold over Cody Callison? What can I do to defeat him? How can I save them? What is my advantage?!" I screamed in desperation at the voice.

"Faith," returned the voice.

"Faith? How can I fight with my faith? My faith has always been so weak! It could never be used as a weapon! What is it I am to do?"

"Have faith."

Without any warning, I was thrust back into the world. I sat up and panted heavily. Adrenaline surged throughout my system, and I could not calm myself. I was still in shock after what had happened. I gripped tightly the armrests of the car. My body was coping, and my mind was not with it.

After shaking and gasping for about ten seconds, I dropped back against the back of the seat. I felt very awake and completely in control now. My breathing slowed, and my shaking ceased. I was back to normal. Completely normal.

I mean to say that everything about me was as it was intended to be. My wounds were closed, and my bones were in place. The only thing I was missing was one of my kidneys, but I had another. I did not feel fatigued nor did I feel in pain. I was in the best shape I could be. It was as if I had never faced Cody. I was ready to fight once more!

Now being able to do so, I analyzed my surroundings. Mikaila sat in the driver's seat to my right. She was silent with her mouth wide open. Outside the car, the scenery no longer flew by us. It was stationary, for we were parked on the side of the freeway outside West City. Feeling safe with where I was, I faced Mikaila again.

Mikaila reached over and grabbed my arm.

"Are you okay, Martin?" she asked with the highest concern.

"I am more okay than I have ever been, Mikaila. I feel better than I ever have."

"Well, you shouldn't. You just died for about eight minutes. You're pretty amazing, Martin. To survive what you have.... That is amazing."

I nodded in agreement as I opened the car door and stepped outside the vehicle. Looking at the burning city only about a mile away, I felt determination rising in my gut. I knew what I had to do. Whatever it took,

I would pay that price in hope of a better life for those who now suffered. I would pay that price because I was the only one who could. I would pay the price because I was stronger.

"I have more than survived. I have found new life. With this new life, I can finally reach my full potential. And if I use this life to save billions of others, then I have reached that potential. Cody Callison has forced a debt on this world; my life will be the defrayal. I am ready to pay that price."

Chapter 22
A New Strength

Looking over at the calamity that was West City, both fear and avidity filled me. How I wanted to help the citizens who were so unjustly attacked! Suffering and despair, once my greatest trepidations, were now my greatest motivation. I had to go and I had to fight.

"The National Guard should be arriving soon, Martin. You will have some back-up in this fight," Mikaila told me as I slammed the car door.

"Their support is very welcome at this time. To complete this mission, I will need all the help I can get. And speaking of help, while I'm fighting this menace, I need someone to help evacuate civilians. I would be very grateful for your support, Mikaila."

"I will do what I can to help out with that. If I can shuttle a hundred people out of here, then I will," she said, seriously devoting herself to the cause.

"Thank you. Just out of curiosity, did you happen to bring any weapons with you?" I asked Mikaila.

Without hesitation, she hit a button on her keys that unlocked the trunk. After moving to the rear of the car, she opened the trunk and revealed tens of high quality weapons. Rifles of many calibers and of all sizes lay in the back of this vehicle, and all were full-auto. Grenades and C4 were stored in 5-gallon buckets. Everything besides the fabled laser rifle, the one weapon I needed most, was here.

"I got a RPG in the backseat, but that's for me. It's not the most convenient thing to haul around, anyways. You wouldn't want it," Mikaila said.

"You may have it. I will be fine with or without it. There are no weapons here that can aid me," I responded, shutting the trunk.

"You're not going to take anything?" she asked me, astonished.

"No, I am going to confront Cody without weapons. I cannot even fight the LIFE Spheres with what I have available now. But if I can get a laser rifle, then maybe I can get some work done."

"I doubt that you can do anything better without weapons than with. Do you really think that is the best plan?" she asked me, hitting the button that opened the trunk again.

"These weapons are not the determining factor in my victory. Don't worry. I will do fine without them," I answered her skepticism with confidence, slamming the trunk closed.

"But you know what he can do, right? This guy's a total monster! You need to find a laser rifle, Martin. At least, do that first."

"I will try, but I have to confront him soon. If I can do anything for this city, it's slowing his killing spree. Getting a laser rifle is the bonus. If I am lucky enough to find one, then I will definitely take it."

"But if it is so unlikely that you could get one, then why do you fight him first? Take out as many of the machines as you can before you go get yourself killed by Cody. That's what I would do."

"Our military can destroy the machines, but there is no way they could ever stand a chance against Cody Callison. He speaks of killing everyone on the planet and he is all too capable of doing so. I am the only one strong enough to stand up to him. Even if I fail, the machines will fall. Only Cody will remain."

She nodded and walked to her side of the car. She leaned on the vehicle and stared at the burning city. I could see the tears welling up in her eyes. I wished that there was a way I could comfort her in these difficult times, but I had no words of that kind in me now.

"You wanna ride on top of the car?" Mikaila asked me, wiping her eyes quickly.

"Sounds like fun," I responded with a kind smile.

She returned a weak smile and opened her door. As she entered the car, I jumped on top of it and held the racks on top of the car. Mikaila started the engine, and we took off along the interstate.

As West City came closer and closer, I could smell the smoke and hear the screams much better. It was the same as Alemande, horrendous. The situation here was dire, and the people were desperate for any kind of salvation. I had my work cut out for me.

Entering the city, Mikaila maneuvered the car through crowds of rushing people. Every face looked the same as they were all drenched in unclouded terror. Not one stood out, even in these large multitudes. No one looked unique anymore. All became the same as they ran for their lives.

Mikaila's hand hit the top of the car and gave me my cue. I leaped from the roof and landed on my feet. I watched Mikaila zoom off to help more people. I was lucky to have her as was everyone in this city. She had a goal that was similar to mine: salvation. We both valued the lives of these citizens equally, and, together, we would take a stand against this threat.

I sprinted in the direction of distant explosions. I knew who would be waiting for me there, but this time I had no fear. I simply would face him; the outcome was irrelevant. If I lived, I could aid the people further. If I died, I could only hope that I took him with me. All I was to be was Cody Callison's worst nightmare.

As I ran, I became the spectator to more death. The LIFE Spheres swooped down from the sky and torched person after person. They were as eagles coming down upon prey, mighty and fascinating, but I was horrified by how this majesty was displayed with such an evil outcome. Mother, daughter, father, or son; it did not matter. All perished here on the streets. Their bodies were burnt beyond recognition. The stench of sizzled flesh was their only remainder.

If only I could stop it! Without a laser rifle, I did not stand much of a chance against a thousand fire-breathing metal spheres. Bullets would only bounce off their hard shells, and my fists would damage them similarly. I just ran, unfortunately not immune to the sorrow of this tragedy.

Far in front of me, I saw military vehicles screeching past. At last, the government had come in to assist the people in a time of need. Sadly, I knew they were still no match for the monster. Perhaps, they could slow him down for me or serve as a distraction. Truly, this was all they could offer.

But how heartless it was to equate these brave soldiers as only bait for my rival! They were the ones for whom I fought. In this field of battle, I lost all sight of the individuals for whom I risked my life. Battle does that to the mind; it numbs it and it loosens the conscience's hold. In the midst of war, a man can genuinely see what lies in his heart, but I would not let it be my destruction. I remembered my past of unsympathetic violence. I would not return to it.

Just as I was approaching the street where I had seen the vehicles fly past, a flaming Humvee was thrown back in my direction. A quick dodge was simple for me, but not for the running soldiers in this vicinity. They were crushed so suddenly that there was nothing I could do. Those trained to keep peace were ended by a lack of it.

Not far from where I now stood, Cody was picking up the Humvees and tossing them as if they were toys. These fiery projectiles so easily met their targets. Cody's strength was beyond belief. I thought I was amazing when I had stopped a police cruiser with my body, but here was Cody, tossing Humvees at his prey. Did I really stand a chance?

I had to remember that no, I did not stand a chance, but it was not my strength with which I was fighting. My God was with me, and no one could stand against me. We would win this war; not I, but we. No, I did not have the strength to conquer Cody Callison, but I had the God.

I noticed that, near his feet, a laser rifle was lying. Further behind him sat the LIFE Sphere, Pilot One. Sitting within was most likely the other rifle that he had used previously. If I could only sneak all the way around his chaos and to the LIFE Sphere, I could possibly get my hands on the weapon that was most important to me. This was my plan.

I sprinted into a building and began navigating towards the Sphere. I jumped over the tables of a restaurant, knocking cups to the floor in my haste. Fearful customers hid underneath these tables, and I did not disturb them. My goal lay with the Sphere and the rifle. That was my only concern at the moment.

To put myself in these customer's shoes would be very difficult for me. I had always been the one who had to take action. I would not be able to remain under a table in fear as the city burnt around me. I had been made with a sensitivity to such suffering and I could not stand it. Never would anyone find me under a table due to fear, and I was glad that this was true.

Zigzagging in and out of shops, I arrived inside the building outside which the Sphere was. Looking to make sure Cody was not watching, I ran to the Sphere. Immediately, I jumped in and grabbed for what I had hoped so desperately. With the laser rifle in my hands, I took the yoke and pushed forward on the throttle. I charged forth towards the enemy.

He had just finished murdering the soldiers when he turned around and saw me. I had the rifle aimed right at his heart. I pulled the trigger and, to the surprise of no one, missed by a mile. Flying by him, I flipped the machine around and charged back at him. By this time, he had picked up the rifle at his feet and now had it pointed at the Sphere. Realizing this with no time left, I let myself fall. As I did this, his blast connected with the machine, and it exploded into a thousand pieces.

Being flung by the blast, I still had enough control to shoot one shot. This time, I aimed for where he might dodge if I fired at his heart. I fired and then I hit the ground. I took up my feet as quickly as possible to see if I was victorious, but the answer was obvious. There he stood, unmoved from where he had been. He did not even dodge. He knew me too well.

As debris rained down, I was looked upon with hatred. He had thought that I was dead. He had thought that I was finally out of his life. He had thought his one rival was finally vanquished. He was wrong and, with his incorrectness, he was enraged.

"How are you here? How could you have possibly survived? Not even a team of veteran surgeons could have saved you from your fate! I could not have failed to kill you," Cody shouted, shocked.

"Can't kill me, my friend," I replied to him with a cocky tilt of my head.

"We shall see. Obviously, I overlooked your advanced healing when I calculated your demise...but I did not! With a multiplier of five, you should not have been able to heal from your most lethal wounds within eleven minutes. Death should have met you within eight. With a three minute gap between life and death, you should have been on the side of death."

"Yet, here I am. Are you ready to surrender?"

"Far from it, Martin. This time, I have a laser rifle in my grasp. Do not think I am merciful enough to not use it. I take no more chances from here on out," Cody said, aiming the weapon at my heart.

"Just know that I shall never give up on you. Simply drop your weapon and you will be forgiven. You can stop all of this. It is your choice. Do you want to bring about the world's demise or..." I was telling him, but was interrupted by Cody's itchy trigger finger. My gut exploded, and I fell to my back.

I let out a scream of pain from the ground. It burned so badly. I remembered this feeling well. Groaning, I looked to my foe only to be frustrated by the look of satisfaction on his face.

"Yes, that is exactly what I want. But more than that, I want your demise. It will be delivered by metal hands. I am going to rip you to shreds," said Cody, moving towards me.

Lying in the middle of the street among deceased soldiers and twisted, burning metal, I listened to the rhythmic beat produced by his tungsten feet. I would have considered it the driving beat of my death song, but I knew better. I would not die here. Today was not over yet.

He was now only several yards from my position on the ground. I pointed my rifle up and aimed for the center of his chest. I was just about to fire when I heard a screeching sound coming from behind me. Cody's focus left me and was now directed on the rocket racing towards him. He moved to my right to avoid the rocket, but not to avoid the laser. I hit him right in the side of his head. That whole side of the helmet burst off, and the heat from the explosion severely burnt Cody's face.

"GAAHH!" screamed Cody, being knocked to his back.

Cody fell as I stood. He, not one to be beaten, regained his feet and lunged at me. He grabbed the rifle and flung it far away. Then, his left gauntlet slapped down on my right shoulder and his knee went into my blown-open gut. When I had bent over in pain, his right fist pounded down on my spine. I was crippled on the ground at his feet. I had made progress against him, but had it proved to do any good at all?

Right before he stomped down on my skull, another rocket could be heard racing towards him. Abandoning me shortly, Cody jumped away from the trajectory of the rocket. Using this brief distraction to my benefit, I dragged myself away from the threat. Looking to where the rockets originated, I saw my ally reloading her RPG. Mikaila was here for me, but, unfortunately, I could not be there for her.

Cody retrieved his laser rifle and immediately fired it at Mikaila's car. Mikaila threw herself behind a destroyed Humvee as her car exploded. I knew she was injured and that she would not be able to run from Cody. That Humvee granted her little safety from the lasers that were already flying. Why could I not help her?

Summoning all remaining strength in my body, I stood up. As Cody fired upon the Humvee, I ran, my heart burning with determination. I threw myself at the foe with no fear. Right before I connected with him, he ceased fire and turned my direction. I could see the astonishment in the one eye revealed by his broken helmet.

I tackled him and began throwing my fists at the uncovered half of his face. Stopped momentarily by the feeling of a nudge on the side of my head, I noticed that Cody had the rifle against my head. When he pulled the trigger, nothing happened. That is when I noticed the fluids leaking out of the handle of the weapon and over Cody's gauntlet. In his rage, he had crushed the handle and broken the rifle. Without the laser rifle, perhaps I had more of a chance than I thought.

Realizing his error, he grabbed me. I continued the assault on his face until he had thrown me away from him. Not at all shaken by being thrown, I returned to his vicinity and continued to fight. His mind engulfed in ire, he threw life-ending punches with little accuracy. My mind stable, I flung weaker punches that hit their mark every time. This was when I knew I actually did have a chance against this monster.

He was fueled by wrath and revenge, and I was fueled by love and justice. My heart burned so many times hotter than his. He fought alone, and I fought allied with the creator of the universe. For the first time, I saw that it was not I against whom the odds were, but he. Alone, Cody could not succeed. No one finds real victory on their own.

My fists hit with more and more strength while his could never find their target. His body strained under the force of every justly received blow. His offense was quickly transitioning to defense as he saw what he fought. The stronger man was losing his will to continue fighting.

Cody Callison, the one who held the power to end all human life on planet Earth, was now retreating from my attacks. His self-preservative dodges kept him inches from my flying fists. He was fleeing, and it was obvious. Nothing he could do would stop me from coming at him. He would have to run for the rest of his life.

Feeling the pressure and needing an escape, Cody reached up to his helmet and said, "All units to Location."

There was no response. The blast from the laser had utterly obliterated all systems of the helmet. He could not call for backup now. He was forced to face me without his army of metal.

Shocked from his mistakes, Cody left himself open. Seeing his vulnerability, I delivered a powerful punch to his stomach. For once, Cody's loftiness was forgotten as he bowed before me. I then threw my knee upwards into his helmet, shattering the remainder of the glass. Cody was knocked to the pavement in all his glory.

I stopped as I saw his hand rise for mercy. He panted lightly, and his deep blue circles were clouded with disarray. I could see the confusion racing throughout his mind. Cody was forced to see me as an equal. Everything he thought he knew was turned on its side.

"You have learned. Never did I think I would be on my back looking up to you. You have shown me that you are so much more than I could have anticipated. My hero has returned," remarked Cody, his words genuine.

"If you see my power, then you can see the futility of your fight. It is time to give it up. You can be forgiven, and everything can go back to how it was," I pleaded.

"Ha! But so returns the fool! You ask me to give up my futile fight, but I ask you to give up yours! You cannot achieve this goal. I shall never surrender."

"Not even to your hero?" I asked, extending my hand down to him.

"I prefer my heroes..." he said, taking my hand and pulling himself up. "Dead!" he ended with his gauntlet sinking into my stomach.

I, stunned, failed to hinder his escape. After punching me in the gut, he sprinted away. I let him go, for I had someone else of whom to take care.

I could only hope that she was all right. She had saved me, and it was my turn to save her.

Running to where Mikaila had hidden, I prayed that she would be okay. Enough lives had been lost today; hers should not have to be included. Flipping the car from its tipped over position, I saw her. She had been crushed, but she appeared to still be alive. I knelt down and shook her, trying to awaken her. Her comatose state filled me with anxiety, and my shaking became more violent.

Finally, she awoke. Her eyes met mine, and her mouth formed a debilitated smile.

"I don't feel that great," Mikaila said, barely breathing.

"Well, you shouldn't. You were just dead for eight minutes."

She showed slight approval for the comment, but then turned her attention elsewhere.

"What happened to Cody?" she asked between coughs.

"He is gone for now. What is important now is getting you out of here. You're done helping people get out of here, and it is time to go. We're going to find someone with a car to drive you out of the city."

"That would be nice."

I lifted her to her feet and helped her walk. Mikaila was so weak. Being crushed by that Humvee had taken a lot out of her. Even in this weakened state, she showed great strength. After I had helped her take a few steps, she waved me away so I could find a ride for her.

Surveying the street, I saw no motion for a moment. Fortunately, a car soon came barreling down the street in desperate attempt of escape. Moving quickly, I put myself right in the path of the racing vehicle. The driver slammed on the brakes, and the tires screeched horribly. The car stopped right in front of me, and I could see inside the car. I did not expect to see whom I did inside that car.

Rolling down her window, Melody, the girl who had helped me get to Alemande after I had escaped prison, yelled at me, "What are you doing out here, man?! Don't you know what's going on? You gotta get out of here!"

"I'm sorry, but I need your help...again." Upon hearing that I needed help, she immediately snapped to attention. She stuck her head out the window more and gave me her full attention.

"Whatever you need, I will try to help."

"I need you to help my friend get back to her house in Alemande. I think you know the address," I said with a slight chuckle.

Melody answered confidently, "238 Paterson Street."

"Thank you so much! You go there and you stay in the basement until all this is over. You will be safe in Alemande."

"We can stay in the basement? Is she okay with this?"

Mikaila, who was slowly approaching, let out a weak gasp for an answer. "Of course she's okay with it. You're saving her life."

"Thank you so much. Shelter is greatly appreciated...especially now."

"Well, thank you, too. You will be rewarded for this. I know you will."

Mikaila reached me, and I opened the door for her. She collapsed into the seat next to Liz and passed out. I closed the door and turned back to Melody. "Thank you once again. I have to go now, and so do you."

"Hey! Where are you going, man?" she yelled at me as I started to run off.

"I have a mission to complete!"

Chapter 23
Whenever There Is Trouble

Searching with urgency through the debris of the battlefield, I ran to where I believed the laser rifle to be. Cody had flung it away from me during our confrontation, but I knew that it had to still be operational. Really, all I needed was one shot.

After combing through the streets for hurried minutes, I found the weapon I desired. It was still in working condition. L.I.F.E. had made these sturdier than I had believed. They were an impressive organization, however evil their purpose was. Thinking of all they could have done had they not gone down the wrong path made me cringe. Such talent. Such good intentions. All wasted because of greed. They could have been so much more.

Incorrect decisions are made every day. I was one to understand this so well. In my past, I had killed and I had hated. These decisions only led to more and more death and suffering. No wonder my life had been like a rollercoaster. Pain would mend my ways, but never for long. I had not learned to show mercy until so late in my life and, even then, I still attacked L.I.F.E.! It took my loss of memory the second time to truly learn the error of my ways. Only then have I been able to succeed.

I could not make those kinds of decisions today. If I let myself make one incorrect choice, then all could be lost. One mistake could doom everyone. I had one focus, and it was to save humanity. I could not fail. This mission was too important for me to fail.

Then, it hit me. I could not fail. It was actually impossible for me to fail, if only I had faith. That was what I heard whispered in the depths of my mind, and it was exactly the advice I needed. With God going before me and fighting behind me, failure was impossible. All I had to do was have faith that He would be with me. Nothing would go wrong, and all would go according to His plan.

With my mind finally opened to the truth, I knew that I would win. I knew that the world would be saved today. I knew that God would not let me fail this day. My purpose was confirmed, and I was ready. Now, I just had to find Cody and end this fiasco.

I raised up the laser rifle and, seeing some of the dreaded LIFE Spheres, fired it. The laser ripped through their shells, and they exploded as fireworks do. They were celebratory explosions. The booms that sounded welcomed in a new beginning. Independence from doubt! I would go now...to the end of death!

It was time for the world to be saved. This menace had gone too far. Evil's decent on this city and the previous were the last straw. I would not let this injustice continue. The monster was entering his final hours and he was not even aware of it.

My feet carried me in the direction in which the monster had run off. They took me through alleys and across streets. My eyes searched for any sign of Cody Callison. All they found was the destruction he had caused in his flight. I was right on his track. I would find him soon.

Exiting another alley, I heard gunshots to my left across the street. Looking there, I saw the justice-seeker I had not seen in so long, Officer Nick Turnbull. He was unloading his pistol into the back of the monster who was further down the street. Seeing Cody turn around, I hid behind the cars along the sides of the street. I needed to remain hidden if I wanted the element of surprise.

Nick reloaded his weapon and resumed fire. It was to no avail, of course, because Cody bent his arm upward and unveiled his shield. The bullets bounced uselessly off the tough tungsten between them. Still, the officer unloaded his entire magazine into the shield. He knew what he was doing.

I moved closer to where they stood. Officer Turnbull had fired all his ammunition at Cody and was now left helpless to face him. Cody approached slowly, looking somewhat pleased at what the simple police officer had done. Nick refused to move. He stared down the monster as the loud clunks of the tungsten sounded off the pavement.

"You stand against me when it is so obvious you will die. Why is this? Are you a simple fool? Or is there more to it?" Cody said to Nick, his eyes gleaming with curiosity.

"You are killing the innocent without reason. You are a murderer, and that makes it my job to make you stop. So I have a question, too. Will you stop or do I have to do everything in my power to make you stop?" replied Nick.

"Ha! That sounds so familiar. You remind me of someone I hate. He does not know his place just as you do not. You two are fools alike. I shall take the second option, fool. You will have to fight me," Cody said, grabbing Nick by his shirt collar and lifting him into the air.

"Then, in the name of the law..." started Officer Turnbull valiantly.

"Put him down!" I shouted, coming out from my cover. I lifted the weapon as Cody's and Nick's heads turned to me. I fired at my off-guard target. He could not move in time, and the blast connected with his armpit, tearing through the armor. He released his grasp on Nick and the officer was flung by the blast. I saw the agony Cody experienced when I fired again. This blast hit his stomach and ripped the armor from it. Cody, now fully aware of my presence, charged at me. For my final shot, I aimed at his head. Just before I shot, Cody's arm bent, and out came the shield again. The blast hit it, and the laser tore through the tungsten with ease. Cody was too close for me to fire again, but I saw that he no longer had two hands.

Right before Cody knocked me to the pavement, I yelled to Nick, "Run!"

In that second, I saw a realization on the face of Officer Nick Turnbull. The man whom he had hunted for so long and whom he had sent to prison was saving his life. He saw a man whom he had believed evil now fighting for the right side. Nick now understood my heart and knew me to not be the man I was once believed to be. I saw him run just before Cody released his anger into me.

The tungsten boot hit me in the gut and Cody's left hand, the one that was still existent, grabbed the laser from me. Here I was in the middle of the road, looking up at the monster once again. "We've got to stop meeting like this!" I said to my adversary, mocking the severity of the situation.

"Cease your quips! It is over for you! Is it not obvious that you have lost?" Cody yelled angrily.

"You have forgotten one thing. I cannot fail," I laughed.

"What do you say? You cannot fail? I do not believe I ever knew this. How could I have forgotten it? And even if I had been in possession of that knowledge, I would deem it as false. You have fallen before me. It is over. Admit defeat."

"Never. I cannot fail," I told him, stubborn as ever.

"Why?! Why can you not fail?! How are you so sure that failure is an impossibility? Answer me!"

"God is with me. With Him at my side, I cannot fail."

"Does God lie on His back under my laser rifle? Because that is where you lie. Is God on the ground with you? Has God fallen as well?"

"Yes, He lies here with me even now. And He won't let you kill me."

"And why would the King of kings decide to aid you, Martin? You are nothing but a fool."

"Because I have faith in Him," I spoke with no doubt in my heart.

Cody laughed mockingly at me before saying, "I am done! I am done with you and your God. I am done with the worthless filth who inhabit this damn planet. I am done! I hate the humans! I hate this planet! I hate God! But above all, I hate you! For eternity, I shall hate you! You may not live another minute, but, forever, you are in my mind. I hate that! If I can never rid myself of your memory, at the very least, I can rid myself of your presence! Admit that you have failed! Admit it so I can finally be free of you!"

"Never. You are the one who has failed."

The screen gone from his helmet, I could easily see the all-consuming rage on the face of my friend. He teeth gnashed harshly, and his whole face trembled. Fiery wrath burned so intensely in his eyes that I felt as if I could feel the heat. He shoved the rifle in my face, his hand holding it shaking violently.

"ADMIT IT!!! ADMIT IT!!! ADMIT..." the monster screamed before the giant metal sphere collided with his body, sending him flying down the street.

His body tumbled down the road, bouncing at least thirty feet each time. He let out outraged grunts every time he hit the road. Unfortunately, I also saw that the laser rifle bounced with him, finally rendering the sturdy weapon useless. I would have no more lasers to assist me in this fight. Good thing that the lasers were not the determining factor of my victory.

When his body stopped tumbling, Cody stood and watched the Pilot Sphere that was racing towards him, attempting another attack. Cody stood his ground as the machine came closer and closer until they collided. Cody was not knocked back this time. This time, he dug his feet into the ground and caught the Sphere. I saw him strain under the force of the machine, but he held his ground.

The two not moving, the man piloting the Sphere decided to attack. Flame shot from the flamethrower positioned directly in front of Cody's face. His shrieks were choked out by fire, but Cody would not be defeated. With all his might, he threw the Sphere into a building on the right side of the street.

The pilot managed to jump from the craft before it crashed through the wall of the building. This was when I knew who had saved me. Dressed in a robe, barefoot, bald-headed, and with Mrs. T in his hands, Tyler landed on the sidewalk below him. Cody, after extinguishing the fire covering him, looked to see who his attacker was. Seeing his identity as I had, Cody ran at Tyler. I, too, ran, but I aimed to save Tyler's life instead of take it.

As Cody was reaching Tyler, I reached Cody. I tackled my foe to the road, and we wrestled for Tyler's life. I threw jabs at the holes in his armor while he swiped at me with the jagged metal at the end of his right arm. My efforts gave little success, but, when he thrust that sharp tungsten into my chest, I felt it.

With me stunned, he stood above me. He picked me up with his left hand and lifted me as he was prone to doing with so many. He lifted his right arm, revealing the hole in his armor. As he held the sharpened metal against my throat, he breathed heavily in rage.

"You have failed. It is over. It is all..." Cody was telling me, but Mrs. T interrupted.

Tyler had fired the shotgun only feet away from Cody. The slug went directly through the hole in the armor and right to his heart. A slug to the heart is an affliction that even a Super Soldier considers lethal. His heart was torn apart, just as it had been on that night so long ago.

Cody dropped me and stumbled backwards, clutching his chest. Blood flooded out of the wound. He turned to Tyler only to have him fire it again into his gut. Blood flooded out from this second wound as well, and in great amount. He was losing so much blood. If he could not get away from us and rest, he would have no chance of ever regenerating that heart. Blood would not be able to reach his brain, and it would stop functioning. He would be dead within minutes.

Knowing my weakness, Cody lunged at Tyler with his jagged appendage. I was not quick enough to stop the shards of metal from entering Tyler's abdomen. I shoved Cody away from Tyler and prepared to fight, but Cody ran off instead. I knew giving chase would only result in letting Tyler bleed out. Knowing this, I decided to grab Tyler and carry him into the building into which the LIFE Sphere had crashed.

I set him on a table and ripped off part of his robe. Conveniently in a bar, I easily found some 180-proof alcohol to soak the cloth. Taking the soaked section of robe back to Tyler, I leaned him forward. I then wrapped the cloth tightly around the hole in Tyler's abdomen. I poured the remainder of the bottle over the wound. Tyler groaned in anguish, but I had to disinfect the wound.

"Tyler," I said, snapping my fingers to get his attention. "You need to stay here and rest. You've done enough for me already. I have to track down Cody and finish this. I don't need you coming along and dying, okay?"

"Heh, he couldn't kill me if he tried," responded the mortally wounded Tyler.

"Yeah, sure. He just about killed you in one hit."

"*Only* just about!"

I smiled down at my greatest friend. His ever-confident attitude always lifted my morale. What a perfect pair we were! We both needed each other and complimented each other to a tee. I was so glad to have him back.

"Kid, could you grab Mrs. T for me? She's right outside," pleaded Tyler.

"Of course. One second."

I left the bar and took a look back at the building. Despite the LIFE Sphere's best efforts, it had not knocked the sign from above the front doors. The sign read, "The Black Hippo." This was the bar at which Tyler and I were when the Vaillancourt had been blown up by L.I.F.E. last year. I looked down the street where the majestic hotel had once stood proudly. An apartment complex had replaced it. Not that it really mattered, for it had been burnt down by the LIFE Spheres. Maybe they could build another hotel in its place.

I crossed the road and picked up the favorite weapon of my lost friend. Mr. T might have been gone, but Mrs. T lived on. I could understand Tyler's sentiment towards this shotgun. To him, it did not represent the wife of Mr. T, but Mr. T himself. Tyler held onto this memento so Mr. T could be with us on all our adventures. Tyler missed him dearly, and so did I.

I walked back into the Black Hippo and set Mrs. T in Tyler's arms. A big smile greeted her. He gave me the same smile and thanked me. "I wish he was here," I said with remorse.

"Me too, kid. That old man cared for you and me more than we deserved. He saw something in us, I guess. He wanted to fight for something and he wanted to fight alongside people he cared about. He got that when he was with us. Now that he is gone....he would want us to keep fighting. So...that's what I'm going to do, kid. You never stop fighting either."

"Never shall I give up the fight."

"Then, go, kid. You've got a mission to complete."

Chapter 24
The Ascension

Following the dark red trail, I searched for Cody Callison. The trail was wide at first, but soon transitioned into a narrower trail. His holes were closing, and the blood was being trapped inside his body. I could not make an accurate estimate on how long it would take for his heart to regenerate, but I guessed that it would take somewhere around fifteen minutes. This gave me little time to find him.

Soon, I was following small droplets of blood that were spaced at far distances. What little of the crimson liquid was left on his suit was fortunately falling to the ground at regular intervals. I knew that he could not have gone too far and that I had to find him very soon. I needed to find him before his body was fully recovered.

As I ran with my eyes on the blood, I almost failed to notice the lack of screams. Stopping my search momentarily, I looked to the sky. I saw very few LIFE Spheres circling the buildings. What had happened to the menace? I got my answer quickly when I saw a whole convoy of Humvees roll by, accompanied by a few heavily-armed tanks. Large caliber bullets knocked down the Spheres and missiles destroyed them. The National Guard had stepped up their effort, and it showed. They would take care of the Spheres; I had my own objective.

I continued following the blood until it led me to the base of the tallest structure in West City. This was the Spence Center. A rich entrepreneur had built this place from nothing, and it served as an educational center for people of all ages. It truly was a shining achievement for West City. I only knew this because, when I was in the mafia, this was a huge target that we hit up about every week. Now, it was being used as a hiding spot for the monster.

I entered through the glass doors and looked around for more blood. I did not look for even a fraction of a second before seeing the beast lying on the floor not far from the entrance. I approached him cautiously, for I did not know whether or not he was awake.

"Come no...closer...Martin. Let me rest...just a moment more," said Cody as I came within ten feet of him.

"You can rest when you are dead. Stand up and face me."

Reluctantly, Cody rose to his feet. I could see the holes in his abdomen and under his arm were no longer existent. I did notice that his body was swelling, though. However strong he was, he, too, would suffer from internal bleeding. I knew that his heart was most likely patched up by now, but that did not mean that blood was not free outside of his vessels.

"I have stood. Am I to face you now?" asked Cody with a grin.

"If that is what you choose. You still have the option to surrender. I know that you think that you're being beaten by surrendering, but it is so much less than the defeat you will face if you choose to fight me. Think of it as an opportunity rather than a loss. Bronze is not gold, but it is many times better than nothing."

"I am superior. Should I not always go for the gold? Would it not be foolish to settle?" he asked me, bracing himself against a wall.

"You said it yourself. You told me that my goals were too great to be accomplished. You said that I should make more realistic goals if I ever wanted to achieve them. Do you not follow your own advice, hypocrite?" I answered him, moving closer.

He laughed, but backed away from me at the same time. His lips formed a giddy smile as he shook his head at me. Having retreated from steps forward, he braced himself against the wall. His eyes squinted at me in disbelief, and then he burst out laughing.

"How the tables have turned! Look who is giving the lectures now! You use my words against me with perfection. Am I to be the fool now?" he exclaimed.

"You have always been the fool," I answered solemnly.

"One Super Soldier's opinion. I know I am not the fool you are. I calculated every variable before ever planning further. I am correct in my stance without a single doubt. There can be nothing but victory for me. There can be nothing but failure for you."

"I cannot fail this day."

"If you cannot fail this day, then you will fail the next. Or the next. Or the next. Or the next. Know that the fool is the one who shall fall on his back in the end. Only then will it be so blindingly obvious to the fool that he never had a chance. Only then will the fool see all his mistakes. Only then will the fool bear witness to the true strength of the one he challenged. I shall be the one to bring you to the end, fool," he said, a huge grin appearing across his face. "Let us begin."

At this moment, I was faced with an ultimatum. He would either end me or I would end him. Cody left me with no other options, but I refused to take his life. I knew that fighting him would get me nowhere and so I decided that ascension was my best option. On the roof where all his evil could be seen, perhaps I could get him to finally open his eyes and witness it. Perhaps I could get him to actually care. Possibly, this could end well.

Suddenly, my adversary flew at me. Cody swung his blunt left and his jagged right with ferocity that I did not return. I dodged quickly, keeping myself always only inches from the danger. While he moved towards me, I ran to the stairs. I had to climb. I had to get to the top and end this. The ascension was the only option I would take.

We brawled through the halls which people of all ages had previously used to seek higher education. Such noble pursuits were replaced by raw violence. Knowledge was replaced with wrath. Self-improvement was replaced with deprecation. This had been a great place before today. Now, it was defiled.

I barely had time to survey for the stairs before I was again ducking under a wild punch thrown by Cody Callison. He went after me with everything he had left. He would not let himself fail. He was different than I. I knew I could not fail.

"Why do you refuse me the pleasure of a solid hit to my jaw? Why do you refuse my solar plexus? Why do you refuse my face? Can you no longer bear to hit me?" Cody taunted me.

"Your own efforts are punishment enough. I shall not punish you further."

"This is your choice. You only make my conquest that much easier without it."

Even more now, he charged at me with everything. Knowing that I would not fight back, he took full advantage of it. He saw that I would not hurt him, so he had no need for a defense. Cody put all his energy into knocking me down. When I was down, he would finish the battle.

As I ran up the steps leading to floor eight, Cody struck my leg with his right arm. I felt the sharp edges cut through all the layers of muscle and I almost fell. I moved upward with all my remaining strength, ignoring pain. I had to finish the climb.

Next, his left hand came down on my back. This time, I fell on my face. Repeated hits to my back were supplied by my foe, but I refused to feel pain. However much pain taunted me to feel it, I would not give in to it. I crawled up the stairs, my arms grabbing the steps and launching me forward. Cody would not stop, so neither could I.

"Will you not give up?" asked Cody, punching my back into the floor.

"Will you?" I responded, still crawling upwards.

"Shall I never be free of your persistence? Let me kill you so I can be free. Do you know no mercy?"

"I have shown you more mercy than is fathomable. You can do without my death."

Reaching the top of the stairs, I managed to escape his assault and sprinted down the halls away from him. I rounded a corner only to watch a LIFE Sphere burst through a window and slam into the wall. Fire spewed forth from the machine, and I did my best to evade, but, weakened by Cody's fist, I could not. The flaming tar consumed me, but I did not stop running. Cody was right behind me.

In agony, I fell to the floor and rolled until I was free of the heat. My armor was almost non-existent now, and my enemy stood above me. He stomped down on my chest and held me down.

"Fleeing was a poor choice. You had enough strength to finish me down on the first floor. Yet, here you are, defeated on the eighth. Why did you elect to climb, fool?" Cody mocked me.

"I chose to climb so you could have a chance. I climbed because I did not want to kill you."

"Do you finally see that mercy has done nothing for you?" Cody said, leaning down until his face was only inches from mine.

"Mercy has done more for me than even I can comprehend. Your lack of it has done nothing but wrong to you," I said, watching the LIFE Sphere float slowly towards us. Cody was unaware of its approach.

"So spoke the loser. I may have had difficulties, but they all end with you. And now..." Cody spoke until the interjection of fire on his backside.

Cody's unique body signature had been programmed into the LIFE Sphere mainframe. The LIFE Sphere, seeking my life source and oblivious to Cody's, shot its flames upon the one between it and me. This was opportunity enough for me to escape. I ran away while Cody released his rage on the infernal machine.

Up to the ninth, tenth, eleventh, and twelfth I climbed. Intervention seemed to always be there when I needed it. However bad anything looked, I would get away. It was becoming more and more obvious that God was aiding me through every step of this fight. Where I was weak, He was strong. Where I was slow, He was fast. Nothing could beat this alliance.

Out of 23 floors, I had climbed 16 before Cody was back on my tail. It felt as if the top was so far away. Cody was always right there behind me. I understood that even reaching the top was not victory. I had to show him everything he had done and hope that he could see that it was wrong. It was my only choice if I wanted to save him. If I could finish this without killing my friend, I would do it.

I wished that the Spence Center had been built by a more conventional architect. The stairs only went up one or two floors whenever I found them instead of all the way to the top. This forced me to find the next staircase on that floor. This small detail made a huge difference in my ascension. I could have already been at the top if only this place was normal.

Up and up and up, we continued. Cody lunged at me whenever he was given the opportunity. Almost every time resulted in a punch to my side and his being slowed down momentarily. As strong as I was, I was breaking. Running with all my strength gave little focus to healing myself. Just as we were nearing the top, I was out of strength.

I burst through the door on the roof of the Spence Center. Having reached the summit, I collapsed. My enemy, his body filled with three times the endurance of mine, walked confidently up behind me. Cody, with more energy than I, picked me up at my neck and walked to the edge of the building. I did nothing as we came closer and closer to the 23-story drop. My death was right there in front of me, and I was being carried to it.

Only feet from the edge, I kicked at him. A new strength filled me and it was the desire to complete the mission. I had come too far to be thrown to my death. I had come here to win, and that was what I was going to do. I flailed until his grasp weakened and then I kicked upward, right into his jaw. His head snapped up, and the beast released me.

This was my opportunity. It was time to show him what was below. He needed to see all of it if there was any chance he would change his mind. I grabbed him with both my hands and pulled him to the edge. I slammed him against the rim of the building and forced him to look down on all of the chaos.

"This is what you are fighting for! You fight to destroy lives! Lives of families! Lives of soldiers who fight just to undo what you've done! They are innocent, yet you kill them. L.I.F.E. is dead, and their evil with them! Give up the fight so peace can come to this world!" I yelled as he looked at all he had done.

"It...is...beautiful. Prepare to join them!" Cody said as he punched

176

through the small barrier that ran along the edge of the building.

He spun around and out of my hold. His leg wound up to kick me over the edge. As the tungsten foot came, I ducked and grabbed his leg. Using his momentum, I slammed him to the ground right before the edge.

Exhausted, I tumbled backwards. Neither of us chose to make a move against the other. We mutually and silently decided to allow each other to rest. There we sat, watching each other on top of the tallest building in West City. We were away from all the chaos below. Only the wind could be heard up here. It was just he and I. At last, we were alone again.

Chapter 25
Revelation

We sat at only a distance of about fifteen feet away from each other. This fighting was starting to lose its value. All day, each of us had fought against the other man's agenda. How many times had I knocked him down only to not take his life? How many times had he done the same? What was the point of fighting anymore?

"I must be the unstoppable force," my foe said, staring at the ground. "You are the immovable object. Never shall I stop trying to kill you. Never will you stop trying to save them. I cannot kill you because you are too strong. You cannot save them because I shall not change. No progress can be made. We shall fight for the rest of time."

"How can it end? Is there any way?" I asked, desperate for a solution.

"It can only end in death. We shall see it end with either the death of every human on the planet or with the death of me. Only those two options will end this fight, but I cannot kill them all, and you cannot kill me. It never ends."

"As long as we are not fighting for now, maybe we can just talk."

He lifted his eyes and set them on me. They fell again, and he returned to a depressed state. He was losing all his will, but it was not enough to make him stop. Still, he wished to listen to what I had to say.

"Words among enemies are the most valuable. Who else but the one you despise to be so brutally honest?" he said with a brief smile.

I chuckled at this and returned his smile. "I am not so sure that is true, but I thank you for this opportunity to talk. What happened to the Cody I used to know that caused such colossal change? That is my first question."

"I have answered this question before, have I not?"

"But now, I am your greatest enemy. You should be more honest this time."

He chuckled and said, "Fair enough. On the day I was forced to kill my parents, I lost my hope. Without hope, I had no faith in humanity. Without faith, I lost my love for humans. Without love, I filled the gap with hate. That hate is what makes me what I am today."

"Thank you for your honesty. What..." I began, but he raised his hand in protest, demanding my silence.

"Stop. You had your question. Let me have mine."

"Go ahead then," I said, gesturing for him to speak.

"I am made of hate, and you are made of love. It must be quite clear to you that, even with my superior intelligence, I cannot understand your ways. What has inspired such love in you? The Martin I knew from before was not like you are."

"That is true. The Martin you knew was without the love of life I have now. I killed almost a hundred people for the mafia. I did not care who they were. If the boss said they were to die, I would supply the death. Even after that, I killed the agents of L.I.F.E. without mercy. I did it because I was angry; because I wanted vengeance. But a seed was planted in me even before I wanted that revenge."

"You give me a vague answer? Then, I request you answer a second question."

"Fine. What is your question?" I asked, laughing on the inside.

"What was the seed?" he asked me, genuinely interested.

"The seed was faith. My family took me to church the two months I was with them, and I learned the grace of God. I was evil, but forgiveness was mine if I asked for it. All I had to do was ask! My whole life prior had been filled with sorrow and guilt, but then I knew I didn't have to live like that. Even when things got worse and worse for me, I always knew the best was yet to come. My faith stabilized my life. I could finally turn my eyes from myself. I could finally care about other people. If a murderer like me could be forgiven, then, surely, everyone could. I understood that taking a life was stealing that chance of redemption that I was given. That is how I learned the preciousness of life."

"While your belief in a deity eludes me, I can understand from where your compassion for the humans has originated. You aim to save because you have been saved. Seeing the benefit of rescue, you wish for all to join with you in it. You are an honorable man, Martin."

"Thank you. Now...my next question. What did you intend to do after killing every human on the planet? What was your life going to be like?"

"There would be peace. Without any opposition against me, for once, I could rest in peace. I would live out my days, knowing that I had accomplished all. I would know that I was the supreme being and that everything was beneath me. Never again would I have to fear evil. The humans would take all of it with them. Everlasting peace was to be my reward for my conquest."

"I cannot understand how that would be enough for you. I think you would find yourself lonely and without happiness in your conquered world. There would be nothing to look forward to and nothing but your own hate in which to engulf yourself. It would be a loveless world where you would never find yourself at peace."

"It would be my world, and that is what matters to me. Do you not perceive conquest in your future? With your superiority, do you not seek to stand above those beneath you?"

"No, that would be impossible. I cannot stand above them because we are on equal footing. Yes, I have been blessed by these unfathomable abilities, but that does not make me more than they are. I am equal with the humans, and so are you. No person is created better than anyone and no person ends their life better than anyone. I don't seek conquest because it is not mine to take."

"A fool's answer. There is not possibility that you could be so blind to your axiomatic superiority. You deny it only to justify your foolish choices. You and I are above all, and everyone but you can see it. Do you truly not believe yourself better than the ridiculously mortal humans below?"

"It is time for my question. And for that question, I ask you about your 'superiority'. How have you achieved such high status? What makes you better than everyone on this planet?"

"I had believed it to be quite evident. I am better because of my advanced strength, intelligence, and skill. I am better simply because I am better."

"You miss the intent of my question. What have you done to earn your higher status?"

"I have done nothing. I was chosen for an experiment, and the experiment worked. That is what makes me better. No, I did not have to earn it, but what is your point? Why should it matter how I got to where I am?" he asked me, showing intrigue and insult.

"You are the plaything of circumstance. If you were so blindly chosen to be better, what stops anyone else from being chosen? By your logic, every single person has that chance to be the best there is. Believing that, you must believe that all are equal. If one can become greater than all by dumb luck, then, potentially, everyone is better than everyone else. Your definition of 'better' is flawed, and so are you. You are not the greatest and you never will be."

"Your logic is riddled with rhetorical situations. Never will so many be chosen as I have. Yes, dumb luck has set me above, but that fact does not affect my higher status. I am above, and perhaps others will rise to my level, but, until then, I shall enjoy my time at the top," he said, turning from me and looking down at his chaos.

"Do you really believe you are better because dumb luck chose you?" I asked Cody, wishing to retrieve his attention.

He turned away from all that was happening below. He then shook his head at me. He was not answering me; he was showing his disapproval for my insistent interrogation.

"I do, Martin. If you do not believe me, then I shall ask you about your success," he said, sticking his finger out at me. "Why is it you succeed? Is it because you are equal with every opponent you face? Is it because you are no better than they? Is it because you cannot be anything more than they can? Tell me why you succeed at all," he challenged me.

"My success is not my own. Everything that goes my way only goes that way because of the tremendous power behind me. God is that power, and He blesses me with that success. It is not mine, but, because I follow Him, I am permitted to share it with Him. I will tell you again that I am no better than anyone, but I will also tell you that no one is better than my God."

"So your god is better than all? Then, maybe you do have a chance against me! Maybe I shall fall today! Perhaps this fool and his god will end this war and restore my faith in humanity."

"That depends. What is the one thing that would restore your faith and bring your war to a close?"

"As I said previously, my death is the only thing that will bring about the end of this war. As for my faith, it is lost to the depths of disbelief. I cannot believe in the humans nor can I believe in your God. Faith is unobtainable and, thus, your only choice is my death."

"I don't want your death. You should know that. You are my friend, Cody."

"And I do, Martin. I understand the compassion you have towards me. You preach that you would suffer many hardships to save me. But do you know what happens if even one of us is alive after today? Do you understand the consequences of your existence?" he asked, knowing that I would not understand what he was saying.

"I am not exactly sure what you are saying. So...that is my question. What are you saying?"

Cody stood up, chuckling at my lack of understanding. He turned away from me and looked down at his war. He shook his head in disgust as if he knew that it was not going his way down there. He turned back to me with a grin still on his face.

"If you do not understand the consequences, then it is justice for me to explain them to you. The humans who are your mission to save are not as kindhearted as you, Martin. They will look upon you in disgust. They will hate you because you are stronger, faster, smarter, and so undeniably better than they. Seeing that power within you, they will aim to obtain it. Nations all around the world will vie for you. Hundreds of millions will fall in the name of their governments just to have the chance at your superiority. Wars will rage endlessly all over your world. More blood than I could ever spill will be on your hands. Greed will end all good," Cody said, slowly showing signs of outrage.

"And what should I do about it? Join with you in killing them all? Is that what you suggest?" I responded, standing to meet his height.

"That is exactly what I suggest. Kill them to be free of their evil. It is inevitable. They all turn against you whatever choice you make. The only difference is that you have the chance to save me. Is one not enough for you?" he said, determined to change my mind.

"Never would I side with your cause. I aim to save as many as possible, and killing is not what I choose. I have explained this already to you, have I not? You seem more insane than I, my friend."

"Stop calling me 'friend'! I am not your ally! I offer an alliance, but you have snubbed it! I offer an escape, but you spit on it! Why I have tried to speak to you at all is beyond my comprehension! Never will you change! You are a fool for eternity!" he yelled with fury.

"This fool will not stand against salvation."

"Then, never will you rest! They will be after you every remaining second of your life! They will never stop until they have you!" He paused and glared at me with those deep blue eyes before finishing, "You think that peace comes when I am gone? Peace cannot come while you are here."

In that moment, I knew what I had to do. It had to end here. Cody was right when he spoke of the havoc my presence would wreak on the world. If coexistence was not an option, then I wished the best for my humans. I only wanted the best for this world.

"If peace cannot come while I am here, then may it come when I am gone!" I declared as I ran at my fellow pariah. My arms wrapped around his body, and I pounded my feet against the roof. His heels hit the rim, and then so did my toes. We toppled over the edge to meet our final destination.

It all happened so slowly. I could easily count the fractions of seconds that passed. I did not miss a single detail. I saw the flames that burned all over my city. I saw the soldiers completing their task of salvation. I saw all the chaos as it was coming to an end. My eyes eventually came to the face of the one with whom I was falling to my death.

I gazed deeply into the blue circles that searched my face for an answer. In those circles, I saw first disbelief. Cody Callison could not believe in his defeat. Next was shown the rage directed fully at me. How could I have chosen this outcome? A blink later, I saw them fling about in an impossible search for escape. When none could be found, tears covered them. Cody's dream of conquest was falling to its death with him.

The last thing I saw in Cody's eyes was what I did not expect. They fell back in line with mine. All I saw now was respect. He had accepted everything I had told him. He now knew how right I had been. He now knew what awaited him and he had accepted it. He had surrendered, and his war was over. Those eyes granted me the victory.

We said nothing as we fell so many stories. My arms were locked around my friend, and I was ready to bring this mission to completion. His arms were loose and held me in no way. He was already dead. Nothing could bring him back. The ground and death had already met him.

Time moved so slowly as we descended. At this time, though it felt as if minutes had passed, we had only fallen 15 of the 23 stories. In this expansive length of time, I noticed the deep blue circles turned to an object not far from us. I turned my eyes to the same object and, with new hope returning, raised my hand. LIFE was racing towards us.

Tyler's timing was perfect as he grasped my hand and I grasped Cody's. Tyler groaned in anguish after catching two Super Soldiers falling from the top of the tallest building in West City. He was forced to lean over the edge of the Sphere just to hold me. This also meant he leaned on the altitude lever, and, thus, we ascended high into the sky.

Tyler, using all the strength permitted to him to save his greatest friend, pulled me up. When my hand reached the edge of the Sphere, I released Tyler's hand and clenched the edge. Tyler fell to the floor of the machine. His arms were surely dislocated, and he was our pilot. Even with that considered and his screaming filling the air, Tyler was not my number one concern at this time.

I looked down at Cody Callison, who was still holding onto my arm. My eyes met his sorrowful ones, and I knew what he was thinking. As he released his hold on my arm, I grabbed onto his wrist. I would not let him fall. Not now that he could finally be saved.

"No! I won't let you die! Not now!" I yelled at him.

"Failure has met me. Death is all that awaits me now," Cody gravely responded.

"No! You have surrendered the war! You have made the right choice! You have not failed! We have won! Together, you and I have won!"

"I have elected to live without victory. I deserve nothing but defeat."

"Don't say that! You can be forgiven for your choices! You can be saved!"

Cody refused to respond to me. His eyes left mine and they focused on the arm which I held. Raising the sharpened tungsten at the end of his other arm, he looked up to me. All I did was shake my head.

He plunged the jagged metal into the arm which I held. Again and again, he stabbed and tore at his arm right below the gauntlet. The armor was ripped as was the flesh. He would not stop, and there was nothing I could do to stop him. I had to watch in horror as my friend performed the amputation that would end in his death.

When he had cut through all but the bone, his deep blue circles rose to me. His face was darkened by the sorrow that he bore due to his lack of faith. Tears trailed down my cheeks as I looked at the little boy by the sea whom I had missed so much.

"May peace come," Cody Callison whispered before he swung his right arm and snapped the bone that held us together.

With the breaking of the bone, he fell. I screamed in terrible grief as I watched him descend to his death. His destroyed arms were outstretched as his body plummeted. He had gone limp just as his mind had gone. He looked at peace, but that was not the truth.

Tyler, recovering, took the controls, and we, too, began a descent. Down to the city streets we would go as well. Our journey was of a different kind than the one Cody Callison had taken, though. We would hit the ground with victory, while he hit with nothing but defeat.

Tears from my face fell with the pull of gravity. It took only fractions of a second before they were out of my vision. Just as the tears fell, Cody had fallen as well, and it was just as quick. How terribly quick it was! The one I had wished to save was dead.

My fingers refused to move from around the wrist of my dead friend. I could still feel the warmth of his flesh, but the soul behind it was gone. Blood dripped the same as my tears. I held the arm even tighter. This was the only tangible part of Cody I had left.

Minutes had passed before my feet finally hit the pavement. Upon meeting the road, they carried me to where I dreaded to go. It was out of my control as I walked the street. I knew exactly where I was going, and so did Tyler. He followed silently behind me.

I came to where he was. His body maintained its shape, but the soul was far gone. Never had I seen Cody without an overabundance of life and energy. It was almost as if I looked down at an entirely different being. This was not my Cody. My Cody was still alive in my heart.

I set his arm back where it once was. He no longer needed it, but I felt it belonged with him. He had used it in attempt to take my life, but I had forgiven him for that. This arm was not mine and it belonged with Cody.

I stood there in silence. The crackling of fire and wailing of sirens were but a whisper spoken in the distance. All I could do was be sorry for the soul who had refused to be saved. In the end, my actions were not the ones that were essential to his salvation. Cody had to choose to accept help and, in the end, he was unable to do so. It was no one's fault but his own, and that was the saddest part of it all.

When I had freed myself from the guilt I faced for the death of Cody Callison, I could see the truth. I had not failed this day. God was with me this day. With His help, humanity had been saved. The pain and suffering from this horrible day were finally over. I could only be thankful to the One who had given me the success I needed.

This tragedy brought me both deep sadness and great happiness. My friend was dead, but so many could now live. I could not save one man, but I could save so many more. This pain would lead to the eradication of suffering. Yes, I was sad, but, oh, how happy I was going to be!

Tyler, struggling with his dislocations, placed a hand on my shoulder. I looked to him, and he granted me a smile. The war was over. It was time for peace. My greatest friend wrapped his arms around me and squeezed as hard as he could, ignoring his pain to help alleviate my own. We laughed and tears rolled down both of our cheeks. Tyler broke the embrace and looked at me with gleaming eyes.

"Mission complete."

Chapter 26
The End of the Old Life

We remained in respectful silence before my dead friend. We were unaware of the men approaching from behind us. Their rifles were aimed at our heads, and they said nothing until they had already come quite close.

"Freeze! Hands on your heads!" yelled a soldier.

Caught off guard, we responded quickly to the order. We fell to our knees and put our hands on our heads. The soldiers swarmed around us, and the barrels of rifles were put against our skulls.

"What are you doing here? Are you with this man?" asked their leader, stepping forward.

"No, we were the ones who brought him down. We don't mean any harm to anyone," I answered.

I looked up at the leader. Analyzing the man, I saw that he was about 6' 3" and, to say the least, in shape. He was a strong man and he had an undeniable presence about him. His sweaty blonde hair gleamed from under his helmet and made his blue eyes shine all the more. His stern gaze met me, and I looked back to the ground.

"How can we be sure you are telling the truth? How do we know you are not like him? You are wearing armor just like he is. Why is that?" asked the leader.

"I wore this so I could fight him. I needed it for protection. You of all people should know what he was capable of."

"If what I know about that man is true, then there is no way you could stand against him for a second. This man has murdered whole platoons of soldiers within minutes. No man could stand against him."

"I am like he, stronger. I was the only one who could fight him and live."

The soldiers perked up and focused on me entirely. I saw them raise their rifles at us again.

"You are like him?" asked the leader.

"I have the strength and ability, but I have a different heart. I mean no harm to anyone," I clarified.

The leader stepped back from me and Tyler and grabbed the radio attached to his chest. Never losing eye contact with me, he raised the radio to his mouth.

"Sir, this is 2nd Lieutenant Munsch. The main threat has been neutralized and is laying dead right in front of me. The Spheres are still mobile, and ground forces are bringing them down. But I have another problem that just came up. I've got two men here, and one of them claims to be like the main threat. He also claims that they were the ones who killed the threat."

I could hear the voice of whomever this man was talking to on the other end of the radio. The voice was not upset or startled, but, instead, was hushed and calm. Whoever it was, most likely a general, was leading well. Listening to the voice, I was feeling myself becoming calmer, and it looked as if the 2nd Lieutenant was as well. Perhaps I had nothing to fear.

"Yes, sir. We will wait for your arrival. Until then, we will guard the..." spoke Munsch, but another threat stopped him.

A LIFE Sphere swooped down and spat flame down at Munsch. One of his soldiers tackled him out of the way, saving both of their lives. The other soldiers sprang into action and moved into the buildings on either side of the street. Bullets flew and then bounced off the shell of the machine. They could not fight it; only I could.

No longer guarded, I took to my feet and ran at the Sphere. My fist flew and knocked it back. Flames attempted to engulf me, but I was too quick. Again, I launched my fists. Though I could knock the Sphere around, I was not making much progress with it. The small dents I was producing would not end this fight quickly.

"Tyler! To the Pilot Sphere! Cody had said something about a control system for the Sphere being in there!" I instructed Tyler.

Tyler ran to the Pilot Sphere while I fought off the metal menace. The soldiers hid within the buildings and watched as Tyler and I saved them. They were helpless in this situation and they knew it. Only I was strong enough to fight this force.

Tyler was busy pushing buttons and flipping switches. He could not find out how to stop the threat. He knew there had to be something there, but he could not find it.

"What do I do, kid?" he yelled to me.

I had not messed with the Sphere controls earlier because I knew that Cody could simply undo whatever I did just by opening his mouth. I had no idea how they worked and could not help Tyler with his task. If only I had attempted this earlier.

The Sphere was beginning to stray from our fight. It could sense the lifeforms all around it. It did not only want me; it wanted all of them. I was struggling to keep the machine away from the buildings and I knew that we needed a solution soon. That was when I had an idea.

Being only about twenty feet from the Pilot Sphere and Tyler, I yelled, "All units: Deactivate!"

The giant chunk of metal almost immediately fell before me. Throughout the city, tremendous crashes could be heard. They were falling! The metal menace was done! Every threat was defeated, and the war was officially over. It was over!

Cheers of joy sounded all over the city. The soldiers left their hiding spots and whooped and hollered. There was undeniable euphoria washing over this place. They threw down their rifles and jumped around. Tyler and I jumped and shouted, too. This was a time of celebration. War was over!

A Humvee pulled right up to our party, and the doors flung open. Out stepped a woman adorned with three silver stars. Yes, this was the Lieutenant General. Immediately, the soldiers stiffened up and saluted their superior. Tyler and I did the same. She was coming right for us.

"Are you the two who stopped this?" she asked us.

"Yes, ma'am. I am Tyler Ishler, and this is Martin Shepard," Tyler said to the general.

"'Sir' will do just fine for me, Ishler. Get in the Humvee, you two. There is someone you need to meet," she commanded us, pointing to her vehicle.

The 2nd Lieutenant approached respectfully and said, "General Nienhuis, what would you have us do?"

"Reestablish peace in the city. Assist the officers already at work and bring the citizens to some kind of shelter. I will leave any other choice up to your best judgment," she answered him.

"Yes, sir!" he said and saluted.

The 2nd Lieutenant and his troops moved on to continue helping the people of this struggling city. There was so much work to do. With good men like Munsch at work, progress was guaranteed. I was glad West City was in good hands.

As we were nearing the Humvee, a man sprinted at us. Bringing momentary worry, I was glad to see who was running up to us. Officer Nick Turnbull stopped in front of us and stiffened just as the soldiers had done. He saluted and waited to be addressed.

"What is it, officer?" asked General Nienhuis.

"General, I respectfully would like to inform you that these men are not criminals. I had once made this mistake. But trust me, they are good at heart and they don't deserve to go to jail," Nick paused, "This one saved my life!" he finished, pointing at me.

"No worry, officer. I know who they are. They are not being taken in for that reason. I am to bring them to someone very important," the general said.

"Then, may I please have a second to talk to them before they go? It would mean a lot to me."

General Nienhuis nodded, and Nick approached us. With the biggest smile I had ever seen, he stuck out his hand for me to shake. I took it and gratefully shook it. Tyler then did the same, and I could see the apology and the happiness emanating from the man.

"I must say that I never thought I would do that," Nick laughed, as we all did.

"Officer Turnbull, I can only thank you so much for your forgiveness. We did awful things in the past, and you have overlooked them. You see us not as we were, but as we now are. I know I am extremely grateful for this," I said to the officer.

"I am, too. I couldn't be happier that you can accept us as the good guys. Know that we were always fighting for good. Even when we killed, we did it hoping for the best outcome. I am sorry for what trouble we have caused you," said Tyler with remorse.

"Your apologies are accepted, and I just hope you can accept mine," said Nick, embarrassed.

"You have forgiven us, so we forgive you," responded Tyler with a respectful smile.

"Never will I forget you guys. Keep fighting for good. Never stop," Nick told us.

"We shall never stop, and I know you never will either. Let us leave each other and go in the name of justice. Officer Turnbull, I wish you the greatest of luck," I said with a tear in my eye.

"Don't give up, Officer Turnbull. We won't stop, and so you can't. Good luck," said Tyler, the same emotions welling up inside him as well.

Tears tumbled down the cheeks of the officer before he spoke to us saying, "I won't. I will never give up. I know you guys will bring justice and I am so happy for that. Good luck to you two as well."

We both hugged the man who once hunted us with such determination. I felt incredibly happy to have this man as a friend. He no longer despised us. Now, the relationship was quite the opposite. To be down one enemy and up one friend, this was a fantastic feeling.

"Officer, I must ask you to help the citizens of this city. They need your service," said General Nienhuis, stepping up.

Officer Nick Turnbull gave each of us a humble nod before he saluted the general and ran to assist the citizens of West City. He ran off at top speed, determined to find and help as many people as possible. He was a good man, and I would miss him.

"Oh! Wait one second, sir. I've got to go grab something," Tyler said, running towards the Pilot Sphere.

I saw him reach inside it, and then he came back toward us. He held in his hands Mrs. T. I was glad he had remembered it. It would have been a great shame to have left it behind.

"I'm not leaving her behind again. I finally got her back, and she's never going to leave my hands again, kid," he said to me. "All right, sir. Let's go meet this person you say is so important."

"Yes, let's. To the Humvee then," she responded.

Tyler and I got into the back of the Humvee, and it took off. I was on the right side, and Tyler took the left. In front of me was the general's right-hand man, and, in front of Tyler, was the general. The Humvee drove down the middle of the road, straight towards its destination.

"Where exactly are you taking us?" I asked the general.

"There is a helicopter waiting for us. You two will board it and be taken to an airport. From there, you will board a plane and be taken to D.C.," said General Nienhuis.

"Why are we going to D.C.?" asked Tyler, leaning forward with wide eyes.

"There is someone there who really wants to talk to you two. Anyone who can stop what happened here today deserves a meeting with the president."

"The president? We are meeting with the president?!" I asked, astounded.

"Yes. Just sit back for now. It is going to be a while until you guys get there."

We both fell back into our seats and looked at each other. We were going to meet with the president! All of our lives, we had run from the law. The government had always been against us, and now we were going to speak with its highest in command. Maybe our difficulties were finally coming to an end.

When the Humvee stopped, we exited and moved towards the helicopter with its blades spinning in preparation for our trip. Before we got there, I was seized by the arm. Looking back, I saw little Liz clutching on to me. She pointed to my right where a car was parked.

"Hey, man! She has something she wants to say to you," shouted Melody.

I approached the vehicle in which sat my ally Mikaila Lamb. The door was opened, and she was sitting facing me, bracing herself on the door's armrest. She was weak, but her strength would not believe it. Mikaila stood when I was but feet from her. Her legs could not support her weight, and she fell into my arms.

"You did it, Martin. You did it," she whispered.

"It's all over, but we need to get you to a hospital."

"They can stay with me..."

I was confused by whom she meant. "Who can stay with you?"

"Melody and Liz. I told them they can stay with me. I have enough...enough to support them. They will...live with me."

I looked back at Melody and Liz. Tears were once again in Melody's eyes, but, this time, they were tears of joy. Melody grabbed Liz and hugged her tightly. She then lifted her face up to see me.

"It's all because of you, man. That morning, I went into work and someone stole some of the money out of the cash register. They all thought it was me, but it wasn't. But that didn't matter. I was fired anyways and sent home. That job was the only thing I had," Melody said, tear-filled eyes locked on me.

"I'm sorry. But how do you mean it's all because of me?"

"When I got home, I sent Liz out to scavenge for food while I laid in my bed crying. I was brought down to the very bottom and I needed help, so...I prayed. I said, 'God, give me one more chance. If I can just have one more chance to make a life for Liz and I, maybe she won't have to suffer as I have.' I laid there, so angry...until I got an answer. I couldn't be sure at all if I had really heard it, but I could have sworn I heard a voice say, 'Help him first.' I didn't know what it meant until Liz came running in, asking for Dad's suit. Then, she brought you in...and I knew I had to help you."

"That's why you helped me? God told you to?"

"Yeah, man. And now that I have, He has given me a new home. A place where I don't have to worry. Where I don't have to be afraid anymore."

Her motives were now clear. She had to learn to help others first. When she had learned this, then she could be helped. She learned an important lesson and gained powerful allies. I was so glad that everything had worked out for her and Liz. They deserved this.

Mikaila grabbed my arm to get my attention.

"Don't forget. You are the true hero here. You had the courage to stand up to that monster. You have rescued us all. The world could really use more like you, Martin."

"I could only have courage after learning whom I had standing behind me. I could only rescue you after knowing God was fighting with me. The world does not need more like me, Mikaila. It needs more of God."

"Then, you should be the one to introduce the world to Him."

"Martin! It's time to take off!" shouted General Nienhuis.

I helped Mikaila to sit back down in the car. I then looked back at the general, who was impatiently waiting for me. I turned back to the ones who had aided me when I really needed it. "Thank you all. I shall see you again." I turned back to helicopter and began to walk away.

I had only taken three steps before I heard little Liz say, "Good luck!"

"Good luck, man," Melody said with the first real smile I had seen from her.

"Good luck, hero," Mikaila said weakly.

I nodded to them and then continued to the helicopter. Taking my seat across from Tyler, I smiled at him. It was time for a new adventure to begin. After all through which we had been, we were ready to start something fresh. No longer would we run. It was time to stand. Tyler returned the same smile, knowing everything I was thinking.

The helicopter took us to the airport where we boarded the plane that would take us to Washington, D.C., the place our future resided. We were treated with absolute respect on the flight. We were seen as the two men who had saved the world. They did not know the full story, but still they knew enough. Never had I known such respect without fear being the motive.

On the plane, Tyler and I were given medical assistance and dressed in fine clothing. Our wounds were stitched, we were fed, and our bodies were covered. I could not be more happy with the service. Tyler surely was quite happy to have a hat with which to cover his bald head. I, too, was glad to cover my shaved head, for they also cut off all the burnt shaggy hair that had been covering my head. We were brought back to fullness before we were to meet the president.

As night fell, the plane landed, and we were taken to the White House. Doors opened for us as if we were kings. Before we knew it, we were outside the door to the oval office. Here it was: the future. Whatever the president was going to say to us, I knew it was going to be important. They had shipped us out here so quickly just to talk to us. A new beginning lay behind that door.

With the opening of the door, I could see the man who led this country. When we entered the room, he stood for us. For two men who, once long ago, brought terror to the streets, the leader of the free world stood. We stood in the center of his office as the president walked around his desk and the door behind us shut. When he and we were isolated in this special place, he offered his hand to Tyler. Stunned, Tyler was slow to take it. Tyler, taking the hand, smiled, and so did the president.

The hand was next offered to me. I was the same as Tyler, stunned. My hand at last moved upward and met the hand of the great leader. Both of us smiled in this embrace and mutual respect we had for each other. We respected his power, and he respected ours.

"I am Rodrick Henry, the president of the United States, and I, as well as all the people in this great country, am forever in your debt."

"We were just cleaning up our own mess, sir. Mistakes made in the past led us here, and it was our duty to fix them. You owe us nothing," I responded shyly.

"At the very least, accept my gratitude. You saved many lives, and, whatever you believe, that was your choice. You chose to take responsibility for your past and you did fix your mistakes. That is more honorable than you know. Both of you, please know that I cannot say enough about how much good you have done today."

"Thank you, sir," both of us responded respectfully.

The president paused and collected his thoughts. There was much brewing in his mind at that second. The two heroes of his country before him, he did not know what to say next.

"Please," he spoke finally, "take a seat. I am sure we have much to discuss."

We sat and, for two hours, we discussed all that had happened. From the origin of my strength to the evils of L.I.F.E., we told him all. Everything through which we had suffered and every trial we had overcome was presented to the one who made the decisions for the United States of America. He patiently listened and interposed with a question whenever necessary. The president trusted us fully and remorsefully accepted the betrayal of the organization he had funded for so long. We told our story and waited for a response from the leader.

"After all that, I know two things: The L.I.F.E. you know is over and a new one will soon begin. A new beginning is what we all need. And at the head of that new beginning, I want you two. Will you take this opportunity to work for the good of all? Will you work for the improvement and enhancement of every life in this beautiful country? Please, will you give us not the old L.I.F.E. we had, but a new L.I.F.E. that we all need?" said the president, standing.

We, too, stood, and Tyler took the president's hand, saying, "It would be an absolute honor to work on the right side of the law for once. I know I accept. What about you, kid?"

"How could I say no?" I took President Henry's hand and shook it. "Thank you for this opportunity to serve. This is what I have always wanted and it is exactly where I am meant to be. Finally, I can use this curse for good. That is all I have ever wanted. Thank you."

"Then, it's settled! You, Tyler Ishler and Martin Shepard, are the new commanders of L.I.F.E., a completely new organization that is separate from the last."

"Just one thing, sir," Tyler spoke up.

"Anything you want," answered the president.

"With a new organization, we need new uniforms. I say that the night's over. The day is at hand! Let's ditch the black and get something a little more our style. I'm thinking white would do the trick," Tyler said, flashing me a smile.

"I agree. It's time for a fresh look. We are different, after all," I concurred.

"Haha! You shall have it then! We will get some white suits for you as soon as possible. Now, only one issue remains," said President Henry.

"What is that? What do you need?" asked Tyler, hoping to assist the one who was giving us so much.

"I don't know what to do about the press. I mean, what do I tell the people? They are going to demand an explanation tomorrow morning, and I need to have one. So much has happened, but they will want to know about what happened today. What can I say? How can I possibly explain all this?" President Henry asked us.

I took a step forward, and they both turned to me. I knew what I had to say. The words so easily sat on the tip of my tongue. It was time for the truth to be spoken.

"You tell them this. Yesterday, two monstrosities of L.I.F.E. fought for the fate of the world. One was filled with hate and, with this hate, he intended to purge the Earth of all who had done evil to him. The other was filled with love and, with this love, he intended to save the Earth so that the people had the chance to be forgiven of the evil they had done. One stood alone and against all. The other stood with the Lord of all and for all. In the end, the one filled with love and with God at his side won, for the one filled with hate and with no one at his side never had any true strength. Let it serve as an example for all: If God is with you, then who can be against you?"

<u>The End</u>

www.ingramcontent.com/pod-product-compliance
Lightning Source LLC
Chambersburg PA
CBHW072109170626
46813CB00004B/1494